SO-BIE-210

HOL... ...ARY

CABRINI COLLEGE, RADNOR, PA.

THE COMPLETE WHITE OXEN

OTHER BOOKS BY
KENNETH BURKE

THE
COMPLETE
WHITE OXEN

COLLECTED SHORT FICTION

of

KENNETH BURKE

CABRINI COLLEGE LIBRARY
610 KING OF PRUSSIA ROAD
RADNOR, PA 19087

University of California Press

Berkeley and Los Angeles 1968

#352586

PS
3503
.U6134
C66
1968

University of California Press
Berkeley and Los Angeles, California

Cambridge University Press
London, England

Fifteen of the stories reproduced in this edition
appeared in *The White Oxen and Other Stories*
(New York: Albert & Charles Boni, 1924)

Copyright © 1968 by Kenneth Burke

Library of Congress Catalog Card Number: 68-17692
Printed in the United States of America

TO

MY WIFE

HOLY SPIRIT LIBRARY

CABRINI COLLEGE, RADNOR, PA.

44917

Lascivam verborum licentiam . . . excusarem, si meum esset exemplum: sic scribit Catullus, sic Marsus, sic Pedo, sic Getulicus, sic quicunque perlegitur.

Martial

PREFACE

WITH the exception of "The White Oxen," the stories that were published in the original book of 1924 appeared in *Broom, The Dial, The Little Review, Secession* and *S₄N*. They are arranged approximately in the order of their completion.

Early items here added are: "A Man of Forethought" (which appeared in *Smart Set,* May 1919); "The Soul of Kajn Tafha" (*The Dial,* July 1920); and *"The Metamorphoses of Venus"* (in the magazine *1924*).

The much later piece, "The Anaesthetic Revelation of Herone Liddell," was published in *The Kenyon Review* (Autumn 1957). In case any one is interested, I would pronounce the name thus: "Herone" is a two-syllable word with the accent *slightly* on the second syllable. The accent in "Liddell" is *strongly* on the second syllable.

In an "Author's Note" to the earlier *White Oxen,* I observed that the sequence of the stories embodies a gradual "increase of stress upon the more rhetorical properties of letters." And with more defiance than assurance, I proclaimed it a "great privilege" to take such a turn "in an age when rhetoric is so universally despised."

"Rhetoric" can have many different meanings. I mainly had in mind an interest in formal and stylistic twists as such, along with their entanglements in character and plot.

Consider, for instance, "The Book of Yul." The story was built around a dream so obsessive that I even tried to make a melody in keeping with it. And despite my tragic helplessness in draftsmanship, I attempted some relevant illustrations. As I see it now, De Chirico could have done

for me the sort of mausoleum city I had in mind, if he
had put in a wraithlike throng here and there.

But my point is: Along with the compulsiveness of this
"content," I was much concerned with what I viewed as
a "rhetorical" element. Thus, the first paragraph is conceived as "annunciatory," and sums up the tenor of the
story as a whole. In its role as a *beginning,* it begins with
the words "While waiting"—and the whole first section is
set up in terms of *expectation.* In the course of it, the
words "thump" and "scrape" are present in one sense—
but they contain an ambiguous dimension that will be
revealed when they reappear later in the story. (Only
much later was I able to discern how superbly Father
Aeschylus had anticipated such intentions, not only in his
general feeling for the formality implicit in a plot, but
also in his specific way of *beginning* his great trilogy on
the very *theme* of expectation.)

Recently, when consulting a library copy of the original
edition, I found in it the clipping of a review by an influential critic-editor of an opinion-making weekly that
was influential in those olden days (and perhaps still is).
The Authority finds "a curious lack of instinct for design." And:

> "Mr. Burke appears to us mistaken in the idea
> that such a sentence as the following is good
> writing:
>
> > 'The various arteries of the city having been
> > loosened by the phlebotomy of five o'clock,
> > the streets dripped profusely.'
>
> "This sentence opens one story and is, presum-
> ably, arresting. The author's preoccupation with
> matters that he also excoriates as the preoccupa-
> tions of modern business men and modern ad-
> vertising offends else . . . ."

At which point the clipping indeterminately ended. So maybe I'll never know.

In any case, please let me add: The title I had chosen for the original collection of these pieces was *Here and Elsewhere* I was talked out of it, but I wish that I had kept it. Yet I don't feel I should make the change now thus belatedly.

A few additional backward-looking pages seem in order: Probably the character of Gabriel Harding (in "The White Oxen") should have been treated without any "inside" knowledge of his motives. Then the sexually ambiguous implications of his role could have been clearer. The "Man of Forethought" item belonged in *Smart Set*. And though it is smart in a way that makes me smart a bit, after much hesitation I decided that it should be included. The editors who took that one came close to accepting the much better story, "Mrs. Maecenas." But I later found good cause to be grateful for its rejection, since its acceptance by *The Dial* marked the entrance of that magazine into my life—and for me that was almost as momentous a moment as the act, or accident, of being born.

"Mrs. Maecenas" was obviously influenced by some early work of Thomas Mann, as well as by Mencken-and-Nathan's enterprise (which had been an adventurous guide for us during our years at high school). The story reflected Mann's gallant error, in the excessive imputing of virtues to the average citizen. Quite a time was to elapse before I began to suspect that Mann's bourgeois-Bohemian dichotomy, for all its twists, too simply divided the realms of the "neurotic" from the "normal." For instance, you are not likely to find many on the "Bohemian" side of the antithesis falling into line with militaristic trends which the average citizen is so prone to equate with love of country.

Or consider the typical prowess of TV commercials, in peddling poisons or arousing absurd fears and appetites, on a national scale.

"My Dear Mrs. Wurtelbach" marks a kind of turning point. Here I was trying to work out a form that would proceed somewhat like the movements of a symphony, with qualitative breaks from one part to the next (as though each were on a different "level"), rather than embodying the kind of continuity "natural" to conventional narrative. While planning the piece, I proposed a bet with Malcolm Cowley. Both of us feeling glum about the literary situation, I proposed to make a bet with him that I could turn up with something formally different from the average. But not only was he to be assigned the role of betting that it couldn't be done; he was also to be sole judge of whether the project worked.

The bet was for $10, which was a lot. Cowley agreed— and later he graciously judged that I had won (but only with the added stipulation that I should not try to collect the ten dollars). From then on, I kept experimenting with that disjointed kind of form which the critic already cited condemned as sheer insensitivity to form (though in subsequent years the experimental "sophisticating" of form has taken so many new turns, my attempts at innovation must seem by comparison almost as neo-classical as a drama by Racine).

The notion of different "levels" comes clearest in "In Quest of Olympus," with its succession of Up and Downward Ways, the final *apparent ascent* actually being (though I did not realize this fact at the time when I wrote the story) an *enigmatic descent*. The ambiguity is discussed on pages 334 to 338 in the essay, "The Thinking of the Body," reprinted in my *Language as Symbolic Action*.

Looking back now on the whole succession of "peripeties," I'd characterize (or rationalize?) the structure thus: (1) Birth, symbolized as climbing out of a cavern; (2) "break-away" stage of adolescence, as the protagonist be-

PREFACE xiii

comes magnified by the chopping down of a (parental)
tree, with corresponding ascent; (3) the protagonist
(whose new identity is marked by his forcefully acquired
change of name) confronts ambiguities of sex in terms of
"pre-forensic" or "magical" conflicts among nature-gods
that stand for a psychology, a cluster of discordant motives;
(4) "descent" (via a dreamer's onanistic spill?) into a
quotidian world of social criticism, here presented in terms
of low-visioned sexual dalliance, under the sign of dirty
dishes in the kitchen sink; (5) compensatory ascent, in
terms of grand natural processes (the incident of the earlier
"nature-gods" now being transformed into a poem that embodies a cult of nature as honestly and piously edified as
the author could make it) ; (6) said compensatory exhilara-
tion proves unstable, as indicated by the fact that a brief
silhouette of perfect bliss in Heaven is burlesqued, albeit
with a touch of nostalgia; (7) Christ's descent into the
dirty everyday world, treated vindictively, in terms of social
criticism; (8) Christ's culminative ascension, a return to
the womb that is ambiguously, or enigmatically, cloacal, as
discussed in the pages mentioned above.*

---

*In this final section (or penultimate section, if one can treat the
last sentence as a four-word movement ending on a four-letter word),
there is a bit of dialogue between "Father" and "Son," and couched
in nonsense syllables intended to stand for a quasi-Edenic "first"
language. As regards this matter, just as I was finishing my Preface
there appeared a story much to our purposes in the *New York Times*
of May 22, 1968. "Glossolalia," or "speaking in tongues," this report
reminds us, "is part of what is broadly termed the 'charismatic movement' and occurs when an individual suddenly begins to pray or
speak in an unknown and as yet undecipherable language." Nay
more, "To a small group of Presbyterians attending the church's
180 General Assembly" at Minneapolis, "the major issue is not the
urban crisis, race or the war in Vietnam, but what the church in-
tends to do about glossolalia." On page 337 of *Language as Symbolic Action* I show how (at least in the case of my story) one example of such enigmatic syllable-wagging can be decoded in terms
of muddled childhood remembrances. And though I'd hardly want
to contend that the issue is of greater importance than the problems

"Prince Llan" turned out to be *au fond* a kind of psychic bookkeeping, a split into two selves, one grown up, though problematically (the "Prince"), the other (Gudruff) representing the vestiges of problematical adolescence, here treated as a separate person who calls the "Prince" to regression. The would-be resolution (Joseph) but re-enacts Gudruff's reflexive cult of sensation on a "higher" level, as suicide. The whole is but decorative, a "masque"; yet in its nature as a doodle it does symbolize a basic pattern of the mind (that was to take a more serious, or even urgent, turn in my novel, *Towards a Better Life*). I have since seen the imagery of infinite doors (one opening, to disclose another; this second opening, to disclose a third, etc.) utilized in a motion picture to represent a mental patient's profound *malaise*. And the principle of fragmentation turns up under many conditions. For instance, when discussing the fragmentation of the statuary in Peter Blume's exceptionally radical painting, *The Eternal City* (see "Growth Among the Ruins" in my *Philosophy of Literary Form*) I try to bring out the *transitional* potentialities of this device. Or consider the observations of the Cambridge literary anthropologists on the "rending and tearing," or *sparagmos,* of rituals that led into Greek tragedy. But though I can find the pattern operating elsewhere in my

---

of our cities, of racial inequality, and of our filthy war in Vietnam, it is at least worthy of note that, at the "culminative" or "apocalyptic" moment in this (enigmatically "Satanic") story, the narrative did (though in sheer fantasy) slip into this perversely "charismatic" kind of double-talk (and right in the midst of mean social criticism, just as glossolalia is "inspirationally" emerging now in the midst of mean social conditions). As regards glossolalia at the time of Saint Paul, there's the likelihood that, in the then prevailing Hellenistic situation when many languages impinged upon one another, the powerful universalizing (catholicizing) strivings of the early Church often made for a kind of "speaking in tongues" that was a naive analogue of Joyce's learned, deliberate (yet compulsive and impulsive), perversely synthesizing contrivances (probably his profound variant of our world's many neo-archaizing trends).

own works (for instance, the last chapter of *Towards a Better Life* or the middle section, on "perspective by incongruity," in *Permanence and Change*), its use at the end of "Prince Llan" owes much to a suggestion by Malcolm Cowley. Among contemporary critics in the United States, Francis Fergusson is particularly sensitive to this "moment."

In connection with "Prince Llan" there is an ancedote that I can't resist telling. I had sublet Hart Crane's room on Grove Street, in NYC. It was on a mezzanine floor, led up to by a broad stairway that split and reversed direction, to reach the second floor by two smaller stairways. At the turn there were two empty niches, backed by opaque glass. In the room beyond them, I had just finished typing the chapter in which the "Prince," fleeing from a madhouse, escapes his pursuers by rushing on board a sailing vessel that was just leaving harbour. The actions of the sailors are described by a deliberate misuse of nautical terms.

Just at that moment in history, my friend James Light turned up, happily tipsy. Some people have read this passage without even suspecting that anything was wrong. But Jim, perhaps because of being an Englishman, could recognize the violations, and they affected him physically. Thus, when the proud author began reading the passage aloud, at each bit of terministic mayhem Jim did not merely applaud; in the generosity of his appreciation he began pounding me and booting me with delight. Though I felt gratified at the thought that my words could elicit so "strong" a response, it was necessarily a mixed pleasure. Besides, as the confusion in the passage mounted, his appreciative pummellings increased proportionately—until I ran into the hall, and hid in one of the niches. As I waited motionless, I heard Jim come stumbling out of the room. Then he stopped, on the other side of the niche with the opaque glass where I was hiding. And just as it occurred to me that, although the hall was dark, my shadow might show through, his foot smashed the glass from behind, and gave me the soundest blow of all. But this step in the development proved cathartic, and we turned next to the sobering subject of payment for the shattered glass.

As regards the last story, "The Anaesthetic Revelation of Herone Liddell," which was written many years after any of the others: I have always had a fondness for what the Germans call an *Erziehungsroman* (the Goethean mixture of *Wahrheit* and *Dichtung,* or the dialectic of Mann's *Magic Mountain,* or the moody treatment of ideas in Walter Pater's *Marius the Epicurean;* and a grand variant, which I came upon late, is Hermann Hesse's *Bead Game*) . I tried a departure in my novel, which was designed gradually to extricate a plot out of aphorism. And my last story in this book is somewhat in the same mode. In fact, there is a sense in which it could be classed as a kind of sequel to the novel; for as the earlier "declamations" courted an affliction, so this "revelation" involves a wan cult of recovery. Thus, when the novel was republished, I somewhat inclined to include the "Anaesthetic Revelation" in the same volume. The "schematism" (to use a deliberately unwieldy word) lines up thus:

(1) The underlying situation: the compelling immediacy of Liddell's *physical* suffering.

(2) Thoughts on the attendant, non-physical realm of symbolism.

(3) Relations between the two realms—culminating in the "gallantry" of symbolism with regard to dealings between male and female alimentary canals (with emergence of a valetudinarian purpose: to the South, and to the Sea) .

(4) Wherein the physicality of recovery by a southern sea builds atop the symbolism of the scapegoat (as Liddell, while nursing his sensations, meditates curatively on the dying of a great poet) .

I cannot argue as to whether or not such things *should* go on. All I am saying is that, in this story they *do* go on. And one might get the point I'm trying to make here by contrasting Liddell's thoughts with the out-and-out fictive account of Brother Angelik's speculations on faith and knowledge in "First Pastoral" (I did not realize at the time that in his bargain he actually "tempts God," thereby personally deserving the fate already determined by the nature of things) , or the narrator's ill-tempered theories, in "A Progression," about the nature of the devil's tongue.

Two words on two embarrassments, and I shall be through:

I grew up in an uncouth age and neighborhood in which it was taken for granted that minorities "normally" referred to one another as Dagoes, Hunkies, Niggers, Micks, Kikes, and such, along with our sound suspicion that we were all minorities of one sort or another. (Imagine the stigma, for instance, of living in Brushton rather than Homewood, or Homewood rather than Squirrel Hill, and so on.) Thus, some of my early stories show occasional pre-Reichstag Fire laxities. Since then, Hitler and his noxious Ism have made it hard even to remember the climate in which such laxities were taken for granted. Gone for ever (and perhaps for the better) are the days when it could be considered good clean fun, at a booze party, if Whitey the goy sang Negro spirituals in a Yiddish accent. I leave the bumpy passages as they were. First, they're not so tough anyhow. And second, I have the firm conviction that my subsequent work makes my position quite clear on the subject of ethnocentric bias, except in the sense of culture as a picture gallery that can liberally accommodate many different kinds of portrait and portraiture.

Of sexual passages in the earlier stories, some were adolescent, others reflect the traumatic survival of adolescent rigors. But in the light of later developments (particularly the cultural trends that have followed upon the Perfecting of the Pill) , I find it a bit quaint when I apologize (and in Martial's Latin yet!) for any "license" in any of these prim imaginings.

K. B.

Andover, N.J., 1968

CONTENTS

WHITE OXEN

WHITE OXEN

PART ONE

1

It is doubtful just what might have happened. But as it was, the inheritance came opportunely — almost immediately after his graduation from a middle-western university, in fact. Marcel Carr was enabled to marry and settle down without ever having come to grips with life. Immensely relieved, he gathered up his minerals—including a valuable agate from Sicily—and placed them down in the house that was to be his home until death. Every fair day he would take his note-book, a small pick, and a little black box which carried five graham crackers and two apples, kiss his wife a meaningless good-bye, and start off with a final assurance that he would be back by six. The day was spent in serious research along the river and among the adjoining hills, for Marcel Carr was preparing a document, a "Mineralogical Analysis of the Upper Ohio."

In the evening he heard Dorothy, his daughter, and little Matthew go over bits of their lessons chosen by him at random, lessons which Dorothy, the mother, had taught them during the day. It was a quiet household, the only disturbances being of little import, as when Matthew cried over his bewilderment in trying to explain Caesar's bridge, or Dorothy, the daughter, answered when her father had called Dorothy, the mother. This misunderstanding, however, was of slight consequence, even though it had gone on for years, since Marcel was not of an irascible nature, and each time the mistake was made he corrected it as though it had never been made before; furthermore, it was all finally settled by Dorothy, the mother, getting up from her Grieg one evening, turning a white, frightened face toward her dozing husband, and sinking dead to the floor.

In their subdued way, there was grief in the Carr household. Old Marcel walked about his wife's bedroom with a steady pace, mechanical even in his sorrow. Matthew moved on tiptoe, a little more embarrassed than sad, and crying only when he saw the forlorn little form of his sister, who kept sobbing as softly as the fall of fine rain.

But in time even quiet grief diminishes. The coming of spring found old Marcel leaving in the morning with his little black box, kissing his daughter as he had kissed his wife, and making the same promise to be home by six. The two children started to public school, where they got along well enough, although they had already become too accustomed to being alone to mix with the other students.

A kindly Mrs. Huntington—the same Mrs. Huntington who was president of the Wilkinsburg Women's Euchre Club before certain things which she found out prompted her to resign—a large woman with a wart on her nose, and nine children, spared the time to mother Matthew and Dorothy for a while, but finding it a thankless task she soon gave them up. From now on the Carr children slowly acquired the reputation of being "nasty." They were left now entirely to themselves; their isolation was made more complete by the widespread report among their classmates that white shapes had been seen at night to dance about the Carr chimneys. Grown-ups explained this by the fact that Carr was one of the few people in the neighborhood who still used coal, but the tale persisted.

Quietly, steadily, as regularly as the beat of a pendulum, old Carr's incompetence lost for him the money he

had inherited, until at last he rounded out an uneventful
life by slipping from a rock and breaking his neck, probably the only vigorous action of his career. Fortunately
for the old man's peace of mind, his death occurred one
week before the arrival of a large envelope announcing
his complete ruin. And when, within two years, Matthew's
sister was also dead, Matthew was left alone, except for
the aunt and uncle he and Dorothy had gone to stay with
in Pittsburgh.

2

There was something so subdued, so placid about his
sorrow, that it was almost a kind of dull contentment. He
spent his evenings — the hushed cool evenings of early
summer—in walking about the better districts of the city;
over Squirrel Hill, where the houses were surrounded by
wide lawns and little clumps of timber, and where the
smell of moist green spread out from the automatic
sprinklers; or out Highland Avenue to the park. Here the
roads squirmed in and out among the slopes; and when he
had attained the northern limits of the park, he could
look out at the Allegheny bounded by the lights of the
towns on the opposite shore. They were dirty little towns,
but at night, when only the lights were visible, thinning
out as the eye went east until the river was lost in black,
Matthew was happy to rest on them. Then he would lie
on his back and look straight up at the tangle of stars.
They would leap to within a foot of him, and then of a
sudden be gone again, billions and trillions of miles away.
A languor of melancholy sifted through his body, until he
felt as though he were softly dripping away. At such times
his respiration became faint, almost imperceptible; his
eyes glazed; his emotions were so nearly extinct, his desires in life so uncertain, that he might even have been
happy over the loss of the three people whom he had
loved.

His days were spent in running little errands for his aunt, in helping her with the housework, or in walking about the city. He loved hot days, with a sun that fell like blows. He would go out through the park, past the zoological gardens to the river, get himself wet and then stretch out on the bank. He said this proved that he was descended from a snake, since he was sure that a snake asked nothing more than to doze in the hot sun; it was the one witticism he ever attempted. He never read, perhaps because his father had allowed him only the best of books, and they did not interest him.

3

One afternoon on his way back from the river he stopped in the zoological gardens, an immense square edifice in the center of the park, approached by a long series of broad stone steps. It had always pleased him so that he was glad it was there, but until now it had never tempted him to enter. Now he was attracted by heavy roars. Two or three people who had been sauntering in front of the outside cages ran into the building. Matthew began taking the steps by twos.

Inside, he looked about him until he caught sight of a group of people standing before a cage at the far end of the hall. It was from that cage that the roars were coming. As he came up with the others, he saw a lion raging five feet in front of him. The animal was pacing in his den, so near the bars that when he turned, his nose scraped against the iron. With each exhalation of breath thick guttural quakings leaped from his jaws, and his loose chops trembled with the vibrations of his throat. The end of his tail twisted spasmodically; his muscles rippled with the advance of each paw. After one louder burst, the roars gradually subsided, until the final two or three were lost in his massive mouth, hardly more than a raucous natural respiration. He ceased prowling, and stood motionless, looking through the corner of his cage at a door far up the hall.

"It's nearly feeding time," somebody said; "the animals are getting hungry." A slight roar at the other end of the hall began. Slowly, mechanically, it increased in force. Most of the crowd bundled off to see the spectacle repeated, but Matthew remained behind, fascinated by this yellow mass of energy in front of him. Suddenly he caught a glance of eagerness; an attendant had appeared, carrying large buckets full of raw meat. The attendant worked down the hall slowly, shoving food into each cage in turn, and followed by a little knot of sight-seers. Now he was at the adjoining cage; a tremor of impatience flowed down the lion's back. Then the attendant was before him. Disdainful to the last, the lion retained his superiority even while being fed. He greeted the attendant with a baring of yellow fangs which gave the impression of sneering; and he snatched the meat from the iron prong with a growl, as though he were stealing it. He kept his eyes on his feeder until he had disappeared, and then began tearing the flesh from the bone by licking it with his rough, scaly tongue.

Matthew watched him until there was nothing left but two white bones. The lion mouthed at these a while, looked out at the world in general, lapped up some water splashily, took a few turns about his cage, and crawled into his little stone house for a nap—leaving as one parting intimation of his attitudes, a tail and rump protrude for the curious to feast their eyes upon.

Matthew walked away, observing the other animals as he went. There were tigers, hyenas, leopards in the same hall. Each animal recalled in him the feeling he had experienced when looking at the lion: a discomfiture at the thought that these living things were unhappy, and a yearning to inculcate into them an understanding of friendliness.

"They are all treacherous," he murmured to himself. These animals could not be petted; they would misunderstand. Or worse, even though they understood they would not care, and would treat an arm stretched to them in sympathy merely as a piece of raw meat. They would snatch at it, and devour it.

Outside, he paused before the polar bear. The poor fellow was lumbering about in his prison dejectedly, incorporating into every movement a complication of motions, as though each part of his body wanted to go in a different direction and had its own peculiar ideas of locomotion. He felt more at home before this polar bear; there was less suggestion of ferocity here. But this animal, too, was restless, nervous, like the ill-tempered lion, or the slinking hyenas. Matthew turned away.

To the right of the zoological building proper there is an abrupt hill, and at the top of this hill the smaller things are kept: peafowls, pigeons, ducks, vultures, coyotes, skunks, foxes, mountain goats, antelopes and the like. Here also, like one calm persistent note in a hurricane, a group of large white oxen added a peculiarly sweet smell to the assembled cloud of pungent stenches that rose from the cages of the other animals.

The birds were in a state of continued agitation, hopping about, trying their wings, jerking their heads, dipping for a grain of corn, peeping. The vultures and the owls, it is true, were quiet, perched stolidly with dull eyes looking out into nothing, as lonesome as dead oaks. But the ugly curve of the vultures' beaks made them more unpleasant to Matthew than even the lion had been, while the sulking owls simply left him disinterested. The coyotes, foxes and skunks were repugnant; they were as lawless as the big animals, but with none of their dignity. The antelopes and the mountain goats he liked. He laughed outright at the self-conscious buck who stood posing on his hillock, scenting the four breezes; the slope of his hillock was quite steep, and gave him much the position of a rearing horse. Head up, nostrils dilating, he held the attitude while some visitors took a snapshot, then descended immediately, as though quite aware of what they had wanted. Matthew moved on to the white oxen.

They were chewing in deliberate contentment. At times they would move their heads to look in another direction; at such times they ceased their chewing, as though disapproving of too many simultaneous motions. But once their head was firmly established in this new direction, their chewing would be resumed. Calm, harmless, sleepy, they lolled about their cage. Each movement of their body went through a graded progression: it was prepared for by an unhurried tautening of the flesh, executed with absolute assurance of the result, after which the oxen easily and imperceptibly settled down again into a state of relaxation. A bit puzzled, perhaps, by man's interest in them, they had nevertheless come to take it for granted, and dozed on secure in their knowledge that food and drink would be given to them at the right time, and that their stalls were ample protection against bad weather. Except for an occasional spring, when an unruly and unmannerly bull was let in for a time, there was nothing in the world that could trouble them; and perhaps even the bull was for the best, since there were certain vague yearnings in the spring which were strangely stilled after he had departed.

Matthew watched them for nearly an hour. Their own tranquility found a response in him. Unknown to himself he was smiling, and trying by means of his eyes to make them appreciate that he was going to love them, trying to pass over to them through the shaft of his vision some intimation of sympathy. He wanted to feed them, but was detained by the memory of the signs scattered about requesting that visitors please do not feed the animals.

But it was late; he began hurrying home. Nevertheless, he found himself taking the roundabout way past the upper reservoir, as though his new attachment demanded a more auspicious exit from the park than Negley Avenue. He came down Highland, broad and sloping, lined with the houses of the rich, and stained an aristocratic black with the drippings of automobiles. The houses allowed only glimpses of themselves through the surrounding foliage. Sober, composed, they atoned for their shallow ancestry by this willingness to remain unnoticed.

Matthew was so contented with them, that he had often been struck by a daring inspiration in passing them, a feeling that it would be quite proper for him to walk up one of those winding gravel paths, ring the bell, and ask for the master of the house. When he was ushered into the presence of that personage, he would announce modestly and quietly that his name was Matthew Carr, and that he approved of—no, not "approved of," "liked," rather, or "admired" — that he admired this house, and forthwith depart. He was sure that the personage would understand, would look at him with a mild and merry twinkle in his eye, perhaps, and say something generous in return. But such wild transgressions were only for reveries.

As he went hurrying by these houses now, their effect on him was a totally unconscious one, and contributed to his elation only in so far as they did not disturb him. He went on down Highland until the big houses were left behind, and he nearly reached the little cluster of churches north of Penn Avenue. He turned to his right into a sufficiently mediocre side street, where an occasional but dutiful poplar gasped in its struggle with city dust. Another turn to the left, and he was home. He entered the kitchen to a sizzle of frying lamb chops. Thank heavens! he was home on time. His aunt was moving about the kitchen.

4

There are only two kinds of women: those who get fat with age until they are convinced that no corset can hold them any longer, and give up the fight against nature and good eating to carry the shape of a stuffed potato sack to the grave; the other is the withering leaf kind, whose skin tightens on their bones, who eat little and sleep lightly, and whose temper with time threatens to become as sharp as their nose. Already the edges of Aunt Maggie's corsets showed across her back and below her hips, protruding like misshapen bones.

"Am I in time, Auntie?" Matthew asked, it never occurring to him that at the sound of the frying meat he had already settled that question for himself.

"Oh, here's Matthew now," she called into the dining-room where her husband was reading. "We were worried about you, Matthew. You must always be careful when you go to the river."

"I am always careful, Auntie. But I stopped at the zoo; that's what made me late." He passed on to the bathroom to wash, calling out a hello to his Uncle Charles.

Uncle Charles, as if it had been decreed that the average weight of this childless family was to remain stationary, was already displaying as many symptoms of corpulence as his wife of leanness. Although the paunch of his stomach was still small, he had acquired the fat man's way of sitting: feet close together, knees spread far apart. He sat now fingering a cigar as he read his newspaper, nervously impatient to be pulling at it; but as it dare not be lighted until after the meal, he tried to quiet himself by toying with it absent-mindedly, much the way a gluttonous baby is pacified with a blind nipple. Good-natured, interested half-heartedly in his business and passionately in the solving of rebuses, he was the kind of man who knew how to throw back his head, open his gullet, and let his stomach agitate up and down with mighty mirth. Nor was his mirth of an exacting nature, so that a good part of his waking hours was spent in pleasant upheavals of the flesh.

That evening at the supper table Matthew's noctambulism came up for discussion. He had asked permission to go to the park again. Uncle Charles looked as mysteriously wise as his pudgy cheeks would allow him, inspected his

nephew steadily through two wee eyes squeezed into mere
slits by the physical tyrannies of his merriment, and suggested slyly in a voice fraught with imminent laughter,
"Starting early, young man, eh?"

Matthew looked bewildered; he never could keep pace
with the vagaries of his uncle's willing wit. "Let's see,"
he went on; "how old are you, Matthew?"

"Nearly fifteen," Matthew answered with something
like relief; here was a straight question which could be
straightly answered.

"Nearly fifteen, eh?" the examiner continued, as though
he had trapped the unsuspecting defendant into another
compromising confession, and was on the very verge, after
one last clinching interrogation or two, of hurling his tremendous accumulation of damning testimony upon the
shoulders of his victim, an impetuous and overwhelming
blow. "When *I* was fifteen, *I* didn't go around — please
pass me another chop, Madge darling." The break was
deliberate; and those who knew Uncle Charles knew also
that when he called his Maggie "Madge darling" there was
deviltry in the air. "Matthew," he went on inexorably,
unaware that his pause, instead of producing in Matthew
the desired sweat of suspense, had merely given him an
opportunity to slip back into his own channel of medita-
tion, "do you prefer light hair, or brown?"

"I don't know, Uncle Charles. Dorothy's hair was dark,
like mine."

"Then she has light hair, eh, Madge darling?"

Madge darling looked at him with disapproval. Sitting
up more erectly, she placed her hands on her hips and
stretched her body upwards to readjust the set of her corsets. "Matthew doesn't think of things like that, Charles."

"Things like what, Auntie?" Matthew had failed to follow the conversation as much through lack of interest as
through inability. He had already become convinced that
his uncle was too deep for him, and once he had come to
this conclusion he made no further attempts to penetrate

into this cavern of forbidding profundity.

"Matthew," and now Uncle Charles employed mock thunder, making it a little less realistic than usual, however, since he allowed for the exceptional dullness of his present audience; "Matthew, I believe you are in love. Boys don't want to go to the park every morning except for one thing, to moon and coo and cuddle up. And I warn you, Matthew, I warn you. . . . If you have to marry her—"

"Charles Bowman!" a curt thrust of shrewish eyes, a glance of all-withering scorn from Aunt Maggie. "Matthew doesn't think of things like that." Matthew, now really troubled, wanted to cry, but the obligations of his fifteen years held him in check.

"I don't know any girls, Uncle Charles."

"It is awful the things you say, Charles. Matthew is a good boy. And you shouldn't say things like that; they're not funny. Let Matthew alone. He never thinks of girls."

Uncle Charles was thoroughly routed. The edge was taken off his enjoyment. But now, although the heart and soul of his little joke had vanished, it devolved upon his dignity to see the thing through. He plunged doggedly on, keeping preserved amid a woeful twitching of his facial muscles a valiant simulation of his former genuine radiancy. "If you have to marry her, Matthew, I . . . I . . ." He stopped because of a sudden terrifying discovery that the conclusion to this hypothesis had been forgotten. "Matthew," he continued the struggle, desperate but smiling, "be good to her. Do not wrong her, Matthew. It is—"

"Matthew, your uncle is making a spectacle of himself. You must not mind what he says. He means to be funny. I hope that hereafter he will succeed better. He knows as well as I that you are a good boy, Matthew, that you would never do anything wrong. And that's right, Matthew, never do anything wrong, and you'll have nothing to repent of. Always be a good boy, and above all, be good to women. Remember that your mother was a woman, and that your sister would have been a woman had our Lord so willed it, and that your aunt is a woman. Your best friend on earth was a woman, Matthew. Please, please, for your poor old aunt's sake, never do wrong. And I know you won't; I know you're a good boy. Only the other day Mrs. next-door said to me, 'Mrs. Bowman, that's a fine nephew you have.' And I know you won't, Matthew; it would be the death of me." And as she felt the big tears detach themselves from her cheeks and plunge off into space, she added, "Don't cry, Matthew, there, there, don't cry." Whereupon Matthew, who up until now had acted like a little man, unloosed the flood gates, wept bitterly and long, while Uncle Charles suspended all psychological operations, resolutely centered his whole life about the distributing of salt over his potatoes by heaping it on the end of a knife blade and gently tapping the blade. . . . After a time order was resumed, Matthew went over to his uncle, the two men shook hands and then fussed over a mechanical trick toy while Aunt Maggie brought in the dessert.

That evening when Matthew started out for the park he went a redeemed man, free of all incrimination, it being explained to his aunt and uncle exactly why he was going, and his uncle admitting frankly and openly that he believed Matthew was going for that reason. But a storm blew up, and it was two evenings later before Matthew saw his white oxen again.

5

It was a calm, moonless night when he returned to them, but the light from the stars and the boulevard lamps a few hundred feet away made it easy for him to see them. They were still out in the open, awake and ruminating, five grouped socially together, one loitering a slight distance apart from the rest. As Matthew stepped softly along the gravel path in the darkness and stopped to lean on the

railing before their cage, they adjusted their heads to observe him, found him unalarming, and forthwith forgot
him. For a time he was content with merely peering at the
half-vanishing forms. Then he began talking to them; his
voice was rich with persuasion, and though subdued it
carried through the darkness by force of the eagerness that
propelled it. But this, too, after a time, was not sufficient.
There was no bond of friendship yet established between
him and them.

He knew the one sure method of proclaiming his concern for them. He must feed them, regardless of the warnings. He remembered a clump of tall grass behind the coy-
ote shed, a patch that the lawn-mower had failed to reach.
He got this grass and shook it against the wire—for with
the white oxen a cage was a mere formality, a few feet of
light wire stretched about them. After shaking the grass a
second time, Matthew drew the attention of the lone ox,
since it happened to be nearest. It approached without
haste, but began eating as soon as it arrived. The other
oxen looked up inquisitively while it ate; finally another
came over to where Matthew was holding the grass. Then
one by one they got up regretfully, and pulled gravely at
the grass held out to them. They pressed their big blunt
noses against the wire, were unostentatiously pleased with
the fresh green food that was given them, but when it was
finished, after lingering a while like polite guests after a
dinner, they went back to the place where they had been
lying, rearranged themselves, and were as unambitious as
the dead.

Very often after this Matthew would come to their cage
in the evenings; they began to recognize him, and would
stumble up at his approach.

Once while he was feeding them, he became careless in
the handling of the grass, with the result that one of the
oxen bit his finger. He jumped away with a little cry; the
oxen were frightened, started back, and then resumed
their chewing. Matthew was not bothered by the incident,

however. He knew the ox had bitten him unintentionally.

PART TWO

1

As the summer went on, Matthew continued his trips to the white oxen. The first eagerness of his attachment had worn off, of course, but he continued his visits largely through an obligation of loyalty which he took for granted. Took for granted, since it never occurred to him that he could simply dismiss the white oxen from his life. They had entered within his horizon, and would remain there until something removed them.

This something came with the opening of high school. When one is not a ready student, it is necessary to devote much extra time to dull and mysterious books. The discovery of this was Matthew's initial realization of the ways of life. He had chanced upon it quite casually one evening when he had risen from his books, turned for his hat, and in searching for it let his eyes drop on a physics book. He had forgotten to study his physics! He suggested to his aunt with mild cynicism that dull people like himself must have a very hard time of it in life. She agreed, and called to witness a boy whom Uncle Charles had in his office. But that poor chap had only a public school education. It would be different with Matthew, if he stuck to his studies, since Matthew would always have a high school diploma to strengthen him in his struggle with the world. And perhaps Uncle Charles would even be able to send him to college, a small college, of course, but a good one . . . a good one. Matthew thanked his Uncle Charles, who admitted his good-heartedness with an embarrassed and preoccupied grunt, a grunt tempered both by his manly pudency at being anticipated in a generous act, and his resolute effort to get his prisoner out of thirty-six cells by taking him through every one once and only once.

Matthew was in his fourth year at high school before making any serious acquaintances; and his first serious acquaintance was Waldemar Jones. Jones was a tall, skinny fellow, of an ethereal build, but in retaliation he could launch forth the voice of a bull, a shout that had come to his rescue in many an argument, a grinding of heavy wheels that made the halls tremble at noontime with the decided opinions of Lowell Waldemar Jones. Universally disliked, he had already learned to carry his unpopularity masterfully by universally disliking; he wafted about him an aura of contempt in general, aided by a massive nose to sneer with and an unusually wide mouth. There might have been germs of promise in Waldemar, but at present certain features were precociously developed while others had hardly begun to exist, so that all in all he was as picturesque as a colt, and just about as established. The consequence was that Lowell Waldemar had set out at this early date to be the sunflower of erudition. An omnivorous reader, he applied his reading inexorably; he wore his learning as his archididascalus, his Lord and Saviour, Oscar Wilde, had worn his green carnation. In Ibsen he saw the protest, in Shaw the flippancy, in Chesterton the machinery of brilliance, in Wilde the perversity, in Meredith the high disdain of ordinary people, in Baudelaire the hashish—in every writer he ascertained with fine eclecticism some superficial and inconsequential fault to incorporate into the great circus tent he had stretched to draw the gaping world. It mattered little that the world did not come; he snubbed the snubbers, excluded the exclusive, and went merrily on hurling his bolts against society, a misogynist, a stormer and stresser, a belcher forth, a striker in the face, and above all—noisy, noisy. It was Lowell Waldemar Jones of all men that had been picked out for Matthew.

The meeting came about one afternoon after school hours. Matthew's Latin instructor, a Mr. Norman E. Wilsey, had detained him to help him with his Virgil. Wilsey had noticed Matthew's earnestness with his lessons, and being one of those wormy individuals who teach high school not because they have failed in something else but because the good God made them to be high school teachers, he had taken an interest in Matthew—which in Mr. Wilsey meant a sympathetic desire to help. But he was a busy man, as restless as the whiskers of a mouse, and had any number of things to attend to before he could give Matthew his attention. Just now he was discussing with another instructor his plan for some charts defending the study of Latin, while he ate the apple which pressing affairs had forced him to forego at lunch-time. Matthew was glancing at a Sallust he had picked up from the desk. Of a sudden he became aware of a disturbance; Jones was entering the room in a frenzy of haste, as violent in his movements as though struggling with some invisible adversary. Seeing that Mr. Wilsey was occupied, he walked straight on across the room, approached a window, continued his ferocious stride until he was within a step of it, and brought his elbows down on the sill with an emphatic thud. For a few seconds he stood motionless; then he moved to another section of the room, where he toyed for a while with a model of a ballista; next he examined a little case of Roman coins; from here he moved to the desk beside Matthew and could at last accomplish his object— he could see what book Matthew was fingering.

"You read Sallust?" he asked.

Matthew answered, "No, I was just looking through it."

"I wondered. It would have been most unusual to find a pupil here reading Sallust, since he is not in any of the courses. Naturally," he added, "I have read him." He went on, "Remarkably easy Latin, I find. What do you think of him?"

Matthew began patiently to repeat that he had not read Sa— but Jones interrupted: "Oh yes, beg pardon. You see, it is so hard to believe. I thought everybody had read

Sallust, just as everybody must have read Tibullus and
Athenaeus. Of course, Sallust is not an important writer,
but one has to have read him, before he can hold his head
up. He is like some of the minor Elizabethans in that
respect, don't you find?"

At this point Wilsey came over to offer his apologies; he
would not be able to keep his appointments with them this
afternoon, as a matter of moment had turned up unex-
pectedly. Matthew began preparing to leave.

"Which way do you go?" Jones asked, and when Matthew answered, he exclaimed with fine irony, "Excellent!
I go that way myself; we can continue our discussion of
Sallust." The two boys left the building together. Jones
now set about to lead the conversation before the mouth
of his mightiest cannon, religion. It was a favourite satan-
ism of his to ask his victim what faith he professed. When
the victim had answered, he would ask about the tenets.
The victim would give two or three readily enough,
stumble through a couple more if he was especially intelligent, and then, while the flame of his memory was
guttering, Jones repeated every tenet of the victim's faith.
But this was only the forerunner to the death blow, the
"No, I do not belong to your church. I am an atheist. An
atheist, you see, is a man who knows all the religions." He
was not exactly proud of this performance, but he accepted
it as an inevitable martyrdom, since he was doomed to find
only stupid people for his enemies.

But Matthew, out of the citadel of his simplicity, hurled
down at Jones a most annoying disappointment. When
asked his religion, he made an honest effort to remember,
and then admitted that he had forgotten. "I am not sure
that I had a religion. My mother used to read the Bible
to my sister and me, but my father didn't believe in
churches."

"Immense, immense!" Waldemar raised an approving
voice to the universe, although secretly disappointed.
Further, he saw that his atheist bolt would glance off with-

out effect, and let it lie back untried. "And so you don't
believe in a God?"

"I never really thought of it," Matthew answered earnestly, a bit worried. What was Waldemar to do? Here was a
quiet Philistine who tore speeches from his tongue as innocently, with the same sweet well-meaning, as a child
pulling apart the wings of a butterfly. He soon found himself defending Catholicism with all the passion of an early
father, glorifying the confessional, emphasizing the beauty
of the ceremonies, and adding—a remark which meant
nothing to Matthew—that any religion was justified which
caused the building of a cathedral.

He made a deep impression on Matthew, who surprised
him at parting by thanking him very gravely, and expressing a strong desire to become a Catholic. That day Lowell
Waldemar received from slow-moving Matthew the first
sobering influence of his life. His technique had failed
him. He was somewhat upset, filled with a sense of re-
sponsibility even. For here was a man—he liked to think
so at least—whose future existence might be radically affected by things said in a moment of idle irritation. He
decided to deliver Matthew over into the hands of a good
Catholic, and wash his own hands of him forever.

2

The next day he introduced Matthew to Edward Car-
roll, a studious, slightly myopic little fellow who went on
steadily maintaining his reputation as the best student in
the school.

"I have brought you a neophyte, Edward. *Ecce discipu-
lus tuus.* He wants to become a Catholic, and I brought
him to you as the most frightfully thorough Catholic I
know."

Edward smiled at Matthew, and shook hands. "I don't
know, Carr, but that Jones here knows more about the religion than I do. He would make a very good Catholic

in——"

"In a world of Protestants," Jones interrupted com-
placently. But he had made a good curtain remark, and
left immediately, grateful for the slight laugh Edward sent
after him.

Matthew liked Edward, and felt very comfortable in his
presence. "Do you play checkers?" Edward asked him.

"A little, but not very well. My Uncle and I play once
in a while; he always beats me."

"I am not very good at it myself. But maybe you would
be willing to come home with me this afternoon; we could
play a few games together." Matthew agreed eagerly, although he had very little interest in checkers. And he
made something like a show of spirit when the physics instructor threatened to retain him.

"I can't stay in this afternoon. Wouldn't tomorrow do
as well?" For a time it looked as though tomorrow would
not do; at last he was told that he could go home at the
regular hour.

Edward met him in front of the principal's office, and
the two boys started on their way to his home. Without
knowing it, Matthew was being lulled in a cradle of quiet
satisfaction, as when he had seen the white oxen for the
first time. The oxen crossed his brain now; he imagined
them chewing dreamily at their cuds. In another instant
they were forgotten, and he had not suspected the association which had brought them to his mind.

When they had reached his home, Edward introduced
Matthew to his mother, a large, stout woman, as homelike
as the smell of the bread baking in her kitchen. He also
met one of the older sisters, and a brother. The two boys
sat down before the fire in the parlour and played five
games, amid a desultory conversation and the interrup-
tions of Edward's mother, who kept him moving about for
this and that. Edward won three straight games, after
which he thought it best to lose the next two.

At the end of the fifth game, Matthew got up to leave,

as his aunt would be expecting him by now. Edward volunteered to walk a few blocks with him, but Matthew would not hear to it. He was glad, however, when Edward insisted on accompanying him.

3

This was the beginning of a strong mutual absorption. At times, with apparently an illogical impulse, one of them would take the other's arm; although there had been nothing in their conversation to occasion such a move, it was accepted as perfectly natural. Then their interest in Elsie Williams, a light-haired, chatty little girl who gave a second glance to neither of them, added a touch of earnestness to their talk, and gave them many a delicious spell of embarrassed half-confessions. When one of them would have a little triumph to boast of, as the way Elsie had said "Thank you" when she had returned an eraser to Edward, it was the time for magnanimous rejoicing on the part of the other, of a resolute struggle against envy, an opportunity to be noble.

Although Edward was in the parish of Sacred Heart, he would often go to the big Cathedral on Craig Street with his friend, or to the dingy old church down-town, since these were the only places, according to Matthew, where he could comprehend religion. And by comprehending religion he meant letting his eyes wander in the vaulted ceiling while the mass drummed mechanically in his ears. He liked the conflict of wood and stone, of lighted altar and shadowy pillars, of Edward kneeling here beside him and the words of the priest floating in from a distance. He was pleased that at a signal, everyone bowed simultaneously. At times he caught the far-off tinkle of a street-car bell, and he listened for the little stifled coughs that started from different corners of the congregation. But the comfortable numbness of the brain which was the characteristic of his happiest moments was gradually becoming dependent upon Edward's proximity; for Matthew there could be no greater meaning to friendship than this.

With the coming of warm days, when the snow was nearly melted, and what little remained was mixed with dirt, there was something of the quality of last autumn in the air. As Matthew's impressions of such weather were linked with the memory of his last struggling visits to the white oxen, he had a strong desire now to see them again. A series of pilgrimages began which increased with the coming of good weather. Moved by a somewhat arbitrary sense of things as they ought to be, he did not invite Edward to come with him; furthermore, there was a secret fear he would not be interested, and Matthew preferred to avoid such an issue.

One afternoon he was hurrying off to them after a miserable showing in his classes, when Edward happened to see him.

"Ho, Matthew, come along with me, will you?" he called out, and Matthew went off with his friend.

But the efficacy of the substitute took hold of him. He understood now with perfect clarity the nature of Edward's appeal. Edward was one of his white oxen! Like them Edward was peaceful, and in repose. Like them, he asked little of life. When taking his arm Matthew had experienced the same warm confidence as when the white oxen shoved their big blunt noses against the wire to eat grass from his hand. He took Edward's arm now, and gave it a little squeeze, happy with his discovery; he had found now that he loved white oxen.

PART THREE

1

AFTER graduating from high school, the two boys went in different directions. Edward started to college in another city. Matthew fought against the kindness of his uncle, who wanted to send him along with Edward; no, he was grateful for the offer, but he felt it his duty to begin supporting himself. His uncle finally agreed to get him a position in the office of a friend of his, with the result that Matthew continued on in Pittsburgh, spending his days in business and his evenings either alone or with his Aunt Maggie and Uncle Charles. He saw Edward only during vacations, and once when he had come home for a week on account of the death of a sister.

But they corresponded very regularly. Edward's letters were filled with accounts of college activities, while Matthew was content to atone for a lack of variety by repeating how much he missed his friend. Although Matthew saw in spite of himself that Edward showed little real need of him now, Matthew watched his friend's letters becoming more and more impersonal, and the protests of friendship becoming scarcer and more mechanical. Still, he could not help clinging to this first of his white oxen, and accused himself of petty jealousy for the way he watched his friend's letters.

Gradually, however, Matthew's letters became more guarded. Now that Edward needed him less, he began to feel less need of Edward. But just as the intimacy of Matthew's letters had very nearly dribbled away, at the very time when he was ready to accept it that he was alone again, something dreadful happened to him, something that seemed to him so hideous, that he was thrown back into treating Edward as being all that he had once been. For Matthew needed a confidant badly.

2

"Perhaps, Edward," he wrote, "you will wonder what right I had to be in that quarter. And I confess it, I was there for exactly the reasons your suspicions may lead you to think. It is hard, Edward—and I know you will forgive me if the words sound vulgar—it is very hard to fight down the taste of sin when you are twenty. I hope you are different. Indeed, I know you are. *You* would not be of so flabby a character. I can tell by the jolly tone of your letters that the filthy needs which have been coaxing me have not sullied you. It may be that I am a monster. If only I had a religion like you to protect me! But no, I am simply exposed to all temptation, with nothing but my shame— and even that has not been very strong!—to keep me right. There is another man like you at the office, Gabriel Harding. Sometimes I look at his kindly, care-free face and feel humbled. Why can't I be like that?" A long passage about this Gabriel Harding followed, a passage of sour comparison.

"For some time," the letter went on, "I have been walking in that quarter, just roaming about with thoughts, more mean in my yearnings than the rottenest of debauchers. It is tenderness I want, it is to cry on a woman's breast, and yet why is it that I walk *here* of all places, regardless of my desire for these beautiful things! Is it my ugliness, so that I feel that what little I touch of woman must be bought? But I can't buy what I want. Realize it, Edward, please understand me, I am not vulgar. I have walked here, I have dreamed harsh dreams about the most brutal of things, but it is something else that I want. Perhaps if I knew that a woman loved me, that would be enough; but with no woman to love me, I have nothing to lift me above horrible things. I pass men on the street, and immediately I think — what? That they are well dressed? That they are going to the theatre? That they are pleasant? No, I wonder whether they have been in those unspeakable places.

"After such nights of roaming I would return to the office the next morning to face the clean, innocent eyes of Gabriel Harding. He would look at me and smile; oh, God, would he smile if he knew what was at the bottom of me! I almost feel at times as though I were corrupting

him merely by letting him smile at me in so friendly a
fashion." Another passage about Gabriel Harding followed a passage of high praise for the happy and the
chaste.

"But my self-respect returned in the most miserable of
ways. I was walking on one of those nightly journeys, wishing, wishing, and daring nothing, when I heard a rustle,
and something like a groan. I looked, and saw a black
shape moving, huddled in a dark corner, the entrance to
an unoccupied store. The street was a dismal one, with the
lamp-posts very far apart. I went over to the dark, moving
bundle, and touched it. It was a woman! I do not want to
tell you the unpleasant details, Edward, of what followed.
Perhaps I might have gone on, but the night was chilly,
and I pitied this poor woman. When I asked her where
she lived, she was unable to tell me. I picked her up and
found her garments filthy with the spew of her stomach. I
would not tell you this, but the bitterness of what happened later is in me, and I want to say it, cruelly and brutally, how impure she was.

"Finding no evidence of an address on her, I led her
staggering and bawling to one of the 'hotels.' Yes, though
I had never been in any of them, I knew where they all
were had often stood hungrily in front of them. I remember now that I felt proud of the look the proprietor gave
me, an understanding look; he thought I was experienced
at all this. Oh, God, to think of being proud of so low an
accomplishment! That any one should want to appear
competent in such matters as these! Now I suffer for whatever squalid conceit I felt then. And I am glad to suffer;
it is a relief to call up every vile act that I have done, a
fierce retribution.

"Forgive me, Edward, and you, my unsuspecting Gabriel Harding, for what happened during the next few
weeks. For we became friends; this woman of the streets
and I became *companions!* She became to me what you
had been when we sat in the Cathedral on Craig Street.

She made me forget poor little Dorothy. And I was indifferent to Gabriel Harding, whom I had wanted before as a friend. I treated her as one of you. 'She is one of my white oxen,' I told myself. That is what I said of a woman of the streets, that is what I said—yes, I will be as inconsiderate of myself as possible—that is what I said of a whore.

"But wasn't there some justification, even so? For you must understand, Edward, that there was a great deal in our relationship to promise well. The vulgar needs of the flesh were gone from me, even without having given in to them. There was nothing impure between us. Oh, why couldn't things stay as they were then! It was a peculiar pleasure, a feeling of being more than chaste, to speak to this woman as I might have done to my mother or to one of your sisters. I loved to think of her as pure, and that thought persisted even though I knew how she was still earning her living. She was very tender to me, and cried once when I brought her some carnations; it had been many a year, she said, since any one had done that for her. How comforting it was to hear her cry, and to soothe her. 'There, there, you are one of my white oxen,' I told her. She listened very quietly while I told her of the white oxen, and kissed my poor ugly face when I had finished.

"As I look back on this time of sweetness, my remorse is almost gone. For there is nothing here to repent of, Edward. To love this woman who had been kind enough to kiss me, to seek something noble here where other men sought a moment's lust—is there anything in that to be ashamed of?

"But even then the dreadful thing was coming. Why should she have done so montrous a thing! Why should it have fallen to *her*, who was continually possessed of other men, to shatter a relationship which I could have preserved forever, although I looked at no other woman besides herself. Or if the laxity of a lifetime had told against her, so that she knew nothing of self-restraint, why should she make so hideous an advance to me? For it was so dreadful that I shall never breathe word of it, let alone place it here on the page before you. Enough to admit that it is unspeakable, that she approached me in a way that neither god nor devil had ever meant for man. And I yielded, sinking back sick with anguish, faint with voluptuosity and horror.

"I know I should never send you this letter, Edward. The vision of my depravity may turn you from me forever. But the feeling of disgust is still strong upon me. I shall never see her again, I swear. The first of my white oxen has failed me, Edward. Don't you flee from me in repugnance now as I have done from her. I need you, Edward, very much."

3

The letter was sent, and for the next few days Matthew was wretched. Would Edward answer him! He hoped at least that his old friend would think enough of their former companionship to overcome what disgust he might feel at the letter, at least to send one last note expressing that disgust. He was sorry now that he had sent the letter.

Edward, however, had dropped into the mail box a greater bomb than Matthew had feared at the height of his anxiety. When Matthew had gone with this boy of sixteen, Edward passed as one of his white oxen mainly because he was undeveloped. His future possibilities were still vague and subdued, probably owing to the awkwardness of expression that is common to adolescence. By now, however, all these possibilities were blossoming gloriously, as Edward's letter testified.

"And so, old boy, you have at last wakened up. Be cheerful; I give you my word that everybody has some such regrets the first time. You were a bit unfortunate—or a bit fortunate, whichever way you take it—in running up against a perversion the first time. It is better to evolve

gradually into that, you know. I showed your letter to a
friend of mine"—the hot blood pumped into Matthew's
face at this—"and he suggested that you read some of the
sex psychologists. You will get a new idea of these things.
He will send you a list of books, if you want it.

"And don't be too hard on the girl, Matthew. Her steady
experience in the usual way of expressing love had dead-
ened her to it. She must naturally, therefore, go a step or
two farther. Go back to her, and—if you won't get jealous
—I'll pay her a visit myself when I return for the Easter
holidays."

There was more, but Matthew did not read it. The letter went unanswered. Matthew had lost two of his white
oxen now, since Edward's congenial apostasy had wounded
him more than his affair with the harlot could ever have
done. He settled down into himself, almost resigned to expect nothing more.

But there was still Gabriel Harding.

PART FOUR

1

THE two weeks after the loss of his first white oxen had
been a graded descent into despair. He had never needed
so much as now the caress of his harlot, or the relief of
writing long letters to Edward; yet the people from whom
he should expect consolation were the very ones who had
brought on his need for it. His Uncle Charles and Aunt
Maggie realized that something had happened to their
nephew, but they both felt themselves awkward in dealing
with so mysterious an emotion as this seemed to be, and
said nothing. Aunt Maggie did, however, suggest a few
general propositions of comfort while they were at table;
we should thank God that we are alive; everything is in
the hands of a Loving Father and will turn out for the

best; we are fortunate that we have our health. Uncle
Charles fairly exploded with brave witticisms. But it was
Matthew's strained efforts to reply to each of them which
finally silenced them both.

As always had been the case with him, his unhappiness
had nothing of triumphant woe about it; there were no
wild fits of dejection. But in retaliation, it stayed with him
longer. When he awoke in the morning he had the impression that he must have been unhappy even in his
sleep. He tried to keep himself busy, since it was no longer
pleasant to let his thoughts wander. . . . This sky could
never be cleared by a magnificent downpouring of rain;
rather, the clouds would hover about until some gentle,
insistent wind, neither too warm nor too cold, came to
blow them away. Gabriel Harding, then, was to be this
gentle, insistent wind, neither too cold nor too warm.

Harding was a neat, middle-sized fellow, well up in his
twenties, with the colourless but beautifully smooth skin
which comes of a good digestion without much exercise in
the open. His forehead passed unnoticed, but his rich blue
eyes were the kindly eyes of a man of sympathies, while
his mouth bore out the impression by means of a peculiarly soft smile. A smile too soft, in fact; when he smiled to
himself while leaning over his ledger, the expression on
the lower part of his face had a touch of weakness about
it. An enemy might have called it a touch of imbecility, if
by any stretch of the imagination Gabriel Harding could
be thought of as having an enemy.

With his soft smile, he approached Matthew one evening as the two were leaving the office. "Carr, you look unhappy lately." Matthew turned questioning, unmeaning
eyes upon him, and he continued, "Perhaps I am being
too bold, but really, I—I can't stand seeing people unhappy."

Matthew struggled for something to say. He saw that
Harding thought his remarks were resented, and was about
to hurry away. He said hastily, "Thank you — thank you

very much." That was all. Harding increased the degree of
his soft smile — it had never ceased flickering about the
corners of his mouth — and went on his way without
another word.

But he had given Matthew something to think about.
For some reason or other, these few words kept returning
to him. And they served to preoccupy him in a measure,
so that his aunt and uncle agreed in whispers after he left
the table that Matthew looked like himself again.

He was no longer the incautious yearner after sympathy
that he had been. He looked back on Harding's approach
with something almost like shrewd distrust. "Thank you—
thank you very much," had been too concessional, he felt.
It was the first step towards placing his happiness again in
another's keeping. He decided to think no more of this
man. The smile had been given in all good faith—Matthew's scent for the traces of human sympathy were too
acute to deceive him there — but so had Edward's letter
been in all good faith, and her . . . but faugh! he dismissed
her. No, he would remain alone. He would learn to be
sufficient unto himself. And he would repel Harding before the man took a lasting hold on him. With this, he
started off the next morning to face the soft, welcoming
smile.

He met the smile, and . . . and answered it.

2

It had been his last protest. Matthew recognized too
well in Gabriel's smile the appeal of his white oxen.
Gabriel began taking his Sunday dinner at Matthew's
home. Then an Italian opera company stopped at the
Alvin for two weeks, and Gabriel took his friend to hear
Lucia di Lammermoor. It was an epochal evening for
Matthew; when the famous sextet was sung, he closed his
eyes, to let the weaving, intermixing voices reach him out
of the darkness. They also went to *Carmen*, where Mat-

thew was vaguely happy over the clean bravuras of the tenor, and the agile, full-throated contralto.

Although Gabriel was perfectly sincere in trying to become intimate with this "quiet, rather sentimental fellow," as he thought of him, it remained for an error to tie the final knot in their friendship. This error was due partly to Gabriel's landlady, partly to Gabriel himself. He had a couple of books which he wanted to send to a friend in another city, but he had hardly begun packing them when he noticed that he was going to be late for work. His first thought was to rush off and let the books lie there; then it occurred to him that the landlady might pack them for him if he asked her. He wrote the address on a piece of paper, laid it on his table, and stopped in the kitchen to see the landlady. She was willing enough to send the books; he told her the address was lying on the table, and rushed out. But there was also a paper on the desk containing Matthew's address, the paper which Matthew had given him the first time Gabriel was invited to Sunday dinner. The landlady saw this paper, looked no further, and sent the books to Matthew.

Although Matthew cared very little for books, he was more touched perhaps, by this useless gift than if he had received something he actually wanted. The receiving of a useless gift is tinged with gratitude that is very near to pathos. Yes, mistaken kindness is a bit pathetic, and as such often earns more gratitude than kindness well placed. As Matthew was always a prey to such naive reactions as these, he was overwhelmed with Gabriel's kindness, so overwhelmed, in fact, that Gabriel could not bring himself to explain the mistake. There was an inkling of guilt in the soft smile which Matthew did not notice; but Gabriel soon effaced this with the consideration that it is good to make someone happy, even if by mistake.

It was soon after this that Aunt Maggie began ailing. Matthew talked it over with Uncle Charles, and finally decided that if he left them it would save her a good deal of work about the house. It was decided that he take a room alone, but when Gabriel heard of this he suggested that they room together. Matthew accepted with readiness; and not long after this the two friends were snugly installed in a three-room suite, two bedrooms and a room to lounge in.

For the first weeks they were both enchanted with the arrangement. They went to work together, ate together, came home together, and spent their evenings together. Then a beautifully-smelling letter came for Gabriel, and he explained that he could not be with Matthew that night. Matthew paid a visit to his aunt and uncle. Gabriel did not get home until the next morning, but as it was Sunday, he spent the day sleeping. Matthew felt grieved at this, but as he could find no legitimate objection to make, he said nothing. Unknown to himself, he had been a tyrant in his unpretentious way, a man who demanded that things be absolutely as he wanted them. What he found disagreeable, he avoided—even if that were his last attachment in the world. But he decided that he had no right to interfere with Gabriel's comings and goings, and that he would refuse to admit any resentment. After all, it was his own fault if he could not offer Gabriel enough to keep them continually together.

Another point was Gabriel's love of reading. Although Matthew had very little to say, he loved to have someone near him to whom he *could* say something if he wanted. But when Gabriel was reading—and he read so much!— Matthew felt singularly left out. Once or twice he had tried to start a conversation. At first he received polite responses, and later responses that were plainly impatient. This again Matthew accepted.

There were other things, more difficult to deal with, as the time when Gabriel had suddenly looked up from his book at Matthew, who was lying vacant on the lounge, and said, "I say, Matthew, you *are* a simple soul, aren't you?" What had he meant? And why had he said it on such an occasion, for no apparent reason? Matthew felt there must be something almost mysterious about his friend, some side of him which he had never seen, and never would see. Those fits of petulance, when Gabriel would hurl something across the room!—Matthew felt somehow that he was the cause of them. After such outbursts, however, there was always a period of renewed warmth, so that Matthew was almost glad of these outbursts. His friend excused himself on the ground of nervous headaches; Matthew was grateful for the excuse, although he suspected that it was not true.

The fact was that Gabriel had begun to be irritated by Matthew. He sensed the dog-like fidelity behind his friend, and it irritated him. But he was ashamed of his own irritation. It seemed to him that he owed Matthew kindly treatment, so that he always felt humiliated after an outburst. But this humiliation, which made things lovely for a few days, was only the germ of another outburst. In order to be on better terms with Matthew, he contrived to see him less often.

The trouble with Gabriel was that he had a refined sensitive equipment, but that he was thoroughly shallow. Such people are given to short-lived enthusiasms, with an acute need of variety. And Matthew of all men was incapable of giving variety. He was a lover of established order, asking nothing more of life than that things remain as they were.

Nevertheless, there were times when the interest that had brought them together originally became operative again, and Gabriel smiled his soft smile. Matthew would forget all the past difficulties between them in the sudden rediscovery that here was one of his white oxen, harmless and kindly. The two would spend glorious evenings together.

3

After about two months, something happened which finally brought the soft smile into its own. Gabriel had been looking troubled for the last few days, and often seemed on the verge of confessing something to his roommate. Although Matthew had tried to make it as easy as possible for him to speak, he had said nothing. The culmination came when he was seen walking into the manager's private office, with the soft smile struggling weakly; he came out again with the smile completely gone. While eating with Matthew that evening he said very little. But after they were back in their rooms he began to stammer out his predicament.

He wanted to tell Matthew the absolute truth, and yet, in spite of himself, with an illogical shame in explaining to him things which he was not ashamed of, he changed some of the details. The start was sincere enough: he needed money, and had made an unsuccessful attempt to get an advance on his salary; he had asked for thirty dollars of the amount that was not due him for ten days. When he intended to go on and explain just how the receiving of beautiful-smelling envelopes can cost money, he suddenly felt disinclined. Another excuse was just as good, and the important thing was *that* he needed money, not *why* he needed it. He found himself inventing against his will the tale of a needy friend. But he was right in his conjectures: Matthew stopped him in the middle of his lying with a cry that he would get him the money. Gabriel was a bit humbled by this; he opened his mouth to tell everything as it really was, but no words came. Matthew went into his own room, returning with a number of bills in his hand.

"I can give it to you immediately," he said, and threw on the floor with a mock-millionaire gesture a sum of ten times the amount asked for.

"What are you doing with all that here, man?" Gabriel seemed almost savage at his friend's stupidity. "Why don't you take it to a bank? Great heavens, who ever heard of a person having so much money in his room!"

Matthew explained that he had been saving ever since he began to work, and had kept the money in his Uncle Charles' safe. Uncle Charles himself had suggested that he take it to a bank. He had brought back the money with this intention, but he simply hadn't deposited it yet. Gabriel snapped out the advice that Matthew get the money safely behind steel doors as quickly as possible. But Matthew was incorrigible; he went on to defend himself, and before Gabriel could stop him had told him where he kept it, appealing to him whether a thief would ever think of a place like that. He was a bit bewildered by Gabriel's anger, but secretly pleased that his friend should be so concerned about him. For the rest of the evening, Gabriel was weak and nervous. He had taken his thirty dollars with hardly more than a dutiful "Thanks."

The soft smile had come into its own; that night he stole the money. For hours he had lain awake, fighting resolutely to fall asleep. Then he caught himself listening to the rise and fall of Matthew's breathing. He knew what that meant! But even as he crept into Matthew's room, he did it with a feeling of faith in himself, a consolation that he might be able to go so far as to touch the money and yet return without taking it. He touched the tin box, and his fingers closed about it through mere reflex action. As he sneaked back with it out of the room, the hope that he would not take it was stronger than ever. He trusted that in some stage of the theft a new emotion would come over him, some totally different current which would enable him to return the box to its hiding place with every dollar still in it. The key was in the lock. He turned it softly and raised the lid. The money was darkly visible, illuminated indirectly by the faint reflection from his white nightshirt of an arc-lamp out on the street. As he caught sight of the bills nestling there in the shadows, a sudden resentment came over him. Why had this man been so stupidly incautious! He began to dress himself, trembling not so much through fear as through the excitement of the unusual situation. This was no time to pack his things; he would take only the clothes he wore. Softly, he took out the money, and tiptoed back into Matthew's room to put the box where he had found it. This might delay the discovery of the theft. How deeply the man slept! He felt there was something brutish about such solid slumber. . . . Perhaps he might not leave at all, but simply throw the box out the window, and set up a clamour; Matthew would never accuse him. But no, he couldn't face Matthew after this. He came back into their common room, picked up the money, and started for the door. Then he returned to Matthew's room, got the box again, and left it lying open on the table. He wanted Matthew to understand immediately. He could not bear the thought that his friend would get up the next morning, find him gone, and begin a faithful worrying as to his whereabouts, without suspecting that he was a thief. For Matthew would never think of the money. The thought hurt, and filled him with admiration for Matthew. He wanted to press his friend's hand, to throw his arms about his neck and hug him. He pitied Matthew, since he realized how much the loss of a friend would mean to him. As for the money, Gabriel knew that if he had asked for it all it would have been handed over to him. He could have had it for the asking, and yet he was stealing it! . . . As he closed the door, he was resentful again. His actions would be misunderstood; they would be taken merely as actions, with no appreciation of the generous emotions he had experienced in doing them. He, Gabriel Harding, was to be the wronged party.

Matthew slept on, unaware that the last of his white

oxen had failed him. But he still had the white oxen themselves.

PART FIVE

1

DECIDEDLY, Matthew Carr was a reliable man. Of good health, he came to the office regularly, and discharged his duties with a gratifying rigidity of scruple. The important thing was that he was steady, a quality which was much more valuable in routine work than wide-awake business acumen. Given something to do, and told how to do it, Matthew was sure to do it satisfactorily.

The other clerks in the office wondered a bit that Matthew said nothing about Harding's disappearance, since the two men had been noticeably intimate. But in the last analysis they accepted it as one more evidence of his quiet nature, and thought no more about it. As a consequence, Matthew never had any explanations to invent, and the secret of the theft remained undisturbed. He came to the office and returned to his room, evidently too wearied to be called sullen, and too meek to be called cynical.

He was now twenty-five, and was under no other obligations than those of eating and sleeping. He expected nothing, and received nothing. When he looked about him, he saw jackals and coyotes where he had once seen white oxen. But he looked about him very seldom. People had no more meaning to him than the pavements he walked on. Matthew was paying now for his lack of clear vision, the inability to learn, by looking at people, what he must not ask for in life. His only way of learning what he must not ask for had been to ask for it, and ask for it with complete assurance that it would be granted him. The result was that his lesson had become an organic part of him, as much an instrument in the conducting of his life as his heart or his lungs. What most people learn of humanity in

a good-natured glance of the eye, he had to acquire labori-
ously by the cudgelings of experience itself. His life had
been the gradual closing up of a shell which was never
quite open.

But there was one attachment left; there were the white
oxen. They, at least, had remained stationary.

2

How good it felt to walk up the long stone steps to the
zoological building, to go around it to the right, past the
cages of the squirrels, up the wooden steps, and out among
quackings, peepings, and flutterings of the birds. They
would be there, down to the left now, in that cage next to
the self-conscious old buck who had posed for the camera
the first day he had been there. Already he could see the
mound where the buck had stood. He became impatient.
He wanted to run down the gravel path. But no; he would
tease himself. He continued his slow gait, almost exagger-
ated it, in fact, He caught the smell of the smaller animals
off to the right. It seemed like a very short time since he
had been here, although it was nearly ten years. Everything was the same. He peered ahead through the haze of
wires to catch sight of his oxen, but they were not visible.
Lying down, perhaps, for the thought never occurred to
him that they might not be there.

A few more steps, and he was in front of the cage. He
glanced about him, recaptured all the past memories at
one switch of the eye. And sure enough, his old friends,
the white oxen, were lying negligently about their cage, so
oblivious to the passage of ten years that they were even
chewing the same cuds.

Of course, they had forgotten him. Two of them looked
at him without concern, and then let their eyes roam on
past to wires, posts, and cages. He meant nothing to them.
But that didn't matter; tonight he would return and feed
them.

He did return, and in a short time the old commerce was restored. They came to recognize him, and rubbed their blunt noses against the wire. He talked to them; they were the one thing on earth that loved tranquility as he did. They looked upon life without question, accepted it with a liquid mind, the way he himself would have done had he been permitted.

One evening as he was feeding the oxen, another human form approached him. As it came nearer, Matthew saw it was a guard. And he expected trouble, since he knew that it was not permitted to feed the animals. But the guard was remarkably considerate, with none of the gruffness usual to petty officials. He struck up a conversation about ordinary things; it was fully five minutes before he came to the matter of the feeding.

"You see, young man," he explained, "it isn't allowed. I've watched you here, and I know you mean all right, but you're liable to be hurting the oxen. All feed is given here scientifically, at certain times of the day, and in certain quantities. So you may be actually harming the oxen by doing this." Matthew agreed to quit. He had never thought of it that way. Perhaps he was killing his old friends!

That was the last time the oxen received grass from his hands. Thereafter, he simply stood before their cage and watched them. It hurt him to see the animals come to greet him at his approach, shove up their noses in expectancy, and finally tired of waiting, return to their favourite lying places, noticing him only now and then with a look of silent rebuke. But it hurt worse the night he returned and only two of them came up to meet him. The next evening not a single one arose; they simply turned their heads in his direction, let their eyes rest on him a moment, and then shifted them stolidly away. He was deserted. Half in earnest, he puckered up his lips, and explained to them in human speech just what was the trouble. But to them, grass was the only way of settling the matter. He determined to feed them just once more, went for the grass, and returned without it. He stood for a long time, looking from one dimly outlined form to another. He rustled the wire, and as they looked up hopefully he was humbled by the cheapness of his ruse. He turned away, and walked slowly down the path. Without consciously guiding himself he continued straight ahead after the path had stopped, crossed a slight grassy slope to the boulevard, crossed the boulevard, and found himself looking down over the bluff into the valley below. It was all like ten years ago. The lights lined the shores of the river, and thinned away as the river serpented off into the blackness of the hills. To the left he saw the steel mills of Millvale and Etna, with their quick flames licking at the sky. Hundreds of feet below him, a cluster of lights was moving regularly with the current. He stood motionless, letting his eyes roam over these miles and miles stretched out beneath him. . . . And of a sudden a feeling of promise came over him, the hope of a boy of sixteen who sees a vision of futurity, of the world before him. He felt an acute interest in what life might have in store yet, a trust that there was going to be a great change, a faith in the proximity of some new vista. For a few moments he was rich with this unreasoning fore-taste of conquest.

Then it was gone, leaving him almost physically weakened. He thought again of his white oxen there behind him. They had none of these painful tilts with life; to them the supreme gift of God was to sleep and know that one is sleeping. He yearned to see things with their dull, slow-blinking eyes, to retire into their blissful sloth of semi-sensation. He yearned to be one of these white oxen —he, the purest of his white oxen.

THE EXCURSION

THE EXCURSION

HAVING nothing to do, and having searched in vain among the notes of a piano for something to think on, I started off on a walk, trusting that I might scent a scandal on the breeze, or see God's toe peep through the sky. I passed a barber shop, a grocery store, a little Italian girl, a chicken coop, a road-house, an abandoned quarry, a field of nervous wheat. All this distance I had walked under God's blue sky, and still without a thought. But at last, after trudging on for hours, I came upon a thought. Miles upon miles I had walked for a thought, and at last I came upon an ant hill.

Idly curious, I stopped to look at the ants. They would go from one place to another and return to that first place again, and for no reason that I could see. Little ants with big burdens, big ants with bigger burdens, and ants with no burdens, the most frightened and panicky of them all. As I watched them they seemed so human to me that my heart went out to them. "Poor little devils," I said.

But I grew tired of watching the swarming mass of them. "I shall watch just one of them," I said to myself after much deliberation. And I picked out one frightened little ant to watch. He went running about unaware of my presence, not knowing that a great god was looking down on him, just as I did not know but that a great god might be looking down on me. And with the toe of my shoe I marked out a rut in his path, so that he had to climb over it. And then I began dropping little bits of sand on him, and turning him over with a blade of grass. "I am his destiny," I whispered; the conception thrilled me.

As the poor little fellow rushed about in terror, I realized how massive his belief in life must be at this moment, how all-consuming his tragedy; my pity went out to him. But my blade of grass was too limber; I picked up a little stone to push him with. I drew a circle. "May God strike me dead, little ant, if you get out of that circle." I took that oath, and the battle was on. It was long and uncertain, with victory now on his side, and now on mine.

The little ant, in a last despairing burst, made for the edge of the circle, and crossed it. I was aroused. "I'll kill the ant," I shouted, and brought the stone down on his body, his passions, his dreams. Destiny had spoken. For an instant I was ashamed, for I had been unfair. He had beaten me under the terms I had made myself. I should have let him go free.

I began watching other ants. They irritated me—they were so earnest, so faithful. Two ants came up and touched. I wondered what that could mean. Do ants talk? Then I watched one of the ants which had touched the other to see if it touched still other ants. For it might be a herald of some sort; perhaps ants do talk.

One little ant was tugging and pulling at a dead bug. Slowly, carefully, I took my stone and drew it over two of his legs, so that he was wounded grievously, and began writhing in agony. My face was distorted with compassion; how my heart bled for him!

I ran the stone across his other legs, and the motion was like a thrust into my own flesh. I was almost sick with pity for the poor little ant, and to end his suffering I killed him. Wide regret came on me. "Perhaps," I thought, "perhaps, he was a poet. Perhaps I have killed a genius."

And I began stepping on the other ants, digging up the ant hill, scattering destruction broadcast about me. When my work was finished, and only a few mangled ants remained alive, my sorrow for the poor little ants had grown until it weighed on me, and crushed the vitality out of me. "The poor little ants," I kept murmuring, "the poor, mis-

erable little ants." And I was bitter with the thought of
how cruel the universe is, and how needlessly things must
suffer. I stood gazing at the death and slaughter about me,
stupefied with calm horror at what I had done. I prayed
to God.

"O Great God," I prayed, throwing back my head toward Heaven and stretching out my hands like Christ on
the Cross, "O Great God"—but I didn't really throw back
my head, for I still kept looking at the ants, and I did not
address God, for at times I even wonder if there be no
God. I didn't do these things, I say, since I was too intently watching the ants. "O Almighty God," I thundered out
in mighty prayer, throwing back my head toward Heaven
and stretching out my hands like Christ on the Crucifix,
"Thou who art Ruler of us all. Now I know why we suffer,
and ache, and I pity Thee, God."

A MAN OF FORETHOUGHT

A MAN OF
FORETHOUGHT

I

CARTER admitted it to himself: his hand was trembling. For after all, there was no reason why he shouldn't admit it; and there was no reason why his hand shouldn't tremble. He was to decide a woman's destiny today, and the woman was atrociously good-looking.

As he stood with his eyes fastened on the dull little penny that lay in his quivering palm, Carter mused poetically on the idea that a mere penny would decide his fate. Any number of people had thrown caution to the various winds when tempted by an obese wallet; he even remembered having read a touching tale of a girl's having gone astray for a pair of shoes; but here he was, the prince of all lost souls, following the dictates of a penny.

Perhaps he had better make it the best out of three tosses. After all, one lone final toss was too sudden, too brutal almost. It was like having the electric light switched on when one had been dozing in the dark. It was like trying to step up one more step than there was, and getting oneself disturbingly jolted. The little penny, as it lay head upright before him, shouted its commands at him, and he resented it. By heavens, he *would* make it the best out of three tosses!

Still, that was unfair, both to himself and the penny. He had sworn on the Blue Book that it would be one toss, and only one. Very well, he would compromise.

He opened the second drawer of his desk and took out a pack of cards. If an ace turned up within the first eleven cards he would take three tosses instead of one.

He shuffled the cards nervously; in his excitement he dropped a couple. They fell face up on the floor, and he saw that one was an ace. He had a sneaking temptation to put it on the top of the deck and begin dealing, but one last spark of manhood held out, and he shuffled the ace out of knowledge into the pack. Then he began dealing.

The fifth card was an ace. He breathed easier. Now he was entitled to two more tosses of the coin.

He took a glance at himself in the mirror and decided that the pallor caused by this excitement made him very handsome. He gave his hair an unnecessary stroke or two. Then he steeled himself for the second toss.

"As before, heads—yes, tails—no; get ready, get set, one, two, three, go!"

The penny sailed high into the air, clinked against the ceiling, fell promptly and rolled under the piano. Carter strained himself to get it out without bagging his trousers. Good—it was tails.

He had earned an intermission. He poured himself a generous drink of his favorite cognac. He paused a bit. Then, made more courageous by the alcohol, he picked up the coin and threw it on his little mahogany *gueridon* with a magnificent carelessness.

Done!

"In God we trust . . . Liberty . . . 1916 . . ." and the serene profile of Abraham Lincoln with his eyes seeking the decanter of cognac.

John Carter cursed *pianissimo*. But his fate was decided —absolutely. Destiny had spoken; and poor dear Clarisse must pay the penalty. For it is the woman who pays; it is not the tempting man but the tempted woman who must suffer. Carter was decidedly comforted by repeating to himself this beautiful commonplace.

But he must act immediately. He knew only too well

his deucedly cautious nature. He rushed to the phone and told the operator in the corridor of the apartment hotel to call a taxi. Then he added a few feverish touches to his toilet.

He reflected with a certain relief that this half-affair between himself and Clarisse was to be settled at last. It had hung on for years now, ever since long before her marriage. Of course, it was a miserable thing to do to Dick. But he had had too much consideration for Dick already. Beginning with the days he had pulled Dick through his Latin at prep school, and ending with his noble stupidity of coming all the way from Italy to be best man at their wedding, Carter's life had been one long list of self-sacrifices for Dick.

Bosom friend or no bosom friend, Carter had at last decided to obey the commands of the tossed penny. He was desperately in love with Clarisse, so much so that he had taken all his other women off the mantelpiece. And such an absorbing love, that might some day spoil his appetite, deserved expression.

The phone rang. Carter swung around with a frightened jerk, and overturned a pile of music. He snatched the receiver.

"Taxi? Yes, be right down. What? No? Oh, pshaw! Tell him I'm not at home." He slapped down the receiver and began picking up the music. He was shaking all over.

"Damn it, I'm too nervous," he muttered. "I'll force myself to be quiet. I'll play something, something of my own, something very gentle. But I have nothing very gentle. I don't turn out things like that. Let's see, there is a soft little thing of Debussy's. But all the little girls play that now after they're through with the 'Dance of the Witches' and 'Snowy Dewdrops.' Grade 3A. The devil. There is a lovely little minuet in one of Beethoven's sonatas. The old masters, something with good solid harmonies . . . that's what I want. Perhaps a good-humored bit of Haydn. Perhaps. . . ."

The phone rang. It was the taxi. He rushed out of the room. What luck, what divinely auspicious luck. . . . he just caught the elevator. Evidently everything was going to go well. He tumbled hastily into the cab and almost whispered the address to the driver. The man looked at him sharply, as though he understood. The insolence! Carter felt himself getting angry. What was the ass waiting for?

"Hurry. I am in a dreadful hurry. I will make it worth your while."

"East or West?" the driver asked.

Oh, so that was the trouble? In his precipitancy he had merely neglected to say which side of Fifth Avenue. How ridiculous of him to get angry when it was all his fault.

"East," and the taxi was off.

As he was jolted about in the capricious taxi, he tried to form some definite plan of action. For decidedly he was a man of forethought. It wouldn't do to stumble in abruptly, drop on his knees, and blubber out "I love you." Yet, on the other hand, this very suddenness might be effective; women are often highly susceptible to that sort of technique. Still, if he began immediately with these sudden tactics, it might lead to something embarrassing. He had better delay until he had made sure no one was there besides Clarisse. It would be just as well, after a mysterious silence, after five minutes of vague and absent-minded conversation, to be *then* transformed into a passionate whirlwind.

But about this "I love you." Here was a problem which always kept turning up, and for which he had never found a solution. Does a phrase, when applied to these ultimate issues, gain by being so hopelessly banal, or does it lose? Women aren't so particular about the brand-newness of a sentence as men are. They are more taken with the impetus of it, and an "I love you," said quiveringly enough, was probably the best one could do. They like to think one is speaking the eternal sentence; it lends a certain cosmic air to their love. Just as the little birdies and grasshoppers have chirped the same love-chirp for centuries and centuries, so this poor man, prostrate before them under the heavy burden of this ultimate issue, must make the same noise as his ancestors, the same meagre succession of syllables must trill from his love-thick tongue.

II

THE taxi, getting suddenly clear of all traffic impediments, took a short spurt, and the realization that he was nearing Clarisse so swiftly stirred up a little panic in Carter. When he had calmed down a bit, he resolved to be less practical in his meditations; he grew ashamed of their cold-bloodedness. He huddled himself into an amorphous jostled mass, and let his mind wander back to the more idyllic phases of their attachment.

The various attitudes he had gone through had purified him, he decided. For the first few months after their marriage he had refused loyally even to lift his eyes to her; he had tried to get her out of his thoughts. What a noble time that had been!

First, in the vain effort to forget her, he had written, and published at his own expense, a book of essays on his travels in Italy, but only to spoil it all by the pregnant dedication, "To C."

Then he had become more desperate, and more noble, and sought distraction among the vulgar beauties of the stage. He was nearly succeeding when his funds theatened to give out, and he was thrown more inexorably than ever into the clutches of his dolorous love for Clarisse.

Then Dick had got it into his good-natured stupid old head that Clarisse and Carter should see more of each other. Carter told him outright that Clarisse troubled him —*intrigued* him, as the Café de la Paix would put it—but the man had simply laughed, and felt a little flattered. Carter thought him a charming ass, but he said no more about it.

Then came the day when Carter saw her with a head-ache, a neat little white cloth tied about her temples. He had tightened his jaw with the sudden realization of how inevitable she was to him. He was proud of the feelings he had had towards her then, for there had been a note of decided Christian cleanness. He had simply wanted to kiss her on the forehead, to advise her, to smoke big cigars and tell her things. It was a period of uprightness, during which he had maintained the most loyal of attitudes towards her and Dick. And most important, it was an excuse for everything that might follow.

But alas, it had only been a period of transition. Slight touches of her skirt as she whisked by him, her smile, the way she said "no," the night she hurt her ankle and leaned against him—these things had contrived to change him. He wished he could have remained the big brother he had once felt himself to be. But things had turned otherwise, until now . . . he noticed with a shock that the taxi had turned into her street.

Another three minutes! Why did he breathe so? There was no danger. Dick was sure to be away, and even if he were at home there were excuses enough. Another two minutes!

The vividness of the prospective scene renewed his zeal. He saw himself drop down before her, and take her hands, and kiss them . . . kiss them. For once in his life he would be wild, incautious. Perhaps it would stir him into a different sort of life, a careless, vicious existence with a maximum of dash, far from his neat apartment with its cut glass, its quiet rugs and mahogany. Perhaps he could write a novel about it. Perhaps . . . another minute!

He saw himself there on his knees, pleading. It was a delightful morsel to dwell upon. But had she been prepared to love him? Had she gone through a period of resolute indifference, then brave sisterhood, then metamorphosed gently into a woman ripe for the love of him? Perhaps she would feel a monstrous disgust at his advances, and turn away from him with scorn, as from something evil and filthy. Or perhaps she would be wounded, deeply wounded, at the insult he offered her, and would run away from him, frightened and whimpering. She was a good girl, and faithful to her husband. He had no right to expect such unworthy things of her. . . .

There was the house now, the one with the colonial portico. What he had been thinking of was impossible. She was not the sort of woman who yields to other men. The calm, smooth life she led permitted of nothing irregular, nothing out of the way. . . . The taxi stopped.

"Drive through Central Park."

"Yes, sir." The driver's voice was puzzling, as though he took a personal interest in all these numerous scandals which he drove people up to and away from. The taxi leapt ahead.

Crushed! Eternally a man of forethought! Carter was thoroughly sick of himself, as if he were a disagreeable food in his own stomach. He would get drunk. Drunk, faugh! What right did he have to get drunk? Drink is for those whose lives are of sharp edges and deafening crashes. The souls that are impelled to drink climb craggy mountains and topple into abysses that are dizzy, very dizzy. For Carter there was nothing; he was ever a man of careful, deliberate, painstaking forethought. He had had the forethought to see that Clarisse was unattainable; he must pay the penalty with his endless mediocrity of action. . . .

Two days afterwards Dick came rushing into Carter's room, savagely drunk.

"She's gone!" he screamed. "The harlot! She deserted me; she's run off with a movie actor!"

Carter promptly left his room, bought a revolver and some cartridges, loaded the revolver, put it to his head and, being a man of forethought, didn't shoot himself.

MRS. MAECENAS

MRS. MAECENAS

1

Ego vox clamantis in deserto.
WORDS OF ST. JOHN

AFTER many years of faithful service, the professor had
become president of the university, taken him a somewhat
scandalously younger wife, and died, leaving a string of
pompous titles to the wind, and a flourishing widow over
thirty to the world. The wife of the head of the physics department, who was usually well up on such things, had prophesied that the president's widow would soon quit the
little town for ever, but contrary to expert opinion, she
continued living in the same house, nay, even maintained
her former connections with the university. The unex-
pressed consensus of opinion was that this woman was too
charming to be beyond suspicion, but yet her scutcheon
was radiant with blotlessness. Propriety had been observed
with a rigidity that was perhaps even a bit dogmatic, as in
the case of her dismissing the chauffeur. And besides, she
was left with a little girl, which was even more reassuring.

After the fitting period of black, and another fitting
period of subdued colours, she gradually drifted into a
superbness of attire which was perhaps not quite so fitting,
but was still within the code. For she never appeared again
in *smart* clothes; in fact, even the most unfriendly had to
admit that she was almost matronly. A big-busted woman,
she carried herself with firm dignity, and talked with a
Southern accent in a voice that was rich and deep, and
might even indicate that she had once been an instructress
in elocution.

Within two years after her husband's death, she had acquired a unique position in the life of the university. There were fussy young girls who, as the expression goes, just idolized her. She was the unfailing chaperon at all school functions, since she had succeeded in the difficult task of both entering in with the feelings of the students and yet making them remember that she was not one of them. If she appeared at any of the games, the students, at a sign from their cheer-leader, would doff their caps, and cheer for her. There is no greater tribute to her tact than the fact that she was honorary head of both the Athenian Literary Society and the Society of Fine Arts, two organizations which were always facing each other with backs hunched and teeth bared. It was as patroness of these two organizations that she acquired the flattering nickname of "Mrs. Maecenas." For of all her interests in student activities, her guidance of "the arts" had been most faithful.

In the course of her five years at the university Mrs. Maecenas had judged twelve debates on the single tax, fifteen on the inferiority of women to men, and nine on various phases of prohibition, state, national, and locally optional; and to her credit be it said that her verdicts were not always the same on the same subjects. Mrs. Maecenas had read a gross of horror stories that had received good grades in English Composition 22, and were written after the manner of Edgar Allan Poe; and another gross or two that had been cribbed from O. Henry. Mrs. Maecenas had gone through thousands of rhymed documents on pubescent and adolescent affections, still in her capacity as a protectrice of the arts. And when the war started, and a big man in the German department had called the French a degenerate nation, Mrs. Maecenas had written a charming letter to the school paper in which she denounced the Huns and spoke very beautifully of modern French poetry.

But the truth is that Mrs. Maecenas was getting weary. She had seen ten semesters of the university, and her hopes of mothering a little renaissance out here in the wilderness had gradually pined away as the engineering and agricultural schools grew steadily more vigorous. Everywhere, everywhere, typical young Americans were springing up, sturdy tough daisy-minds that were cheerful, healthy, and banal. How could art thrive here, she asked herself, in a land so unfavourable to the artist's temper! These lusty young throats that cheered her at the football games, they were miserably sane and normal. And Mrs. Maecenas found herself entertaining uncharitable feelings towards these fine young men and women who thought so much of her.

Under the plea of ill health, she began to appear less at school festivities. Also, her child was getting older now, and the need of giving it more attention added motivation to her retirement. She became less kindly in her opinions of the stories and verses she was given to criticize, until this burden had decreased almost to a total nullity. As a consequence, within another year Mrs. Maecenas was hardly more than a widow with a little daughter. An occasional attack of her old weakness for genius-hunting would lure her now and then to one of the literary clubs, but she usually returned from them with such a feeling of exhaustion and disgust that she wondered how she ever could have stood it.

Mrs. Maecenas settled down to be the voice of one whispering very quietly in the wilderness. The great machine of the university could dump its annual output of standardized "leaders of America," could ship them off every commencement day labelled "with all the advantages of a college education"; the alumni could put up a sun-dial or a gate, or an iron railing, every year in sacred memory of their dear Alma Mater; the great auditorium could tremble with cheering and shouting when big Dick Halloway, handsome blond-haired Dick, the hero of the university, shot the winning goal; all this could go on if it would— but Mrs. Maecenas got farther away from it all, and nearer

to her books and her piano. The university became health-
ier, and she quietly blushed for the future of America. . . .

And then it was that her genius came. By the purest
chance she had gone to the Athenian meeting. She found
the room peculiarly astir. Little groups were talking quite
low together, glancing now and then towards one corner
of the room. In this corner, with his back turned towards
the members of the Athenian, a rather gawkily formed
young man was reading a yellow paper-covered volume
which Mrs. Maecenas recognized to be a French novel.
There was a slight smell of whiskey in the room.

Mrs. Maecenas knew she had found her genius. Yet at
this time Siegfried was barely seventeen.

2

*Ecce quam bonum et quam jucundum
habitare fratres in unum!*

PSALM 132.

Siegfried presented himself at the home of Mrs. Maecenas late the following afternoon. He was just as gawkily
formed as the night before, and another yellow-covered
book was in his hand, but his breath this time smelled
strongly of coffee-beans. In spite of the coffee-beans, however, Siegfried had had no more whiskey; with peculiar
astuteness in these matters, he had realized that it would
probably be a false step to exhale the same shocking odour
of the previous night; but on the other hand, to exhale the
standard destroyer of this odour might give the precisely
proper variation. Siegfried selected his breath with as
much care as less imaginative souls give to their neckties.
The door was opened by the widow herself.

"Mrs. Maecenas, I believe?"

"Oh, Siegfried, won't you come in?" She had always insisted on calling the students by their first names.

He stepped into a dark reception hall, and then followed her to the left into her library, Mrs. Maecenas having dispensed with the small-town parlour. "I am very glad you came to see me, although . . ." and here she laughed with her widow roguishness, "although I'm not so sure that I ought to be."

Siegfried was startled. He had not hoped to be taken so freely. But he skimmed the cream of the occasion, and cast away the yoke of his youth in the quality of his equals-to-equals answer, "Throw all caution, etc., I implore you, Mrs. Maecenas, and be less churchly and more Christian. I have come to you as a last hope; deliver me from this American captivity." He began looking over her books without further formality. Mrs. Maecenas sat down tentatively on the piano stool, facing away from the piano, and her two arms stretched back on the keyboard.

"Your remarks might lead me to conclude that you are not an American yourself, my dear boy, but nevertheless I'll risk my life that you, like me, were raised under the tutelage of the chopped-down cherry tree." At this Siegfried turned suddenly, like an ill-tempered dog.

"Ugh! My father was an alumnus of this university. Is that credentials enough?" And then just as suddenly cherubic again: "But you have them all, every one! I might think I was by the Pont Neuf."

"The books? Yes, and I should be pleased to lend them to you, if you should ever want any of them."

"And no George Sand! And no Sandeau! And no Bourget! Why, Mrs. Maecenas, I am in the library that *I* shall own some day. Oh, please let me come here, in this modern *thébaïde,* in this elevation above the chewing-gum and sarsaparilla of our beloved country men. God bless them, they have carried their Monroe Doctrine into culture. And what a beautiful set of Flaubert!"

"Shhh! *Et les bouquins! Viens!*" With mock caution she led him by the hand to a corner where something square was standing, covered with a drapery of dark purple. She lifted this slowly, disclosing another bookcase. "Popery!"

And she slipped out two heavy breviaries, with black leather bindings, and rich gilt edges. She opened one of them at random, and displayed a beautiful front of red and black, with illuminated capitals. Then she pointed to a Dutch edition of Boethius' *De Consolatione Philosophiae,* in the russet-leather of the seventeenth century. There was the Vulgate in five volumes, the *Peristephanon* and *Psychomachia* of Prudentius; Siegfried's eyes followed her hand as it brushed along the books. "I must admit," she said, "*I* did not collect these. They were my husband's. We spoke of them in secret, as though they were the limbs of a child we had pulled apart and stuffed up the chimney." There was also a copy of Huysmans' *Sainte Lydwine de Schiedam* in Gothic type, Remy de Gourmont's critical anthology of mystic Latin verse, and Saint François de Sales's *Introduction à la Vie Dévote* in a paper cover of ludicrously innocent blue.

"Popery, bah!" Siegfried exclaimed. "The de Gourmont gives you away. And that, down in the corner, that Petronius! Madam, you are a pagan, for who but a pagan would own such lovely tomes? Nay, you are worse than a pagan; you are a lover of art. I am scandalized. I shall expose you before the world!"

Mrs. Maecenas laughed. "Art was once loved; then it was tolerated; and now it will soon be prohibited, so that we must express our devotion to it in secret, deep in the catacombs. Those are, more or less, the words of de Gourmont. And so you must come here often, Siegfried, and we shall kneel together before the clandestine altar."

After this, they knelt together no less than twice a week. Although Siegfried was more cautious, Mrs. Maecenas plunged headlong into her epithets, and described their evenings as "something rare and wonderful." Love, art, death, renunciation, the beautiful—the two of them drank long draughts of these deep-red vintages, for they each loved art eloquently. Huddled darkly in the crypt, they would discuss all eternal and universal things, and he would read his prose and verses. She didn't write herself, but what a warm critic!

Perhaps no evening was more wonderful than that sleety night before the holidays. Siegfried had struggled against a persistently vindictive slashing of hail, and arrived with his overcoat feeling like a hulk of iron. As he turned from the street towards the widow's home, he saw the subdued red of the drop-light, "their light," glowing in the window. He felt so deliciously conscious of his health, of his strength, as he stamped on to the porch. Mrs. Maecenas opened the door before he could ring.

"Whew!" he exclaimed, "how many enemies I have out in this night!" He knocked the drippings from his hat, and shook his coat, then stepped into the warm hallway. "I was hardly more than a primitive out in that storm, battling savagely with all the little gods."

She took his coat. "Ah, you have noticed that? It is so easy to understand when one is fighting a storm, just how the original man had to imagine the world peopled with demons. A cutting wind in your face soon seems like a challenge aimed at you personally, just as a fist in the face might. And you can't walk against it five minutes without squaring your jaw, or even shouting as though you were a fiend yourself."

Thus was the platter handed to Siegfried. He returned it graciously as they stepped into the library: "And then, to continue the same viewpoint, think how extraordinarily secure this original man must have felt when he had gained his cave, where there was fire, and light, and warmth to reassure him that he had outstridden the demon. . . . Perhaps that is why I feel so peculiarly comfortable now as I see those logs where I can warm my hands." He laughed. "Congratulate me; I feel that I unwound a pretty statement there. . . . But as to the warming of hands, it is a pleasure to warm them before a log fire even when they are not cold."

"Once the hands are warmed before the fire of logs, we

can then warm them before the fire of life," and the widow had acquitted herself.

"Ah!" After which, for no defined reason, he thought this a time to summon all his boyishness in a toss of the head, and a patent carefree laugh. "How fortunate it is that Landor is not popular."

"Yes, if I were deprived of that lovely quatrain! How *right* a thing to compose on one's seventy-fifth birthday!"

"Isn't it? It must gratify a man to evolve so perfectly concomitantly with his years, to write patriarchally when he is old, to be so complete an entelechy."

"The entelechy, I always felt, was one of Aristotle's most valuable conceptions," Mrs. Maecenas fell in, thereby advancing the conversation another stage. They were gratified with the way they were talking this evening; already they had, by logical steps, moved from the storm to Aristotelianism, and Siegfried's feet were hardly warm yet. And this in the light of the fact that they had begun with the most deadly of conversations, the weather. Nor had either of them failed to note that the weather itself had been done satisfactorily.

Siegfried was worthy of his task. "Aristotle came centuries too soon. If the divine chronology were in perfect ordination he should have come now, after man had flopped and floundered for so long and so distractedly. For if he came *now*, and offered his massive sanity to the world, men would open their eyes with wonder. But as it is, this astonishing cure for dark thinking was propounded before we began to think darkly, so that we are still *waiting* for someone. If the world should——"

"Pardon me for interrupting you, Siegfried, but I have been watching you. I have been watching your eyes. Siegfried, do you suffer from headaches?"

Siegfried was content; the interruption was significant. Remarks like this had been an ever-swelling note in their song of late. But one must be cautious. "My eyes—yes—Aristotle . . . oh! Do I suffer from headaches? Why, I sup-

pose they are headaches. I had an aunt who went mad, but
I don't suppose . . ."

"No, no, no—nothing like that. Don't say it, Siegfried!"
And Mrs. Maecenas stopped her ears, so that Siegfried
noticed her full white arms. . . . There was a lull in the
conversation, as was fitting. The big clock in the hall suddenly became important, and flooded the library with its
ticking. Siegfried looked lugubriously into the fire, relig-
iously observing the ceremonies of the situation. After a
time, the widow ventured a timid triad. It was delicious to
be pampered this way! Siegfried was basking in the warm
sun of sentiment. Then, as if putting aside a great burden,
she broke the silence: "Did you bring anything to read to
me this evening, my boy?"

"Some more of my Bible. I did good work on Chapter
37 of the Second Epistle of Josephat. And I have the Forty-
first and Forty-third Psalms of Obad. But the latter are
too rough yet. You would accuse me of excessive youth. I
brought only the Josephat."

"You have been working hard, Siegfried." And she
closed her eyes in voluptuous expectation as Siegfried
opened his brief-case.

Siegfried returned and sat down by the fire. He prepared to read, then put down the paper again to clear his
throat. He cast a quick glance in the direction of the
widow; she was ready:

"Second Epistle of Josephat.
Chapter 37, Verses 9 - 17.

9   And the prophet Mehovah, when he was come out
of the dry places of Arabia, lifted his voice before the multitude assembled, saying:

10   Many are the sorrows that beset the ways of sinners
and those that trespass against the Lord, for His eyes of
vengeance are manifold, and His wrath endureth forever.

11   He shall slake their thirst with salt, and feed their

hunger with the dry bones of His laughter; their bellies
shall be empty, and the tongues parched of those that have
sinned against Him.

12   He shall smite them until they cry out with mad-
ness, and gape and blubber at the sight of seven moons.

13   And they shall be made to run naked in fields of
thistle, where the thistle barbs shall prick them, and strike
out at them like hissing snakes.

14   And they shall wander in night as black as their
iniquity; in the blackness of night, beasts shall brush
against them, and unknown things, and voices shall whine
out of the funnel of darkness.

15   And they shall wend from the valleys up into the
mountains, and from the tops of the mountains back into
the valleys, and find not what they seek; no, not even shall
they know the things they are seeking.

16   All these evils and many others shall visit the sons
of Belial, and Belial's daughters, but for those blessed with
righteousness there shall be playing of harps and dulci-
mers, and an abundance of honey.

17   And when Mehovah had said these things, he
turned again into the desert."

"Excellong!" the widow cried out immediately. "Let me
have them. And you recited so beautifully!" Siegfried
handed her the manuscript. Glancing through it, she
made her criticisms. "The delicate irony of the prophet
coming up out of the desert just to deliver a speech of
about a hundred words, and then going back again, is the
kind of thing we love to find out for ourselves. France
would have loved to do it. And how much more capable
your prophet was of imagining tortures than bliss; the
point is ferociously well made. But, Siegfried, I am afraid
of you, with your eager *sadisme littéraire*. Your mind is so
gloriously unhealthy, so à la Baudelaire. If *Le Mauvais
Vitrier* were not already written, I am sure you would do
it sooner or later. Or some of de Gourmont's *Oraisons*

Mauvaises. You are an incipient Giles de Retz. And—pardon me—so young! But why aren't you younger still, Siegfried, so young that I could throw my arms around you and kiss you for this magnificent performance? Siegfried, you are going to redeem America in the eyes of the world."

Siegfried nursed the moment in silence. Mrs. Maecenas went on. "But there are things lacking yet, Siegfried, *big* things." Thoughtfully: "If you can do this much without experience, on air, as it were, great Heavens, what will you come to when you have lived! Sometimes I feel it is my duty to—to—*aid* you, Siegfried, to be a—a *real* Maecenas, or a real *Mrs.* Maecenas rather." Then explosively: "Oh, Siegfried, my poor, dear boy, the wonderful things you are still to learn." Abruptly: "Think, Siegfried, you haven't even been in love yet!" He said nothing. "Have you?"

"I'm not sure, but there's a charming little prissy in one of my classes whose delicate-pink cheeks I should love to slap."

"Faugh! How young you can be at times! Not to know more about oneself than that! You will begin by loving an older woman." With a laugh: "But we both know that you must find out all these things for yourself." And with the echo of this interlude still rumbling in the far valleys, the conversation again turned to art.

As he ploughed back through the slush that night Siegfried attempted to place his relationship with Mrs. Maecenas, and finally contented himself with the conclusion that the general was leading to the specific. Or there might be room for some sort of a syllogism somewhere: he needed *Experience;* Mrs. Maecenas wanted him to have *Experience;* ergo . . . but that didn't quite fit together. In any case, on the whole the thing had a slight *savour* of the Aphrodite-and-Adonis, with him playing Adonis merely because he didn't know how to play anyone else. He hated to be so frank about the thing, but it *did* look as though the day was approaching when he could face the sun stolidly, and proclaim with firmness, "I have become a man."

But the important thing was that these evenings were excellent, and it was delightful to be so worried over.

3

*Nemo mundus a sorde, nec si unius
diei vita ejus sit in terra.*

BOOK OF JOB.

A week later. The dim red drop-light was burning in
the window, which might have told the world that this was
one of Siegfried's nights. Outside, a soft snow was sifting
quietly, making a mystic haze about the street-lamps. Siegfried had just finished playing the *Moonlight.*

For a moment he sat motionless, still facing the piano.
The big clock in the hall, ever on the alert for such times,
promptly loomed up again. The flames of the gas-fire
climbed noisily over the asbestos. He turned slowly towards the widow. "And just think, Mrs. Maecenas, one
isn't allowed to like the *Sonata Quasi una Fantasia* any
more! . . . But who knows? Perhaps I shouldn't either if
it were literature and not music. . . ." She was looking out
the window, and made no answer. He let a few moments
go by, then instinctively, he plunged into another direction. "You are looking out into the night? . . . It meant a
lot to me to come to you through a night like that. It felt
as though I were stealing to you. Or as though I were here
by the special dispensation of a good fairy who had warned
me that I must be home again by the stroke of twelve. . . .
The night is full of whisperings about Cinderella. . . . I
had to play the *Moonlight,* you see. But I am silly? Yes?"

"A little Siegfried — but pleasantly so." They both
thought her answer had a sweetly Shakespearean flavour.

"But you should forgive me. We who have not had the
big things of life yet, you will find that at bottom we have
a horrible amount of silliness; silly little dreams, silly little
expectations, silly little longings. Perhaps we are not so

pure as the little girls in a convent, but we are every bit
as silly.

> 'Little Doris of twelve, what is sillier, Dorrie?
> Is it you, or is it I,
> Or the silly little morning-glory?'

Yes, they are mine; but I never brought them around. I
never dared to."

She turned and faced him, having contrived dexterously
to keep the divan from creaking. "You should have, Siegfried. I was coming to think of you as a monster. And after
all, are we not peculiarly close in our present predica-
ments? You have not had the things of life, and I . . ." with
an uncertain sigh, then explosively, "I have passed them
by, I suppose."

Siegfried was sure the flower was in full bloom, but in
spite of him, Adonis answered: "Yet we always hold back.
There is some sickly longing in man to deprive himself of
those things which mean most to him. We are proud, not
when we have been happy, but when we have wallowed in
misery. *If any one have anything of which he is especially
fond, let it be taken from him.* That was, I believe, one of
the rules of the Benedictines. It is a sentence that is very
beautiful to me, and yet there is no sweeping simile, no
brilliance of epithet, nothing but bare bleached bones. It
is its sheer austerity which makes it alluring, the mere
conception of these self-flagellating temperaments so eager
in harvesting their tortures. . . . We no longer have religion, if by religion one means the hierarchy of the angels,
and a *Janitor Coeli,* and a God to sit massively on his
throne, but ah! . . . how appealing the *instincts* of religion
still are to us! I could take the vows of an anchorite, not
to attain some ultimate Kingdom of the Blessed thereby,
but merely through a vague urge towards asceticism, even
though I have nothing for which to be ascetic. For we are
all tinged a bit by the stench of holiness, *sanctitatis odore.*

. . . Perhaps I might be ascetic for my art, but you tell me that the artist must *live*, not *flee from life*. Blind mouths, as Milton has put it. Blind mouths! We are like frail little kittens hardly a day old, nosing around for the mother's teat." Siegfried was dissatisfied for once, even though his rhetoric had been faultless. Still, he had ended the flight happily enough, it might prove.

There was a long silence. Then the widow began speaking very slowly. "My eloquent child, my baby Nestor, have you ever seen Thackeray's cartoon of Louis XIV? You remember the one drawing of the silly runt of a king, old, sallow, dried, hideously devoid of kingliness. Then steps forth Louis the Great, the official Louis, Louis the Emperor Augustus of France, Louis the State, the King of Corneille, of Racine, of Molière. He is stilted, and bejewelled, and sumptuously robed. He is draped and decorated. He is magnified with scaffolds. And behold, he is Regal! In the same way, Siegfried, I should love to make a cartoon of what you have just said. For you have done nothing other than Thackeray says was done to Louis. You have taken a condition that is devoid of interest and value, and you have decked it with royal purples. . . . No, Siegfried, you can say what you like about the beauty of asceticism; but after you have perverted and twisted and beautified to your heart's content, at bottom the original thing remains. . . . For your art's sake, for *America's* sake, you must get up and move. . . . The Muse is a woman, Siegfried, and the formula is that the worse you treat a woman the more she loves you. You may find that if you forget art long enough to live, your art may be all the stronger for it afterwards."

Siegfried was content. He found it pleasant to be exhorted, and pled with. But he wished for a way to get off this Adonis strain. He cursed himself for his praise of asceticism; it might have been too discouraging. But while she was making cartoons, why didn't she make another, showing his true attitude towards Experience? Taking the royal purple off his "urge to asceticism" might reveal an urge of an entirely different sort. Siegfried had no essential objection to being Experienced. But, hell . . . there was plenty of time. Yet it was disagreeable to think so practically about these things.

"But the play, Siegfried! We have wasted all this time, and I am determined to hear the entire play this evening. The little snatches you have told me of it . . . I am mad to hear it all. Begin it immediately."

Siegfried rose from the piano, and went out into the hallway for his brief-case. Mrs. Maecenas pulled a chair up to the light for him, and fixed herself on the sofa, with eyes closed. Siegfried returned and took his seat by the light. He paused. Mrs. Maecenas readjusted her pillow, glanced down at the white of her exposed neck, and then over at Siegfried.

"But, Siegfried," she cried out in sudden horror, "what is the matter with your face?"

He looked up in astonishment. Then he thought he understood: she was pampering him, no doubt. "The paleness? Am I unusually pale tonight? I was smoking a lot today."

"Uh . . . y-yes. Why, yes, the pallor." Then she seemed to recover. "But that is not unusual, I suppose. The artist's temper . . . nervosity . . . pallor would be natural."

Siegfried understood now. It was not the *pallor*, then, but the *redness. Nemo mundus a sorde;* nature is *such* a tyrant. Yesterday they had broken out, and today they were all over his chin. But how annoying that she should react so to pimples!

A few more sentences were offered. She seemed very tired. Siegfried decided tentatively to remember an engagement. "Oh, I am awfully sorry, Siegfried." She would let him go so easily, then? . . .

A few months later they passed on the street, and she nodded to him very sweetly. They even exchanged a couple of words.

She hoped he was getting on well, she said.

THE SOUL OF KAJN TAFHA

THE SOUL OF
KAJN TAFHA

NOBODY knew when Kajn Tafha had been young. Old
Kajn was like the great trees, which in their turn are like
the great angry rocks. The point of his beard extended
down to his navel, and the hair of his brows grew over his
eye-sockets like shrubbery about the Poison Cave. Nobody
knew anything about Kajn save that he was as wise as the
little animals and that he ate no meat. The lobes of his
ears had been torn off; some say it had been done by a
passing demon who tried to whisper false counsel, and bit
at him when angered by his indifference; others say the
priests had done it as a punishment when Kajn called it a
sin to throw she-babies into the Ganges; but no one knew.
Mothers frightened bad children by telling them Kajn
would get them, and yet when people were sick unto death
they called for Kajn. Kajn was very wise, so wise that it is
horrible to think about.

Then one day, just before the last bleeding agony of the
sun, when the dirty brats were gathered in front of their
own homes, and every one was tired, Kajn appeared in the
midst of the village, and lifted up his voice in prayer to
his own gods.

"O ye miserable gods, you have made me wise, until I
can foretell the darkening of the moon, and know to fear
not the quaking of the earth; nor do I fear the heavens
spewing fire and turmoil. For years I have walked upright
with the awareness of my wisdom, and now that I am wise,
what has it gotten me? The ignorant children about me

pull back their lips from their teeth, and I know that is a sign of laughter, which is a sign of happiness. I would give my soul to be one of them. The weary toiler of the field comes home and looks at his woman, and the look is one which, with all my wisdom, I cannot understand, but which I would give my soul to be able to practise for a day. Last night, while I read of imminent spirits, and told myself how wise I was to know of them, I heard the voice of a young girl swell above the noise of the little animals, and I was made uncomfortable, and wanted things. And for those things I would sell my soul. Like a seed fallen on the rocks, I am withering away; I am dry and useless, like that seed. I turn against you; I will sell my soul."

And thereupon Kajn spat, and walked out of the village.

And the story went through the village like a wind of sudden death. And when Adab Teegal heard it, he said:

"I am only an ignorant pariah; I know nothing of the things that Kajn knows, but I have made two stocks of wheat sprout where my father had made but one, and I have seen the ocean. I must find Kajn Tafha." And he walked out of the village in the direction Kajn had walked.

Outside the village, Kajn came upon a rich merchant who was riding on the howdah of a white elephant, with tusks that were carved with sacred inscriptions. His servants carried caskets of rugs and far ivory, and opium brought from a great distance. Occasionally one of the servants would stumble under his excessive burden, and the merchant would order him beaten. At such times his cries of delight were louder than the servant's cries of anguish.

"I would sell my soul," Kajn called up to the merchant as he lay back on this rolling mountain of flesh.

"I will barter with you ivory taken from male elephants that live beneath the earth, and which breathe out fire and pestilence. I have rugs that were woven by monstrous spiders bigger than oaths, and opium which will make you dream of nine evil women. Here is the crystal of Confucius; if you gaze into it you will know all things but one. And here is a potion made of the eyes of live virgins which will teach you that one thing. The man who rubs this stone will live though vast throngs wail and die about him. And here is a magic fruit, which you can eat for ever."

"I would sell my soul," Kajn answered, "and I will sell it for one thing—youth."

Whereupon the merchant became angry, and jabbed a goad into the elephant's ear, until the animal roared with pain. Then he began laughing disagreeably. "Listen, old man. When I have passed out of sight, move the first finger of the hand on the side of your heart, move it so fast that it drops off. And when it drops in the dust, you will be young again." But Kajn, who was wise, knew that the merchant was toying with him; he continued on down the road without moving his finger.

Then Adab Teegal came upon the merchant, and addressed him, saying:

"I am only an ignorant pariah, but I own two houses where my father owned one, and I have seen the ocean. And now I am looking for an old man, Kajn Tafha, who is very wise, and passed down this road, and wants to sell his soul. And I wonder if the magnificent stranger has seen him." But since he was a pariah, the merchant did not answer him; one of the servants, however, furtively pointed down the road, and Adab knew that Kajn had passed.

In the meanwhile Kajn had come upon a very golden pathway leading from the main road. It was the pathway to the Beautiful Woman. He entered, and found her watching two naked servants at play. Their game was to wrestle before a table of gorgeous foods, and each was to prevent the other from eating. The Beautiful Woman lay watching the snake-jewels the merchant has just left her. They writhed in her hand, and tried to crawl between her fingers. When Kajn appeared, she laughed, and sang, "What do you want here, old man?"

"I would sell my soul," Kajn answered, "I would sell my soul for youth."

"I don't buy souls, old man. I sell my own."

And Kajn went on down the road.

Then Adab Teegal came upon the very golden pathway. He first prayed for protection, and then entered. The Beautiful Woman was teasing her flowers. She would dart a glance at them, and they would blossom and give forth delicate odours, for they loved her. And when she looked away, they would close up again, and lose their fragrance.

"I am only an ignorant pariah," Adab Teegal said to her, "but I have had two wives where my father had but one, and I have seen the ocean. And now I am looking for an old man, Kajn Tafha, who is very wise, and passed down this road, and wants to sell his soul, and I wonder if the Beautiful Woman has seen him."

"It is late, and will soon be dark. The night will be restless with prowling things, and spirits that whine. Perhaps the stranger may care to lodge here until sunrise. For I have seen no old man pass here." But her jealous flowers cried out that she lied, and Adab Teegal hastened on down the road.

And in the meantime Kajn came upon another old man who was standing on his head in the middle of the road. And when Kajn Tafha asked him why he stood on his head, he replied, "If I stand on my feet, my reflection in the Sacred Lake is upside-down. But if I learn to stand on my head, then I shall exist properly in the Waters of the Gods."

Kajn marveled at his piety, and was ashamed to tell him that he wanted to sell his soul. They blessed each other, and Kajn passed on down the road into the gloom.

When Adab Teegal came upon the pious man it was so dark he could scarcely see him. "I am only an ignorant pariah," he said, "but I have prayed to two gods where my father prayed to one, and I have seen the ocean." And when he asked the old man about Kajn, the old man told him to hurry and he would catch him, for Kajn had only just passed. Adab plunged into the squirming darkness.

Finally he heard faltering footsteps ahead. "Kajn Tafha, Kajn Tafha," he shouted, and the answer came back out of the blackness, "Yes, I am Kajn Tafha, the wise man, and I would sell my soul, and if my ears are honest, I hear the voice of Adab Teegal."

"I am only an ignorant pariah, and not fit to talk of learned things with Kajn Tafha, but I have seen the ocean. If Kajn Tafha will tell me where he is in the darkness, I will lead him home."

"Onward I go, Adab Teegal, for I would sell my soul."

"I am only an ignorant pariah, but I have seen the ocean twice where my father saw it but once, and maybe we can't sell our souls, and maybe we don't even have souls to sell."

Then Adab Teegal heard such a horrible shriek in the darkness that he ran all the way home, and nothing was ever heard again of Kajn Tafha.

OLYMPIANS

OLYMPIANS

AFTER the Wilsons moved from Edgewood, their house was left empty for nearly two months; at the end of this time it was occupied by a Mr. Beck, who put a little black and gold sign in his window, "J. J. Beck, Instructor in Music." Also, Mr. Beck joined the Methodist Church on Braddock Avenue, and gave five dollars to the local ball team. When asked to become affiliated with the gymnasium, Mr. Beck said they were doing invaluable good towards the upbuilding of healthy American manhood, but that he personally was denied all violent exertion, owing to cardiac rheumatism. He gave full assurance of his moral support, however.

Within a year Mr. Beck had convinced everyone that he was an asset to the community. As a member of the Christian Entertainment Committee he had applied himself with an earnestness that was not easily forgotten, and already he had piloted seven little girls and two boys safely through Czerny, both elementary and intermediate. The Howardell's eldest daughter Dorothy, was even playing the "Valse" by Durand, and the "Scarf Dance" by somebody, but she had taken lessons before Mr. Beck taught her, and was unusually gifted anyhow. Besides, she was older, now being nearly fifteen.

A disagreeable incident took place in the basement of the church once, when a chapter of the Boy Scouts was being organized. One little ruffian nominated Mr. Beck as scout-master, causing a subdued titter to pass around the room; but he was afterwards reprimanded by the minister, and his own father as well. A younger and sturdier man was elected scout-master, of course, and no further mention was made of the matter. It is even doubtful if Mr. Beck ever got wind of it.

Aside from this one incident, which was of no importance as it was occasioned by a mere child, Mr. Beck was treated everywhere with consideration and respect. The minister's wife used to invite him now and then to speak at one of her teas on "The Appreciation of Music," or "Music as a Factor in Education," or some such subject, where he always charmed his audience with his astonishing modesty, a certain lovable shyness, and a wealth of anecdotes taken from the lives of great musicians. And nothing is more illustrative of his goodness of heart than the fact that, although he was by far the best musician in the community, he refused to hear of replacing the church organist.

Perhaps the quality which went farthest towards Mr. Beck's popularity was this pathetic modesty of his. Although he knew so *much,* he seemed to be continually apologizing for his presence. One might almost say that he was timid. When he was introduced to anyone, he stuttered noticeably, and retired from a conversation as soon as was possible within the bounds of politeness. He was tall and thin, which with his ailment, the cardiac rheumatism, gave him a very *fragile* appearance, so that one would inevitably treat him with a kind of tenderness almost without knowing it. As a result Mr. Beck always brought with him into the room an air of peace and mildness, and anyone who talked to him for any length of time was left with an impression of how lovely life can be if we but choose to make it so.

So that Mr. Beck was sweetly and inexorably removed from the class of eligible men, and looked upon as a kindly institution. With an unquestioning docility, he walked in the path that was laid out for him, shielded his failing soul with umbrella and galoshes, kept it sufficiently warm with the horrible respect of his acquaintances. The facts of his own flesh and blood, however, caused him to suffer a mild degradation, which made all of his contacts with life awkward for him. This was the cause of his timidity, or his *fragility*.

All of which agitations culminated when he was teaching the Howardell's eldest daughter, little Dorothy, who was now nearly fifteen, and was his favourite pupil.

Three times a week she came here with her music-roll, corrected her *expressivos,* practised her fourth finger, and when Mr. Beck praised her, fed her joyous little ego with satisfaction. To Dorothy, Mr. Beck was simply a nervous "Good morning, Dorothy," a pulling of a chair up beside her at the piano, and a voice in her ear that made suggestions, with a queer licking sound in its throat after it swallowed. To Dorothy, none of this was especially pleasant, but it must be gone through before one can play before visitors, and was therefore beyond question. Miss Sweeny was a Catholic, while father said that the teachers down-town charged too much. Then again, she really preferred Mr. Beck in a way. For Mr. Beck meant music to her; the taking of lessons was clearly associated with Mr. Beck; when she went to Mr. Beck, she was performing one of the functions of all the music students in her Sunday-school class.

This morning Dorothy was with him again, had come out of the first spring day and into the dark parlour with the picture of a man with side-whiskers over the piano. One of the windows was open a little, so that the spring air, and the soft noises outside, and the notes of Dorothy's "Witches' Revel" had commingled in a way that caused Mr. Beck to feel a mild and uncertain despair.

A few houses farther up the street, some boys were playing marbles, shooting against the curb-stone; while directly beyond, the Wrights' washerwoman was standing in the doorway, leaning, her bare arms crossed gloriously on her breasts. The grass on the front lawns was soppy with the last of the melting snow. Dorothy had finished. "I want you to learn that well, Dorothy. . . . You know, you are my favourite pupil."

Dorothy was his favourite pupil. Dorothy his favourite pupil, and it was spring! That urge, then, was to awaken in them? The tender urge which lends poignancy to "The Barcarolle" and perpetuates the funny little grasshoppers? Were Dorothy and Mr. Beck to *sing* together? Mr. Beck's heart, already weakened as it was by rheumatism, fluttered irregularly with affirmation. The Olympian was rising within him, along with the sap in the trees outside. Apollo was stirring; Balder . . . But Dorothy had fastened her music-roll; she was leaving. "Good morning, Dorothy."

The next time Dorothy came for her music lesson, Mr. Beck felt strangely unfit. She stepped into the parlour, laid her hat and coat on the settee, and sat down at the piano. She was now ready for the voice to buzz in her ear, and make the funny licking sound when it swallowed. But Mr. Beck experienced a sudden fling of insolence. "It is going to be a wonderful spring, Dorothy." He was comforted with the tenderness of his own voice.

Dorothy spread out the "Dance of the Elves" before her. "Yes, Mr. Beck," she answered, obediently. Mr. Beck understood fatally that she had not responded. Somehow or other, he had expected something of her. There was a pause; Dorothy glanced with unconscious significance at the piano. Mr. Beck found something strangely disproportionate. It was as though he were walking arm in arm with a midget, or riding a puppy-dog on his back.

"Let me play you something, Dorothy." The piano became a lovable instrument. Dorothy arose from the stool with a puzzled "Yes, do, Mr. Beck." He seated himself in the place she had left; it was warmed! He ran a scale, and was astonished that it was so *brilliant* a scale. "I shall play a little *Albumblatt* of Beethoven." Here was he, and here was the piano; he felt very professional; yet he was trembling as he began to play.

He was elated by the daintiness of its arabesques. Then came a miniature *crescendo,* with its insistent bass, followed immediately by a clean chromatic descent in triplets. It transformed again into the arabesques, and was finished. . . . Mr. Beck left the piano with a feeling of surprise. He had taught this piece probably fifty times in his life, and never realized until now that it was so neat and white. Dorothy broke in with a dutiful "How fine it was, Mr. Beck," and that was all gone, too. Without spirit, he gave her her lesson.

After Dorothy had left, Mr. Beck was frank to himself about any number of things. The scene he had just been through made him weak with humiliation. And to have played for her; as though he had stood beneath her window as a *troubadour.*

Out of this unaccountable disgust, Mr. Beck tried to reach a determination. He must annihilate Dorothy from his head. For at best he could only awake her out of a dead sleep; at best prepare her for some coarse, brutal youth.

It was late, and they were returning in a street-car. Dorothy was trying to hold her eyes open, lulled by the low groan of the motor. In another fifteen minutes, thank God, Mr. Beck would leave her at her doorstep; she would go to bed without cleaning her teeth. Mr. Beck sat beside her, his eyes working over the other occupants of the car. Everyone was dull, and detestable. But in Mr. Beck there was still a disturbance from his memory of the opera. The duet is so *bold;* the voices of a man and woman in harmonization, adapting themselves to each other, intertwining. The car jerked and groaned through the deserted streets. And they passed dark houses, shutting away all manner of things; houses that stood out frankly and openly, but within their walls, what slinking possibilities; houses with black corridors, with furniture and people in the shadows. These were sleeping houses, and as secret as caves.

SCHERZANDO

SCHERZANDO

As I entered the room, he was reading one of his poems to a very moth-eaten person. *"Catalogus Mulierum,"* he grunted at me, and went on with the poem. From which I assumed that the title of the thing he was reading was *"Catalogus Mulierum,"* or "A Catalogue of Women."

> "Yes, I know the old ones who have had their day.
> I have observed them.
> Those old wrecked houses;
> Those dead craters."

The next I do not remember. Or rather, I do not want to remember it. It was detestable. And the stanza following. . . . The moth-eaten person clucked after each, and murmured something. When he had read another stanza, I left, while the moth-eaten person clucked—whether at the poem, or at me, I do not know.

> "Then there are the little girls,
> Recently able to become mothers;
> Packages wrapped securely
> In the admonitions of their parents."

Why must men be hog-minded like that, I say. Great heavens! have we exhausted the play of fresh morning on a lake? Have all the possible documents been written of a star near the horizon? I have seen him sitting monstrously in his chair and leering at me as though I were a whole world to leer at. I remember him in the distillation of my

memory as a carcass, so many pounds of throbbing flesh
with the requisite organs stuffed in, growling over the raw
meat of his ideas.

Is there some gigantic cancer for us to sap with wells,
and where we can descend
on ladders? Could we
spend our holidays here,
on the edge of the decay-
ing flesh, with our wives
and children? I used to
grind my teeth at the mere
thought of him, until I
had diseased my liver, and
I ached from escaping
juices.

Ossia: There has been
Christ, and the saints, and
whole libraries of sanctity,
and yet there was no law
to exterminate this man!
What darkness of dark-
nesses have we been plunged into, when pestilence is
invited among us, suffered
to sit at our table and fester
our tongues? But the critics are coming, and the sat-
irists. Soon a wide plague
of caterpillars will cover
all the green leaves. There
will be nothing behind
them but naked trees and
the scum of intestines.
Prepare for a lean season,
made meager with exces-
sive insects.

I have sat opposed to him, and remembered the sunlight
with a bursting gratitude. I remembered a little town
sleeping in the foothills, with a bright clay road working
across the country-side, and a green pool with the shadows
of trout. I remembered the long, drooping fingers of the
chestnuts—for the chestnuts blossom late, and there was a
scattered frost of them even though the beards on the corn
were already scorched. I remembered all this, while there
spread about me the cool, dank mould from the cellar of
his brain.

Coda

Let us construct a vast hippopotamus to the glorification of our century. Other ages could have constructed hippopotami of equal vastness, but ours will be superior in this: That it is exact within as well as without. A steam heart will beat against the brazen ribs of the brute, and the ooze of the kidneys will have been studied accurately. On the bolsters of his folded hide we shall have blotches and sores proper to the hippopotamus. And when we have finished, we shall have constructed a vast hippopotamus, which will cast its shadows across the plain, and disfigure the sky to the glorification of our century.

PORTRAIT OF AN ARRIVED CRITIC

PORTRAIT OF AN ARRIVED CRITIC

ALFRED closed the door softly behind her. He would send her lilies. This must not be forgotten . . . lilies . . . to Adelheid. Or perhaps just one lily; more laconic, and therefore more damnably effective. But he had seen an ad somewhere: "Say it with flowers." He must not be department-store. Still, he was *not* saying it with flowers; he was saying the exact opposite, in fact. The exact opposite; poor little Adelheid! He wrote on his calendar "L. to A."

As to this matter of the artist, "precocious cry-babies, all of them." That might be an effective tune to hum. But that was rude rather than pessimistic. One may as well be an early martyr as be rude. . . . *Condiebar ejus sale;* "I was pickled in the brine of Christ," Flannagan insisted on spitting it out the other night. Flannagan had outshrieked St. Augustine by a note in translating it that way. But Flannagan, of course, was invariably rude. A simple Freudian case, since his abstinence was notorious. Flannagan was revolting, a tongue dripping meconium, a mess of *caca*.

"Precocious cry-babies," then, was Flannagan's province. Alfred put a fresh sheet in his Corona. "Let us, rather, be kindly disposed towards the artist. Let us realize just how pathetic are his bronzes built against time and the universe. Consider the true misery of the poor devil who deposits his treasure, squeezes a tear of joy over his under-

standing of its significance, and dies. And we, if we do not
like it, forget it; and if we do like it, we examine it, and
punctum. It is astonishing, but true, that there are men
who fill their stomachs and burn their oxygen for the sole
purpose of perfecting a work of art, although even while
they are doing it they are aware that a generation is mewl-
ing in the cradle which will have a new idea of perfection."

Flo would complain that he was bitter, and he *would*
grant her that he had been "severe." A letter was sure to
come from somewhere out in Ohio. If only Flannagan
stayed sober! A drunken Flannagan would bawl disgusted-
ly about "parlour pessimism" and "bows to the ladies."
Why, of all people, had Flannagan chosen to track *him?*
But anyhow, neither Flo nor Adelheid could bear Flannagan. "Or even those who feel that it is not perfection
they are after, but mere crude expression, the proclaiming
of their own ego, the thrusting of their personal wants and
ecstasies on posterity—perhaps their lot is more unfortunate still, since their message, being more individual, is
therefore all the harder to convey to the future, let alone
the present."

To be making the artists in general provide his comfort
for him! It had never occurred to him, during that
wretched adolescence of his, that he could have obtained
such easy terms with life. Not even a toothache. . . . Furthermore, if he *had* attained a certain competence in
things, it was an active intelligence which had got it for
him. He had gauged life correctly, and that was nothing if
not admirable. Yet there was always a discouraging lot of
detestation in the world for someone who had succeeded
—which was unfair. Origins should be taken into account,
although they never considered origins; if they found a
man at *astra* they were inclined to resent it, forgetting his
per aspera. . . . Adolescence would justify everything; *then*
he had *plainly suffered*. Out there in that ridiculous cabin,
with the wide nights and the big days to handle, with sym-

phonic storms to wail with, and long stretches of dead summer, and his father reading fairy stories . . . all that meant that he must either burst or get a grip on life. Hallelujah! he had gripped it!

"There are two million seven hundred and fifty thousand ways of writing a given poem, and yet some greasy waif will knock his head against the stars because he has stumbled on one of them. And even while he writes, the wheels of the universe are grinding him towards oblivion. What an interesting phenomenon it is, that the poison of his genesomania is *always* the stronger, that he strives for immortality in the most fragile of substances, art!"

The artist, however clever he was in the use of his medium, lacked a certain astuteness, a kind of cultured shrewdness, in looking at life and relating it with himself. The disappointing thing was that people admired this lacuna, although *no* lacuna should be admirable. If being a complete man precluded being an artist, the artist should be properly discounted. He could see nothing divine about myopia. There was room here for a less temperamental Nordau. . . .

To put himself over against Flannagan, to make the contrast screamingly evident, that little incident on his first night with Flo was excellent. When he had laid the umbrella and the broom side by side on the bed, and breathed a pun about the "bride and broom," and then let suggestion run its course. Ten minutes later Flannagan had come in, as drunk as a pig, shouting "confessions," a vile vomit paraphrased from Huysmans, something about "I tore open the bellies of little children and sat therein." Flannagan was distinctly a minor character, to be utilized in a romantic novel like a Bowery tough or an Irish washerwoman.

"Couldn't we, in the last analysis, divide the intellectuals into two significant categories, the artist and the compleat gentleman? The artist, disorbited, unoriented, reeling with the mental tipple of his talk about unattainable beauty, unrealizable ambitions, ineffable innuendoes, slashing blindly, without discrimination or dignity, at an escaping colour or a half-heard note, distressed in a manner highly romanesque because he cannot express things which were never there to be expressed, irresponsible, childish, unwashed; and the opposing nature, the unit that is perfectly aware of the contracts of society, alive to the subtleties of human relationship, that tiptoes about the world with a discerning and critical caution, likes and dislikes with a mildness born of the obligation of generations, and knows that everything is subordinate to the regulations of life, the compleat gentleman. . . . But we must have artists, so long as there are walls to be covered, and Pullmans to travel in; as we must also have ditch-diggers."

"L. to A." He must not forget the lily.

DAVID WASSERMAN

DAVID WASSERMAN

Ita fornicatur anima.
St. Augustine.

1

"You have it all," Wright had said. "To begin with, you are a neurasthenic, or at least, you have just recovered from neurasthenia. You are a Jew. You have the memory of sex, although at present you are continent; also, you are in love. And the twenties is naturally a restless period anyhow." Was Wright being decent for once? Did he mean that just as he had said it? The bastard!

Cynthia must be watching how his hands trembled. That was the neurasthenia. Or she should think so. And damn it, it *was* so, anyhow. If Mendelssohn ran up the scale to *si,* and then was called to dinner, and got up in the middle of his soup to strike *do,* it wasn't that he absolutely *had* to. He wanted to, simply, and did it. Yet it wasn't an affectation, because he sincerely and without forethought *wanted* to. In the case of the hands, then, if the neurasthenia was there, why clamp it in a vise? Let them tremble, and perhaps even encourage them a little.

Hell with such considerations!

Why not cut clean of all that and plunge right straight on? Just rip and tear, like kicking through a newspaper on the sidewalk.

"I love you, Cynthia. Yes, I love you, even though you *are* a Yiddish vampire." Cynthia smiled meekly, and continued existing there, two feet in front of him. "I love you,"—and she existed; "I hate you,"—and Cynthia *still* existed. At times when he left her, he knew all the time that over in Brooklyn, Cynthia was existing inexorably. *"The memory of sex."* At times he had tried to bludgeon her with that, too, and was answered as usual with the quiet fact of her existence.

"The war. I'll get you yet. Gaping on a battle-field in France. Can't you see me there, my face all twisted like a piece of an old tree-trunk, a gun tossed somewhere, and my guts oozing out; can't you see me?" Cynthia, with nothing else to say, admitted that yes, she could see him. Monstrous!

With a snarl; "You, my dear, ought to live in some Arcadian province where women are disposed of more summarily. Biceps,—that's the way to court *you*. Like this." He stepped against her, threw his arms around her, pressed her backwards with his chin, and began heaving her to the couch. His knuckles scraped against a chair. The divan reached, he dropped her on it. "Stop it, David!" She laughed, and pushed away one compromising hand of his. Wassermann panted, felt ridiculous. "Straight business, with annoying difficulties and injuries," he thought in the style of Wright as he paid attention to the smarting knuckles. She rearranged herself, with no thought of a recovering hen; the things that slipped by her!

"She smells like a horse." He added aloud, "Perhaps I should have brought Wright with me? . . . She *stinks* like a horse. How is it possible to love such a woman. For I can't lie out of it, she *stinks*. But I *want* her to stink. It is *my* way of having my guts ooze out. That ought to cure me of her, but it doesn't. But this for consolation: my urge is at least proved to be straight lust." Cynthia had answered something about Wright; he would not ask her what it was.

"I suppose I shouldn't resent these failures," he began argumentatively. "We are still walking in our origins. It continues to be a matter of Apollo and Daphne, where if women can't turn into laurel trees any longer, they turn into logs. But then, you must not forget you are always open to the charge of being undersexed, which is scandalous." Both laughed. "Still as I say, you are only acting within the nature of things if you resist. Be as fair yourself, then, and admit that I, too, am acting within the nature of things when I *per*sist." But what an ass to justify her. He should deplore her without end. Never to weaken on the thing. To *know* that she must give in. And never begin defending himself; it should go without saying that his position was fitting.

He pointed upstairs. "Listen: it's sisters, and mothers, and fathers. Great God, what chance do *I* have! Even if you were insane to give yourself, those noises would keep you pure. How could a man *ever* seduce such a woman; with so many thunderous generalities to combat? As I just said, you are protected phylogenetically; with those noises upstairs you are protected socially; and worst of all, you are protected by these damned cerebrizings of mine. Oh tender Gibraltar!" . . . Cynthia was listening intently. "But that's all the wrong tack, Cynthia. Let's *faire table rase.* Why not begin all over again? I am glad to know you; weather and so forth; yes, I know Harry; Ibsen *is* a bit demoded; do you really think so? Come on, Cynthia, let's sing a duet; if we can't agree on love, at least we both believe Shaw is right about the war, Shaw with his rare common-sense."

"On the whole we think reasonably alike, David."

"Yes, we *think* very much alike. Our minds are in perfect copulation. But *corporeally.* Damn it, I have more important things in this world to do than niggle around with sex. But so long as you hold me up on this one score, I am worthless. I am kept in an endless state of dispersion. I'm just a *waldschrat,* one always-swollen————. . ." The people upstairs! He saw it in Cynthia's eyes, and subsided, the harsh word unfinished.

Five hours of this! He left her, kissing her at the door.

Within ten minutes Cynthia was undressed, and had walked to the bathroom in her nightgown. Wassermann caught the subway to Times Square as Cynthia was brushing her teeth.

Wright to Wassermann: "The fact is that you simply *must* stick to this much-ado. If you drop it, you have nothing left. The . . ."

"I refuse to swallow any more of that, do you understand? First Cynthia, and then you; it's too much for an evening, just a l-i-t-t-l-e too much. You and your composure, bosh! You say I am histrionic. But it never occurred to you that your immovable front is another symptom of the same disease. If I am a stage neurasthenic, then you are a stage Stoic."

"Wait a minute. I am not fighting with you, I am *diagnosing* you. Cynthia hears that sort of thing as long as you are with her; can't you listen to one sentence of it?"

"It isn't the diagnosis I object to, it's the flatness of it. You say I have nothing but my agitation, my noise in other words. What am I to answer? You simply kill all chance of discussion with a sentence like that. What are its merits? Is it astonishing? Is it clever? Is it subtle? It just stands out there like a big face fat with a bad liver. If you want to *penetrate* me, I am willing to listen. I am *anxious* to listen, in fact. But if you're going to fling hunks of statements at me like mudpies, I want to make it clear that I am not interested."

"Go on."

"I have said what I had to say."

"No!"

Wassermann snorted. "You're getting weak, Wright, if that's the best comeback you have. Or I've gone the length of you, and am leaving you behind. You must have been frantic for a last word if you could grab at such a shabby little straw as that." Wright said nothing. "Quite in character, you say nothing. That is expected to wither me, to

dry me up and blow me away. But this time, it doesn't."
Wright smiled encouragingly, said nothing. "I'll give you
credit, that works. It gets on a man's nerves, especially a
man like me. It would be highly admirable, if it weren't
so easy to apply. Another trouble with it is that it is inclined to become too pat. It fits roughly in too many cases
to be nicely adapted to any of them. And in time it blunts
a man, since it gets him into making a broad division of his
sensations: this thing I recognize, this thing I am silent
about. With the final result that you become inarticulate.
You forget how to carve neat slices off a big steaming idea.
You become no better than an amoeba, approaching what
is pleasant, and retreating from what is unpleasant, without intelligent observation."

"There is a lot to what you say, Wassermann. But I
must be going now, if you'll let me leave without calling it
a last bit of blunt technique. The fact is that I *do* have to
go. We'll see each other tomorrow night."

A dirty way to defeat a man. Wright's going left him
bound. The bile must drip back into his stomach, and stay
there poisoning him until tomorrow night. They were
monsters, both of them, with Cynthia a little worse because she was a woman, and loved. They were two suns for
him to race around; they stood still, and let him break his
neck. But the devil; what a superb martyrdom anyhow. If
he saw things, and simply *had* to say them, it was worth
seeing and saying them at any cost. Not so bad to be a
victim of too much clarity. He was a fly-eye.

"Waiter . . . waiter." The waiter came on the run. "I
ordered *black* coffee."

2

"Everything in the world's one more little devil's tongue
for me to bleed on. If it's a chair, I'll stove my shins on it
in the dark; if it's a razor, the relation between us is an
immediate possibility of my hurling it out the window; if

it's a person, it'll say 'How are you,' and I'll nearly pass
out apoplectic with pounding sentences. Don't you ever
get that? An egocentric attitude to life, with nothing but
you and God, and God making the world to plague you?
No, of course not. Roman therms, resignation, either no
God or a *laissez-faire policy* on the part of God; ah, how
Walter Pater, how Parian marble, how off in the mountains to meditate. But I know there *is* a God, with a swag-
ger, and an ugly leer, and a quid of tobacco in his cheek.
However, my friend, damn you. You are driving me into
this. I was unusually conciliatory this evening. Even a bit
reminiscent, in fact." Wassermann stopped; Wright
stretched and yawned with a miniature embarrassment.

"And then to this: '*D'ordinaire, insinuante et im-
périeuse, elle violait doucement, intéressée par les capitu-
lations successives, jouissant des retraits et des sursauts de
la pudeur des mâles qui n'est vaincue qu'au moment où
elle devient inflexible. Son jeu était serré, sûr et astucieux;
délicieux insecte d'aventure, serrant autour de sa proie les
spirales de son vole, elle chantait comme une abeille; puis,
soudain l'abeille se taisait, buvait, les ailes calmes, la vie
de la fleur humaine. Mais aujourd'hui, peureuse, elle se
laissait dévêtir avec la patience d'une orpheline; sans autre
désir que d'être agréable aux mains de son ami.*' What a
velvet touch! He caressed those sentences as he would have
caressed Mauve herself. For God's sake, man, give over that
truck and read literature. Have you ever seen *Le Miracle
des Roses?* No, you haven't. Then why talk about French
literature to *me?*"

"By that time we were all pretty well soused."

"And then to this: '*Ou pouvaient, songea-t-il, se recruter
de telles vocations? Quelle corne, sonnant dans la nuit,
sonnait assez haut, pour assembler un troupeau d'aussi
lamentables femmes? Donner toute sa vie à la mort, n'avoir
d'autre souci que la toilette des cadavres, la veillée soli-
taire près des corps rigides et des faces froides où l'ombre
du nez marque une heure immuable sur la putréfaction*

de la joue!" All the bigger Frenchmen have places now and then that run like rivers."

"*You* know that little hotel, too? The west rooms give you all you want of the Hudson in the morning. And no questions asked."

"Oh, no, I take it back, Wright. You get up in front of me like a big stupid face to be punched, and I am always just a little too off my balance to punch it. Some day I'm going to look at you, and promptly break into little pieces. You and . . ." . . ."And now it's Up-Swallow, Fifty Cents Gone. You couldn't get rid of money faster throwing it down the . . ." . . ."Cynthia are two marvelous forces to have drawn up in either direction of a man. It's as though I were in a big gloomy hallway, with an Italian carved grandfather's-clock on one side of me, and a family portrait on the other. Dull gold face and dull gold frame,—it's worse than if my two shoulders were sinister, had worms in them, and I could see them out of the corner of my eyes. You're like two big boats, dull black in a dull grey harbour. You're problems, like all static things.

"I had more promise during adolescence, right hand and all. Then these damned problems of human relations hadn't pulped me. I was a shrieking, battling *I*. At night I used to wander through the cemetery, and if I didn't get scared, I'd scare myself. I'd throw my arms around a tombstone, and listen, and then start to blab and blub as though I was mad, until finally I would be half-mad. And then I'd walk slowly away, with my back to all that darkness and pale white, and when I got out of there I would be sick. Once I vomited on the sexton. *Then* I was . . ."—". . . I wanted to kiss Minney and light my cigarette, and instead I put the cigarette in her mouth and nearly kissed the match. Did you hear that? I wanted . . ."

"But that's all different now. A man is worth something when there are women in general, not specific women. While there's a world of women, there's possibility; but what can I do? Flap and flutter and squawk myself over the hedge. Go on stirring the brew to keep it from sticking. Rattle at my brain with words until I've numbed it. Thank God, there's always some satisfaction in a precise diagnosis. So long as I can chart my defections, I at least have the intellectuality of the chart to encourage me. And when I die, I'll know exactly how I'm dead. Hamletism is a remedy worth talking of. Especially Hamletism on the proscenium. For the hamletically inclined, there is always pause enough between the wound and decease to drop a cosmogony and a couple of attitudes on life. And how conciliatory it may be to pass away with a properly modernized *adsum*.

"Oh, hell, oh, hell. Out of this kitchen-pot of fairies, and kikes, and lounge lizards, and Spearmint stenographers, and fat old breeding machines on the East Side, out of these five million pancreas and livers, why do I have to moon over Cynthia! Why can't I get back into the swirl of things, and embrace the city in general? If I could plunge forward into some dawn or other. Or if the city could occur to me like a sudden revelation, with me shrieking, 'Fish! Fish! Jesus Christ, God, Son, Saviour!'

"If religion is the sublimation of sex, where's *my* breviary? I'm nearly bursting with sex, and yet I just have enough religion to be mildly blasphemous. Why don't people shout at me when I walk along the street; why don't they lock their doors, and pile furniture against them, and watch me from their second-story windows; for I'm one unceasing swollen possibility of rape. I'm satyriasis stalking nymphomania. And yet if an auto were to run against me accidentally, I could call a policeman and have the driver arrested.

"But I have been too honest with myself. A man's a suicide if he insists on clarity. Beyond knowing what's right and what's left, and what's up and down, clarity becomes a grave nuisance. Intelligence is a parasitic growth, and saps the body like a cancer. It endangers the silver medium. The brain was once a mere implement of the body, functioning solely to add to the body's welfare, like the kidneys. But now it is threatening to usurp an entity of its own. It demands certain foods and amusements which can be indulged in only at great inconvenience and often with danger. *Comme on pisse les chiens*, one must walk one's brain. And it is still so young, that one's attentions to it are frequently of a disgusting nature. And so, I have stuffed my brain with rich, oozy clarity, with the consequence that I can see every pore in every nose, and catch the smell of every armpit. And when you see that way, you have two choices: you can be either a dervish or a pig. If you're a dervish, you shrink from it all, and drown yourself in denials and negations, and spend sinister years trying to rub the filth out of your carcass. But if on the other hand you see it all, and *refuse* to deny, and are determined even to *glorify* and *wallow in*, then, friend, you are a pig. That is what clarity does for you. A sweet little virgin who grows up in neatness, goes to school, is courted tenderly, and finally married; there is modesty, refinement, loveliness for you—and intellectual muddiness, and passional stupidity enough to drive you wild. These women are perfectly functioning units, developing logically and infallibly towards the grand culmination, marriage. Thus we see how orderly and social things are without clarity. But *with* clarity, you must be either a recluse starving on God, or a cur with his nose under a tail."

Wright's eyes edged toward the centre of the room. Gutzkow, like a monster shadow, was holding a jug. Beside him was a university student with a small moustache, a watch in his hand. "Get ready—get set—Go!" The butt of the jug was raised a little higher, while Gutzkow's lips wrapped themselves surely over the mouth. The liquid began seeking its level. Gutzkow took it amply. It was all like a fire-hose spurting into a sewer.

"Fifteen—twenty-twenty-two seconds. You take the money." Gutzkow had won.

3

"I suppose if you picked pins off the floor fast enough you could get out of an *idée fixe*. I'm trying to forget my captivity with battling around the cage. *Cynthia!* Christ, what a Muse! Between—it's a nasty bell to have ringing in your head. Booze, dope, sweating, socialism—they're the only four escapes, and I've tried them all. Dope is the poorest; I can't go that way. I can thump and pound until I burst, but I can't fade away. And booze is only an accompaniment. It's just a steady bass to an agitated treble. Sweating is at best Tolstoyan. It's a grand theory that dies with a whine, like a pig-balloon. And at worst Jean-Jacques Rousseau. Weary brawn at sunset—a tender department store master. Toiler with his pipe; open fireplace; wife and cradle; work basket on lap; sunset visible through window. And as for socialism, it's either bums or double-lens spectacles.

"I joined the 'Red Flag.' Recommended as trustworthy by a dear and intimate friend. The great night finally approached. We assembled in a rathskeller. 'Would you kindly leave the room, while the matter of new members is being discussed?' 'Certainly, certainly.' I went up to the bar and had a beer. Another beer, and I was summoned before the committee. 'Mr. Wasserman, before you pledge your word, you must understand that this is a grave matter. We are part of an organization forming over the entire country to resist the forces of reaction. We are an underground organization. The cause is greater than our life. The pledge binds you to be subject at any time to perform anything which is found necessary.' 'Mr. Chairman, I am not prepared to go blindly to such an extent. I am anxious to ally myself with the principles your organization stands for. But I cannot forswear the freedom of disposing of myself as I may see fit at any time. And to me my life is more important than the life of a community however great and oppressed.' 'Mr. Wassermann, you are a serious-

minded man. You are no doubt earnest in your radical
sympathies. But I fear you are not ripe for the cause we
represent.' I am rejected, but my dear and intimate
friend, who is one of the chosen, enjoys to this day the
privileges of this dark organization. Once a month they
give a dance, he tells me, and with the yearly dues of five
dollars they are able to keep up a pleasant little clubroom,
with translations of Russian novels, and three volumes of
Schnitzler in the original. Also, I believe, there is a book
by Karl Marx. . . . I was too mild.

"And again I am thrown back on Cynthia. . . . Scotch?
Beer here. A Scotch and a beer, professor. . . . Why can't a
man have a real opportunity? Or an arrangement whereby
we can be of some use—consumptives, decrepits, and poor
devils like me. I want to found a headquarters where all
people can come who are going to die. Take a suicide, for
instance. He comes into the office, with reliable credentials
that he is a paranoiac; he has decided to kill himself. I look
through the card index system; and find that so-and-so has
been responsible for another half-cent rise in the price of
sugar. My suicide receives a full description of this gentleman, his habits, where he lives. Then goes out and mur-
ders him, explains publicly that it was owing to the half-
cent increase in sugar, and kills himself. Or a consumptive
could have done it, and spits his lungs out the following
week in prison.

"But it's coming, men," Wassermann ignored Wright,
and addressed the people at the next table. "The greatest
hope of revolution in America came with the passing of
prohibition. The American still has the instinct of the
Boston Tea Party in him; he must have something trivial
to revolutionize about. You can starve him, rob him, drive
him among the cogs of a machine, or explode him, and
he'll merely grumble. But step on his corn, or call him a
bastard, or kick his dog, and by God, he'll murder you. . . .
But I am afraid the ruling classes know this as well as I do.
They won't force the issue too strongly, and as a result of

this yielding, social unrest will disappear behind the aegis of mean prosperity, the ability to earn a good enough living, to marry and provide your wife with an effective douche. The Bismarks and Von Moltkes of America will be more successful than their prototypes, because they possess enough English blood and English diplomacy to add hypocrisy to the rest of their dirty equipment. And the idealism of America is always low enough to enable the purchase of their chosen leaders. So we can expect every Sam Gompers of the future to appear in the best of society; we shall hear talk of great prosperity; of America's colossal commerce overtopping that of Great Britain; of America's stupendous merchant marine; of American banks in every third-rate city in the world. Everything will be 100 per cent American, made in America, *Amerika über alles.* Competent experts will be despatched at the government's expense to study foreign markets, and the ways of eliminating foreign competition. Do you see what I am doing? I am prophesying the rise of another Prussia." With the word *rise,* Wassermann rose himself, and swung his right arm at the crowd that had gathered around his table. "I am depicting our development for the next thirty or forty years, when all of a sudden we shall awake to the fact that the armed forces of three-fourths of the globe are steaming toward our ports, to conquer another and a greater Prussia in another ghastly 'last war.' Perhaps I am ill-disposed tonight, ladies and gentlemen, but that is what I see tonight for this great stronghold of free speech, constitutional rights, and making the prisons safe and so forth." Someone began to cheer, and the others took it up at once. "Shut up, you swine," Wassermann bit at them, and they shut up, causing a dead quiet. Outside, an elevated train rumbled past. Wassermann recommenced in a low voice. His peroration.

"Debs, we don't want you. Our constitutional liberties came too easily to us for us to defend them. Regardless of a country's constitution, it gets the sort of government it deserves; and we evidently deserve a government of hypocrisy, low-mindedness, under the species of eternity, the dollar. We don't want our constitution, Debs, we want salved nonsense, and sleek respectables, and greasy ward-bosses. And if you try to restore to us something we don't want, into prison you go, judged by twelve of our own good and true. To the dungeon with you, Debs, and if you attempt to do anything for us again, we'll lynch you, in accordance with another of our highly democratic customs. Do you hear? Like the friends of good government and humanity we are, we'll squeeze your neck till your eyes bulge and your tongue hangs out, and then we'll let you dangle there as food for the crows and approving editorials in the *Times.*" He picked up his glass of beer, put it quickly to his lips, and took it at a gulp. Then with a sudden snarl, he flung the empty tumbler against the ceiling, where it smashed into bits, and fell on the heads of the listeners. He turned about viciously, and burst through the swinging doors, Out Into The Night.

* * *

"Why, Cynthia, must you insist on walking on these noisy streets? I want to break down to-night, and cry, and have my tears kissed, and all that. Cynthia, I am terribly miserable."

"What did you say, David? The cars, you know. It is hard to understand you when you speak so low."

"My God, my God. Everything is monsters! That damned fool speech in the saloon was a monster. My life since leaving you has been one monster after another. This situation to-night is a monster. Monsters, MONSTERS,— did you hear that?"

"Yes, David."

"I quarreled with my father to-day. He wanted me to learn that dirty Jew business of his. Why must all Jews be either pawnbrokers or in the clothing business! I left the house. . . . That was another monster. And I went into a public comfort station and saw montrous phalloi scribbled on the wall and one drawing of the female parts, just the hips and the thighs. The wretch who did that had a direct mind; Rops was never madder; Cynthia, I love you!"

They were already on the Manhattan Bridge. Cynthia said nothing. *"J'eusse aimé vivre auprès d'une jeune géante.* Thank God, Baudelaire understood. I wonder if they know what they are doing, these mild college professors who put that sonnet in their anthologies." Cynthia said nothing. The lights along the shore revealed dim shapes. The thick girders of the bridge itself were dim and far above their heads. "I could take you now, and hurl you away down there into that black water. Couldn't I?" He cackled. "Eh, couldn't I?" Cynthia shuddered as she felt his arms on her hips. "Oh Christ, oh Christ!" he moaned. "I give it up. Cynthia, will you marry me!" Cynthia's heart gave a bound, but she thought it advisable to say nothing. They stopped, and looked down vaguely into the water. Wassermann brooded wearily on the realization that he had proposed marriage, and was no doubt accepted.

4

The candle was nearly out. (Cynthia had insisted on candles. She seemed to take it all so comfortably. The candle gone, leaving the room heavy with irregular darknesses; the fire in the grate a mere sullen glow; the cold drawing its circle closer and closer about them, and forcing them nearer to each other; his head resting on her knees. Wright wondered if she accepted all this without question; and he suspected that she was perfectly at home.

"Our last night together, Cynthia."

"And our first!" There was a hint of a sigh. Wright winced. My God, how women loved this sort of thing!

Men *have* to hate other men, considering what must be said to women. Would she mention Wassermann? But he must quit gauging her; he must dip into this thing with heart. What nasty complications arose . . . his virginity, and her own. Did she know he was watching her? Do women suspect the *calculating eye of the male?* The spider and the fly . . . trite again. Why didn't he rebel? Why couldn't he send her home, even at this late hour, and load his lungs with the cold fresh air of a good book? No, he had but one of two choices: he could pass this by and be as incomplete as ever, or he could keep her here and put up with the tarnish. It was tyrannical, yes, but inevitable, that no matter how far one has gone with reading, life must begin at the beginning. But wasn't this, too, a cheaply romantic judgment to confuse life with sex? Like that little Jew back in Ohio who used to go down to the whore-district to "see life." But damn all this ergotizing; no wonder so many eager little girls can go so long untouched, if men must spend their time in straying from the highway. . . . But women demand some sort of ceremony; just as their sex is distributed all over their body, so the sex urge is less localized, less immediate. With men, philandering is cowardice; with women it is a completely accepted component in the formula of love. . . . Still, he yearned for a direct statement, and trusted in its efficacy, if he could ever find a fitting one. . . . He took off one of her shoes, and hoped to God that he had done enough. As he must have, since she kissed him a moment later, and went into the alcove, where he could hear her undressing. She had only dropped in for a few minutes; really she couldn't stay; and now here she was undressing in his alcove; he felt weighted down with experience, for he knew that *all* women would be this way.

"Good night, Lambert!"

"Good night, Cynthia. And don't worry about me. The little cot out here will be perfectly comfortable." All part

of the ceremony, as they both knew; ten minutes later he
was crawling awkwardly into bed with her, after rinsing
his mouth with Chartreuse.

She cuddled over against him, and a little song of happiness began singing within him. This thing on his shoulder,
—it was lovely, it was *sweet*. Her cold nose was against his
ear.

"Listen, little Cynthia; here is a speech on what people
remember: People remember different things. Some
people remember the names of everybody they went to
school with, and some remember when they had chicken-
pox, and some remember their Latin, and some remember
the first time they saw the Eiffel tower, but I remember the
tumult of her breathing in my ear." Thank God, he had
delivered it! He had walked up, and laid down his brick,
and walked away. But Cynthia was sleepy. . . . He lay there
helplessly, and let her slip away from him; tender, brutal,
weary, rebellious—one by one his moods changed color,
and all the while Cynthia drifted more impregnably into
sleep. He loved the little twitchings of her legs. And last
of all, he decided to forgive her, and surely girls do not
realize they are cruel. Cynthia was asleep.

He must be *thin*, he must be woefully *one-stringed*, to
suffer this with such resignation. And poor little Cynthia
would unconsciously take advantage of this. Yes, she was
safe. Ferociously, then sentimentally, and then wearily he
admitted it, she was safe. She would go to Wassermann
with all the technical requirements fulfilled.

*   *   *

"You dog, you can sit there and smirk me on my way
into matrimony. I confess, I have failed. It was marriage
or nothing, and my nature abhors a vacuum. I'm done for.
Wright, this is my epilogue, these words I am saying to
you now. Or is my epilogue the ones I say five years from

now, when I'm a Jew with a nose and a fat belly?" He approached a sneer. "Do you know, do you realize, man, that I have patched things up with my father, that I am to be his junior partner, and that we are going to enlarge the firm? The Wassermann Clothing Company becomes the Greater New York Clothing Company, a growing organization, you see. Wish me luck, and hope never to see me again."

AFTER HOURS

AFTER HOURS

THE various arteries of the city having been loosened by
the phlebotomy of five o'clock, the streets dripped profusely. The general tangle among the directions of the
pedestrians gave an illusion of hastiness, as though the
speed of the street were the aggregate of all the individual
speeds. The vehicles also added—especially the Cross-town
car which Howard took. He had attained this car between
a channel of automobiles moving like blocks of ice. He
had paid his fare behind a pregnant Italian woman who
still emanated the odor of this morning's garlic, while a
Jew pedlar from behind had collapsed his hamstrings by
the unexpected impulse of a bundle. He stepped into the
orchestration of breaths, sat down, and waited.

The car tugged ahead unevenly. The car filled disgust-
ingly. The inmates, paddled by the conductor's shouts,
flowed halting toward the front of the car. Three shop-
girls entered, pushing past a fat woman who really should
not ride at this time of the day. Their complexions were
not yet ten minutes old, having been renewed at five minutes to five. Two girls dropped nickels; as the third paid,
pennies were heard chasing one another down the glass
chute.

"Hold on there," the conductor yelled unnecessarily at
this third girl with the chasing pennies. Howard looked
at her and decided that she was a war horse. "Come on
with the rest o' the money."

"What do y' mean the rest o' the money?"

"I what do y' mean that y' on'y put in three cents!"

She said she put in fi' cents; the conductor said she on'y put in three; she said she put in fi'. Finally the conductor wouldn't argue no longer, and he turned the crank until all the money was out of the box. Then he held it up in his hand, and when he had taken all the nickels and dimes, there was nothing left but three cents. He showed this to the fat woman, who grumbled with disgust, and to the two other girls, who sniggered, and to a plumber who had just got on the car and who felt embarrassed; he also showed it to two other men whose occupations were uncertain. The girl paid the two additional cents, and whenever the car stopped after that you could hear her telling the other girls that she put in fi'. All sorts of people kept glancing at her and the conductor; the plumber stayed on the platform and looked at the headlight of the car behind.

Out of the newspaper sticking upside down in the overcoat pocket of the man in front of him Howard learned that

NING SCHOOLHOUSES
PECIALTY OF FIREBUGS
ee Destroyed Recently in West-
moreland County, Pa.
obe, Pa., Nov. 10.—A firebug

The damned guy moved his arm like an idiot. Howard fought hard over the thing, but the jerking of the car was another handicap. Then the man moved unconsciously further up the car. Howard observed with satisfaction that the lower half of a woman shifted into his immediate vision. He began thinking specifically of this lower half of a woman. The whole idea became preposterous. . . . Howard observed with profound guilt that he was riding past his stop. After all, it was worth a gambler's chance. Her knee . . . sure enough. After one entire extra avenue, she moved away. Howard left the car with resignation, and walked back in the face of a cold dark wind.

AFTER eating in a chop house with steamed windows, Howard went on down to the Village. Finally he got to the house he wanted, went up the stairs slowly, entered. Various hellos. Howard sat down. Problem: sociability. ". . .'s Baker doing now . . . new girl . . . that so! . . . devilish cold . . ." Fire is agitated. Edna is tweaking Lynch's nose; they shouldn't get off by themselves that way, it breaks up the party. Howard and everybody took everything with silent heroism. Everybody gravely watched Ramsay poke the fire unnecessarily. ". . .'s Charlie doing . . . for a coon's age . . . I don't . . ." Howard watching Edna's foot; it tapped, tapped, tapped hinging at the ankle; it had nothing whatsoever to do with Howard; he fingered a book and said things about it. Other people answered things. Differed and agreed. Intellectual conversation. After five minutes it had petered out; two voices started up, and fell together; everybody gravely watched Ramsay worrying the fire. The wind suddenly attacked the three inches of open window; somebody ran and closed it; somebody else said, "Whew . . . hell!" Then Englander arrived with the booze, and the evening was saved.

Howard felt his stomach recoil as the first slug of the vile stuff hit it. But after that the battle was won, and Howard poured it down without further discomfiture. The emphasis changed; that is, when Ramsey poked the fire once more before forgetting it for the evening, only a couple of people noticed the manoeuvre, and one of these was appreciated for saying "How sadistic!"

Somebody suggested poker; Howard heard people shout "Yes, poker!" and "Hell with poker!" and he heard himself shout "Yes, poker!" There being a general shove, he shoved, and learned a few seconds later that he was fighting for a chair. He attained a chair, and sat down, and began beating on the table for poker. Poker came. Within two minutes the cards were sticky with port, and the banker was still distributing chips. Howard won the first pot; somebody updumped the table; the game was over. Howard snapped a drink into him, threw back his head with such a jerk that part of the liquid trinkled into his ear.

He swerved about the room with the subconscious realization of many things: the stove in the corner; millions of miles away, Neptune was plunging through space, cold and deserted; it was only a question of time until Edna left Lynch; that queer time in the street car—he would say nothing about it; drink it slower, old man, slower. Everyone was frankly in his own orbit; they called out to each other from a distance and in haste, as though they were going in opposite directions on railway trains. They reeled within one another's recognition, and out again. Howard was grateful when spoken to, and answered with overflowing emotion. Frankly, he saw no disgrace in repetition. At times, however, when someone drunker than himself approached, he looked at that person and registered with clarity, "You are drunk . . . you dirty slobbering cretin, you are pig-stewed." At times he even said this, and the remark would secure him a staunch temporary friend.

Edna came up to him. "Hello, Howard dear!" They began to talk. They didn't talk about much, but they talked soberly. Howard became embarrassed and dropped his eyes. Not because they talked soberly, but because he remembered distinctly once when they had ALMOST. Her husband was in the room now, and Howard had just told him he was pig-stewed, and yet with this woman he had once ALMOST. He was overwhelmed by her unheard-of brass. He wanted to crawl away from her. That was why he dropped his eyes.

The independence of his orbit grew more pronounced. Howard went over to a window, and looked out on the street four floors below. Snow had fallen. He lived for a while in the sweetened haze of the swaying electric light

on the corner, and watched the shadows adapt themselves
irregularly in the snow as the light vacillated in the wind.
Little strips of cold air whisked against him. He laid his
hot head against the cold pane, and then took it away to
observe the grease marks from his nose and forehead. He
sat down on the floor, and dropped his head on the seat
of a chair. He watched the left wall continually beginning
to get higher than the right one. Being experienced, however, he accepted the phenomenon with confidence. He
slipped full length on the floor, and felt things revolve
uncertainly. Then, of a sudden, a powerful conviction
came over him. He understood now that he was going to
be nauseated. He left the room reeling, but with a set
determination; leaning over, he suffered the fulfilment of
his nausea.

THERE had been a cat. Howard had gone out into the
kitchen, to get a drink, and seen this cat, and spoken to it
without enthusiasm. The cat had looked at Howard with
large, moon-steady eyes. Howard had first spoken to the
cat, and then caressed it abstractedly, and then swept it
off the table. Then he had splashed water on it, and left
the room.

And now it was not the *os innominatum* which those
two were trying to solve. The *os innominatum* is a bone.
Os: bone . . . *innominatum:* . . . . The geometry
proposition is *pons asinorum.* They were not trying to
solve the *os innominatum,* then, but the *pons asinorum.*
Howard lived through it all meekly. He accepted it re-
ligiously that it must be proved that a^2 plus b^2 equals
c^2. Englander drew a triangle on the white woodwork of
the door, and he named the sides a, b and c. Then he
made little squares on all three sides. And then he stopped.
Pons asinorum; he stopped. Howard labored with a half
conscious anguish. What next! Englander did not know;
Howard did not know; nobody knew. When Pearl began

talking to him, he felt himself lean his body with relief to listen to her, while Englander fumbled angrily at a^2.

Pearl talked a lot of stuff. Pearl pulled things about breaking away and "wasting yourself magnificently" and "the good things of life." Howard synthesized it thus: Once you used to live with me; you don't live with me any more; why not live with me for tonight? Howard understood all this with meekness. Somewhere off on the borderline of his consciousness he debated the practicality of seeing this thing through; without perfect awareness he decided that the scheme was impractical. If Pearl's man was getting too old for service as any thing but a pocketbook he, Howard, could not. . . . He had been dropped once; it would be a lowering of his dignity now. And besides, you never know just how much of this kind of thing is real, and how much is a mere feeler to satisfy a woman's vanity. Howard worked at these problems slavishly, and said, "Since I have been married, Pearl, I have received another outlook on life. Tonight, you find me drunk, and therefore as I used to be . . . apparently . . . but in reality I am as different as (gesture) . . . as . . . the world." Pearl followed him. People were disturbing him by their movements about the room. But this was evidently a time for solidity. Howard became more staunch; "You cannot understand, Pearl. I almost love you for it, I confess. But with a man, there is always the dreadful temptation, to use your terminology, to fall into tergiversations against all that he once exemplified. A woman is what she is; a man is a composite of what he is and the negation which that essence predicates. The more pronounced ego-centricity of the male results . . . or better, this way . . . no man is a worthy saint who has not been a hell-raiser, and hell-raising is infinitesimally insignificant except when it is found in one who has renounced the Faith. And so I have attained my apotheosis in that I am different from that which I formerly signified.

And frankly it is almost pathetic to one in my situation when he finds that a person whom he once loved has not tergiversated with him." And Pearl synthesized that it was all off.

Howard collapsed into glazedness, still vaguely appreciative of the heavy blocks of his diction. He weighed them all over again, one by one, and catching Englander's eye, he smiled. He forgot the smile in the middle, although it wore off gradually, his facial muscles were so stiff with weariness. Then he got up, consciously put his hat on crooked, consciously let his coat drag, and started home.

When he finally got home, he woke his wife while crawling into bed; she cried a little, then they both went to sleep.

MY DEAR MRS. WURTELBACH

MY DEAR MRS. WURTELBACH

1

WHAT if he had known Wurtelbach since the days when they had a tent in the back yard and played Old Maid if it rained? It was in the company of Wurtelbach that he had bought his first beer. Furthermore, he had roomed with Wurtelbach at the university. But as to Mrs. Wurtelbach, he had taken her limp hand and been assigned to a chair once, and another time he had been informed that her husband often spoke of him. As a consequence, the letter was written thus:

My dear Mrs. Wurtelbach:

How can I express my sympathy with you and little Dorothy over the loss of husband and father! I heard the terrible news this morning for the first time, and since then I have felt the need more and more strongly of writing a few words, however much they fail of conveying my deep condolence. At such times one is painfully aware of just how cruel fate can be, and how we are all called upon to bear our load of suffering. But surely it must be some consolation to you in your sorrow to realize that there are so many who knew and loved your husband. And then again, you must strive to remember that he himself would wish those whom he left behind to be as happy as possible.

My mother asks me to assure you in her behalf how greatly she, also, enters in with you in your affliction.

Wurtelbach dead! Wurtelbach pig-stewed . . . dead. Wurtelbach addressing the Chamber of Commerce with that artificial seriousness of his . . . dead. Wurtelbach sneezing . . . dead. All the little untied ends of Wurtelbach's experiences had just stopped being there to tie. In some closet or other the baggy trousers were hanging which Wurtelbach was going to put on next Sunday morning. His wife and child were probably crying in Sewickley.

Charles did not cringe at sending the letter, any more than he had cringed at eating breakfast. If it had been Charles who had died, Wurtelbach would have sent a similar letter to his mother; indeed, somewhere in the letter he might even have situated Charles comfortably in Heaven and hinted that it is selfish of us to grieve the loss of one who has been Called Home. Charles realized that he could write it, and mail it, while the fact of Wurtelbach's death would remain on his hands in exactly the same way.

The time he and Wurtelbach had . . . dead. Like lead, in bed, his dull, dull head (pause) . . . dead (one, two, three) . . . dead. "Hello . . . yes . . . oh, hello, Alice. I hoped you'd call. Yes, I got home all right . . . dead . . . rather late, of course, but I had a good night." Now, concerning this matter of the Chicago Awto-Lite Company, why not write them and tell them to forward the photographs in any case, and if we found that we could not run the illustrations, we could either return them forthwith or hold them for a future article our editors might get up on accessories. Hanging up there lopsided in the closet, all ready for next Sunday. The pump stopped; it's all over when that convulsion stops down there under the ribs.

Once, with a sudden freezing, Charles understood that he had lost dear old Wurtelbach.

2

First Esther had stepped over the log, and then Miss Anderson had stepped over the log, and then Myrtle and

Wurtelbach had stepped over the log, and then, after a long interval, Anne had stepped over the log . . . and then . . . over the log . . . the log . . . log. . . . Then they were all gone. They had all gone ahead, leaving the log behind them, and fresh rips in the ferns growing out of the rotten leaves. Wurtelbach had avoided the cow-flops, as well as the eyes of the girls. What if he were to eat a cow-flop; Christ, what a stir! The girls' legs carried them up, up the hill; Wurtelbach considered the masterful working of these mechanisms.

Esther was a kid; that's why she was first. Or more accurately, Esther was still a colt. Esther went on up the hill, without the least suspicion of the night Wurtelbach wanted to eat her. Esther was as useless as a sparrow. Her unhappy body was without significance. Wurtelbach agreed with a certain guilty awkwardness while she talked of climbing Hawkbill and yelling across to Chestnut Ridge. He was willing to drop behind.

Myrtle, gentlemen, was Queenly. With all her bones comfortably buried beneath a half-inch cushion of warm flesh, Myrtle could take up as much of your time as she cared to by talking deliberately. Myrtle could bathe in spring water without suffering; but the irrefutable fact remained that there was frequently a strong odor which came from Myrtle's armpits.

The general picnic spirit continued. They would be at Buckeye Spring in fifteen minutes. Oh, look, the columbines were still *perfect!* And they had seeded in the valley two weeks ago. The bull! The bull! . . . Wurtelbach promptly advanced, while the girls crawled back under the barbed wire nervously. The brute kicked up clods of grass and dirt over his swaying rump. Wurtelbach collected rocks with an inward emphasis. Then he began throwing, until one rock hit the bull on a protruding shoulder bone. The bull retreated back among the trees, vibrating and sending little pebbles rolling down the hill. Wurtelbach continued to throw, thus assuring safe conduct for his women.

Then came half a mile of tangle, where the trail was nearly lost, until it broke into full view of the mountains. They rolled away blue-black, like the faithful backs of elephants. From across the valley they got the broadside of Craggy. Everyone waited for Anne, and when she arrived she was chagrined at being waited for. You could plunge words deep into Anne. Some little half-uttered sentence with the man-and-woman about it . . . you could let it drop and feel sure that it would be picked up. Anne was like a deep pool: you could throw in a pebble . . . there would be a little ripple . . . and then the pebble would lie there. When Anne went into her room at night and shut the door, you felt that it was being shut with sullenness. Anne was not good-looking; it was generally agreed that she would never marry.

When they reached the Flats, Wurtelbach sneaked away to observe the ridges. Thirty-seven could be seen from here on a clear day. Wurtelbach counted twelve before he thought to close his eyes. When he opened them again, he picked one little white roof five miles down the valley. Then he sailed from here to there in a bee-line, and among the ridges. The thin, dead air made him feel the pulse-beat in his ears. Two months after this Wurtelbach was dead.

3

For a few notes the band chugged in unison, and then it broke away again, all the little parts flying off independently. That was jazz. The piccolo wobbled on a three-bar spree; the violin tumbled down three octaves. The pianist bounced alternately from bass to high treble. (No use; everybody just ate.) The trombone saw its chance, and drawled blurtingly. The trap-drummer let loose all over, drums, bells, bones, cymbals. For a while each player ran his own little circle around the melody, existed by himself, felt recklessly assertive. (Five hundred crab meat salads were removed simultaneously, and five hundred roasted second joints of capon were brought in their place.) The band stopped to change the score, and there would have been dead silence if every one were not hearing his own jaws.

After the nuts had been passed around, however, and breadcrumbs had been brushed secretly from the knees to the floor, and the cigars were lighted tentatively, one dealer from Buffalo, seated at table 36, offered a joke about a very stupid and very typical Englishman. This Englishman, while visiting his American cousin in California, being greatly impressed by the extended cultivation which was going on, had asked, "But bah Joove, ah say, what do you do with all this produce?" And the American had answered. "Oh, we can what we can, and what we can't can, we can." Now the Englishman was inordinately tickled with this, but later, while trying to repeat it back home, he blundered with characteristic stupidity, "Oh, we can what we cawn, and what we cawn't can we put up in tins." Table 36 laughed the fitting amount, and a dealer from a small town outside of Buffalo told one about a rather fast woman; and what is more, he followed it with one about a woman's parts.

Table 36 was now in a pleasant frame of mind, and when the band jazzed again, everybody joined in the chorus. Two men came out—fairies probably—and sang something or other. The five hundred gentlemen assembled did not listen. The two fairies melted away, and forty women appeared, which explains why certain tables were upset in the yowling rush toward the center of the floor. Yaaing, these babies stood upon ladders, and oscillated the jelly of their breasts.

For an hour, then, this tingling meat was examined. And when it left, the president of the All-American Corporation gave a speech:

"Gentlemen . . . As I look over this glad assemblage . . . of more than five hundred . . . this evening . . . it takes me back nine years to the first annual banquet held under the auspices of the All-American Corporation. . . . Stop to consider, gentlemen, what really tremenjous strides the All-American has made in these nine short years. . . . Transport yourself back to those uncertain days when our organization was making its first struggle for existence. . . . If I remember correctly, there were just . . . one . . . two, there were exactly fourteen dealers present at the first annual banquet of the All-American Corporation.

"How little we expected then, when Mr. Hemmingway talked of moving his little hub factory to a larger city, that nine years from that day we should have . . . not *one* headquarters in a large city . . . not *two* . . . but representatives distributed over the length and breadth of the en-tire world! Little did we think at that time that civilization would develop such an insatiable hunger for our commodity.

"Little did *we* think, I say. But that statement is unjust; for even at that early date the faith of the founder of our organization never wavered. For Mr. Hemmingway was a man of vision, a prophet, a seer. He could foretell, where we could not, what a great demand was to be created in the world for his invention. And today, thanks to the vision of that undaunted genius . . ." THE WORLD IS WITHOUT A TOY. Romance, realism, the inquisition, the City of God, geo-centricity . . . they have left us nothing . . . nothing but a wobbly art trying to hit us on the head with a club. Is there some life beyond the mucous membrane? Is there some significance beyond a little suburban home? As an adolescent, I carried vague possibilities in my groins; and now there is nothing left but to look at people. Christ, they have even burned out our pessimism!

Ah! to have gotten up in the night, and to have noticed

the door open and the light lit. And to have passed down the corridor . . . and nothing . . . nothing . . . to have returned, unchanged.

What are we to do with the growing trees? And Mrs. Buckhorn yelling down the dumb-waiter shaft? Let me rise above . . . let me maintain . . . let me affirm . . . There is the epigram, and there is the epic . . . and I have squeezed big theoretical tears. If there is one pure joy left with us, it is to pass a tight jobby.

David, my little man, sling your pebble at the universe.

THE DEATH OF TRAGEDY

THE DEATH
OF TRAGEDY

PART ONE

Argument: From our eagle's nest above the century, we observe details scattered beneath, finally pouncing upon Clarence Turner as a likely bit of carrion.

In following the road to Lynn, where Paul Revere summoned our forefathers—spiritual at least—to guerilla warfare, note the excellent facilities of the Standard Oil Company for purveying gasoline at exorbitant prices . . . and on the return, fill your pipe with the aid of the tobacco trust, for you can smoke on the after-deck of the railway combine's ferries until the pilot turns and goes the other way, thus making the pipe illegitimate since it is being smoked on the fore-deck. Believe us, it is all built on a healthy basis of Garfield niggers stoning Frogtown dagoes, and Saturday afternoon amateur baseball games in the suburbs, and especially back in them grand days when papa got over his bun just in time for Sunday dinner. (Recalling the game which wound up the season, Brushton against Homewood, and our boys got licked twenty to one oh Jeezuz. In the last half of the ninth, when Humpty Haas came up to the plate, they hit his bat with a lemon. That same evening, however, the pitcher of the other team got drunk and strayed into town somewhat boastfully. And our boys showed what they couldn't do with baseball they could do with their fists.)

My aunt once told me, if I wanted to be healthy, to read

Science and Health and eat an apple at bedtime . . . but now the country is going to the dogs, and it is all candy laxatives. Great God, if a volcano came upon us suddenly, and preserved our subway signs for future excavations, surely the archeologists would conclude that the rites of visceral purgation had something to do with our religion. In fact, as enlightenment spreads more and more among us, are we not coming to realize with continually increasing clarity that a man can not put in a good day at the office without his once before breakfast and once before going to bed?

Some day we shall surely own half of England, and have our own taps draining the hearts of the natives of India, to feed fresh blood into our patriotic barrels. Further, Mrs. Purdue, noting the mysterious quiet which suddenly fell upon her son's tent out in the back yard, peeped through a crack to observe six little boys sitting around with their peeties hanging out, and her son was one of them . . . the same one in fact, who later went to avenge the rape of Belgium.

Herein lies wisdom: If we have had so many years of the Democrats, let us go Republican; and when we have had so many years of the Republicans, let us spit upon them, turn our backs upon them, and go Democrat; and when we have tired of being either Democrats or Republicans, let us repeat the process under different appellations. In this way we can always be assured of an abundance of sinecures for our Irish-American population, while we shall seldom make the mistake of electing a mayor without a wad in his cheek . . . like that perfect product from Pittsburgh who, being introduced among Pittsburgh high society, on preparing to make his speech and noticing that Mrs. Eitelbaum was talking, shouted good-naturedly, "Hay there, you shut up 'r I'll throw y'out." As is evident, he won the élection because he knowed how to mix with the boys. A similar situation will be observed in Denver, or Charleston, and other cities.

Our rich and powerful country also possesses certain songs, and we rise when those songs are played, because certain of our countrymen are getting control of the entire meat-packing industry of the Argentine. Millions for defense, but not one cent for tribute; my country, right or wrong, my country; we shall have peace, if we have to fight for it; remember the Maine; by God, we are bound to be great, for we can find the right sentence. (In contradistinction to the much more accurate Germans who always find the wrong one; as to wit, the scrap of paper.)

There has been kite season, and commy season, and roller-skate season, and baseball season, and swimming season, and roller-skate season again, and football season . . . and then in the evenings a fire is lighted in an empty lot. There are earnest, unhappy souls who observe these fires from a bedroom window or an automobile, and suddenly feel like going out for a walk in the cold fall air. Forms, half red, half black, disappear and return; there is a gush of sparks. I have at such times heard a horn blow out of the darkness, and one voice from the fire answer "Allright," thereupon the circle about the fire being diminished. By ten-thirty no one remains but one orphan, one boy whose father works at night, and one other. The fire is allowed to languish; eventually it burns a sullen, characterless red, left alone in the black field.

Also, there are the nice houses. What has been said for the clean, dead houses on a terrace, with father returning a little after five in the summer, slapping his paper against his knee, and being met on the front steps. There are mists from the river which come after dark to lie over this part of the city. In a slight wind, the arc-lights sway on the deserted corners, making the shadows of telegraph wires climb up and down the walls. Occasionally the Polish maid entertains on the back porch.

The great lump of the country rolls on, with Howard swiping apples out of the cellar, and a high school sophomore pimpled with pubescent love, and elderly men dressing up to apply for jobs, and unexecuted rapes . . . and thieveries dead in the planning . . . . . . half-ambitions . . . . fractional insights. . . . . while as for Clarence Turner, his book —thank God!—had already reached its eighth edition, and there was the reasonable possibility of his play appearing on Broadway. The success, in fact, had been immediate. Not that Turner was low enough in the scale of jackals to have actually pandered to the public tastes. On the contrary, he had written in all sincerity, and it was simply a lucky accident that those subjects which were nearest to his heart happened to scratch the itch of the muck and glut of America's reading public.

If, climbing upon the ruins of America, we have reached Clarence Turner . . .

PART TWO

Argument: Or rather, having cast about for a theme, we came upon that of Clarence Turner. It is, perhaps, worth further development.

ON the third floor he stopped at a room which was done in purples; Florence was lying down, appropriately. "Ah, then you *can* come to see me, Clara!" she said to him with a certain commendable richness. He went over to her, and kissed her: kissed her, and all the memories of her. Glancing at the mantelpiece, he noticed that the lion's head had been restored to its place. (Once, he had gone over to touch it, calling forth from Florence a startled cry, pretty but honest. Another time, when he was looking at it steadily, she walked between them. But Clarence got the thing laid out quite clearly after a while, as is evident from this: While they were taking tea together, he had blurted out quite inconsequently, "It strikes me that the lion's head has a most fatherly look." The next time he came, the head had disappeared; and within a week he had attained her!)

"Yes, I *can* come, and I *dare* come, in spite of your loveliness," he answered in tune.

"See what I was reading? Your book . . . again and again, one chapter! You can not tell me that that chapter was not written to me . . . oh, you know the one!" Not being quite sure of the one, Clarence bowed his head in mute acknowledgment that he knew it, oh, too well. Then a trembling came over him, and he ate her hand with kisses. (But above and beyond the fact that she had set Rimbaud to music, and had even published songs of her own in which Turner figured indubitably, above and beyond the yield of her kimonos and the genius she had for draping shadows about a room, there was the fact that she slid as gracefully into other arms as into his own . . . which explains after a fashion why he suddenly broke off the affair, marrying someone of a less accomplished quality in her voice. Soon after this, as a divine vengeance, came the success of his novel.)

Suddenly she arose, and then, significantly: "But we shall have tea." He looked at her deadly, and let his head sag into his hands. She sang three or four weak little bars of a song of hers, and wrapped her kimono more tightly about her. These little touches had been almost brutally definite; each understood just what had been given and taken. It was, roughly, this: "But we shall have tea" equals "What, Clarence, you think I can be put down and picked up again at will! I shall break the whole trend of our emotions with the irrelevant tinkling of the tea things." . . . His sagging head equals "I accept it, Florence, perhaps after a fashion even welcome it; not too proud to have you see me desolate over the loss. Look, I am frankly miserable; our friendship has meant so much." . . . Her timid little flurry of song equals "Still, you dear, dear boy, it must be that way, if our memories are to be retained in all their purity. Oh, God, to see it of a sudden, just what we had, and what we have lost!" . . . And the wrapping of the kimono equals "But all that is settled now; snap, it is finished. There is a wall between us." Silence for a few moments, while they listened to the far echoes of a relationship which was irrevocably gone. (It was all quite sympathetic to his mentality, this thick aura-of-soul which in the course of centuries has come to interpose itself between the agent and the feminal.)

The silence continued all during the preparation of the tea. Over against the general formlessness of their emotions came the definite clinking of the china. Clarence's eyes worked earnestly about the designs in the carpet.

Then she nodded, and he pulled up his chair. Their feet met beneath the table; she did not withdraw, but looked at him steadily. How far their relationship had retrograded!

She laughed after a time in anticipation of a sentence which she was going to say. "Ha, it almost seems," it had been only the littlest laugh, "it almost seems, Clara, as though you will not really be here until you have left." Then she became agitated. "A history of tea! A history of tea! Is there anything but walls and beds which has seen humanity more intimately? Indeed, I vote for tea, Clarence, for here the great organ-notes of our passions are turned into the neatest, tiniest little cameos. Think of a murder across the tea-table. What a lovely hokku the whole idea would make! . . . It should be done, of course, with some sort of poisonous needle, held out along with a very properly turned compliment, and barely scratching the skin. . . . And the final death; would the victim fall across the table? Would the tea-things come rattling to the floor, the destruction of a miniature empire? Really, it is all very lovely, don't you think?" (Both being very conscious that Mrs. Turner could not do this sort of thing at all.)

And then: "But let me put away the tea-things. I must put them away now. For I shall not be able to bear it, seeing the room all cluttered up by you. And I must rearrange the chairs." Without ostentation, Clarence took the ends of the cigarettes which he had lined along his saucer —there should be no fetishes!—and carried them to the grate, threw them out of his life, and hers.

It was all so plain that this day was his last hold upon their intimacy. Now he could still go to her and take her in his arms; but after leaving this room this day . . . when he met her on the street, he would touch his hat, ask a few words about her brother, tell her some recent anecdote, and then hurry away.

He resented any distraction as a sin against this woman

in front of him. Yet his wife would surely be expecting him from now on. He felt subconsciously that he should offer Florence a pure immersion in the present, in the emphatic this-ness and here-ness of their parting. Their parting, since that was certain. Everything that had happened this afternoon seemed to leave some little broken end. He arose abruptly, went to his hat and coat, and threw them across his arm. Walking to the door, he opened it, and paused with one hand on the knob. Florence dripped into her chair, looking at him without meaning.

On her little writing-table the phone began ringing. Once, twice, then with a nagging impatience. Tacitly, however, they agreed to rule it out of the scene. Still, it *did* increase the tempo of their leave-taking; for he began to close the door with a jerk of sudden decision. She leaped from her chair, bolted toward him. He received her with a groan, crushing his hat between them. Then he turned and went stumbling blindly down the stairs, while the phone peeled forth one wild, unbroken plaint.

Reaching home, Turner hurried straight to his room, where for some hours he wrote feverishly.

PART THREE

Argument: Becoming impatient, the author finally wanders elsewhere, and seems in the direction of a positive beauty, when the old subject returns like a gastric juice in the throat.

HE fell asleep in the early morning, and when he awoke again at eight he found that the life had faded out of him. He went down for a walk, bought an orange at an Italian fruit-store on Sullivan Street, and ate it standing on the corner. A drayhorse had fallen in the slush; Turner watched the agony of its feet as it struggled to rise, while its team-mate looked about with indifference. Finally he surrendered himself. He accepted it more or less consciously that he had given time enough to the burial of his love—taking the term, that is, as a technical expression, by which is meant that love, like potato farming or marine insurance, is developing a specific nomenclature as the manifestations thereof are becoming more standardized with the help of education. Now, if our more prominent novelists, of the type of Turner, could have taken two years of the classics and then two years intensive study in amoristic engineering, this fact could have been put upon its right basis long before now. A graph of the human heart, for instance, by a senior A. E., could have traced the curve from Seeing Her Pass, through Poignant Night and With Her Alone, ending perhaps with Burial of His Love. To look upon this as a scientific terminology, that is, so that the phrase "burial of his love" should not be dismissed as banal, but rather accepted as the accurate dictionary equivalent for the thing itself, and sanctioned by the consensus of the leading minds of the nation.

The steady rumble of every-day had gradually reclaimed him, so that he turned from the drayhorse—Christ! after Florence could not his wife even be called a drayhorse! Stand up the sorry thing and look at her. He could do that; that was his trade. The brute, walking along these streets; exciting no interest, and yet tearing the last strip of dignity from the woman he had married. Consider all the little pulsing hearts, too good for other pulsing hearts, but not good enough—oh, God! how short-coming—for *one* pulsing heart, our hundred millions are composed of. What sewer-cleaner's daughter would marry the son of a honey-dipper? Yet Clarence Turner . . . after Florence . . . his wife! Added to a sleepless night, it is not hard to understand his bitterness.

When he reached the apartment she had already left, which was a show of delicacy that he had not expected of things. The furniture sat about, peculiarly irresponsive to his emotions. Going to his room, he threw himself upon the bed, and sobbed.

Lying there sobbing, and the stars *do* go around the earth. He has read any number of volumes on the play of the mucous membranes. Let us erect a dirty little monument to these intellectuals. There is even the possibility that we shall be driven into the Church by the scurviness of our free-thinkers. Building upon the sound foundation of this low-visionedness, there are those who, coming from Ohio, own the loss of an "r," while others, friend, can pronounce certain words with the accent on a different syllable than is customary. Such observations are really of value, since they may contribute to the happiness of still others.

On the other hand, oh, God, on the other hand, we shall sail easily across an enthusiasm of contours. To the south, the broad back of a hill curved down slowly into the plateau. And still farther south, an opposing curve swelled up and stretched away in the haze. While the lake fitted itself silently into the basin which the glaciers had scooped out for it some thousands of years ago. Or, off against the sky, consider the little meadow lying beyond a V of two hills. Or trees banked up the mountain-side like clouds, and at irregular intervals the black-green firs jutting out like a city of church spires.

While there are, for those who love such things, rains which come ripping along the valleys, attacking whole forests, bending around gaps between the mountains, driving things before them. Further, there are patchy rains; they piddle for a while, then pour, then even cease entirely, so that the sun gets at the landscape here and there in shafts. And there are still other rains which you go on the porch and exclaim, "Why, it is raining!" they have sneaked into being so imperceptibly. While after any sort of rain the woods are even smellier than usual.

Oh, vomit of loveliness! Let us rise in the night and give thanks for the pure horizons that remain to us. Exult, for the heavy hills are patient to be climbed upon; willingly they suffer us to paw at their necks and sit across the peaks of their ears. And looking down from them, we see the valley, as it dips and waves, and how the shadows of the clouds . . . the shadows of the clouds, there being any number of clouds that day, though there was also the night when I went to the door/ and found the whole world snuggled away under snow/ that spread off and over the hills/ blue in the full moon/ sifting softly against the fences of the meadows/ and drooping from the fir trees.

Addenda

Turner's convalescence was hastened considerably by the intelligence that his play was really to appear on Broadway; he also became wrapped up in the consequences of a note which had said among other things, *"Je te désire."*

THE BOOK OF YUL

THE BOOK OF YUL

PART ONE

WHILE waiting, two men carried on a conversation that flapped and fluttered like an old newspaper. And a third was silent. Finally, the conversation gained in intensity, culminating in some disagreeable figure or image. Whereat, the third man rose and left the room. With us following, for it is he who conceived of Yul and the eleventh city. Thus:

Three men in a room, towards night. Two of them sat in the cold, sprawled somewhat, and with their overcoats on. The third was huddled in a Morris-chair, knees up to his chin, looking down over his toes at the vague carpet. "Do you think she will come?" one of the other two asked. He swallowed, and noticed that his throat was getting sore. For a while they shifted slightly, in silence. (As the room grew darker, no one had moved to light the lamps.) The sounds outside came in dampened by the snow.

"We should have started a fire when we first got here," the first man said, yawning. "If we're going to wait around here we might as well be comfortable."

"Too late now, she'll be along any minute."

The man hunched up in the Morris-chair sniffled three or four times, and then blew his nose. "Ah, what a bitter world!" one of the others laughed. "Look, the poor devil had to move." . . . A heavy clock, in another room somewhere, or upstairs, or in the hall, sunk seven strokes into the room. Outside an automobile stalled. They heard the scraping of the self-starter several times before the motor began working again. Then the car jerked ahead; then stalled. After a few minutes, however, the motor thumped with a solid regularity, and the car passed on down the street. Out of the high windows the snow could be seen falling diagonally across a street lamp.

"This waiting outside the gates of Heaven is cold business."

"Why in the name of God do you call it the gates of Heaven?"

Somebody could be heard walking. Thump, thump, THUMP louder . . . then THUMP, THUMP, thump fainter. "Probably the people in the next house." Listening intently, they could even catch a grumble of voices. Off up there, on the other side of the wall somewhere, people were no doubt sitting around talking, before a big fire, in a room full of light, eating, or maybe drinking something strong. Like those conceptions of perfect luxury which are inserted in the upper right-hand corner, the rest of the picture being devoted to a boy in rags, starving to death in a snowy alley.

A wind caught in the chimney in such a way as to disturb the burnt rubbish in the grate. The smell of rotten apples blew out into the room. Two girls passed outside, laughing, and hurrying with short, sharp steps. The man who had swallowed a little while ago brought up some saliva and swallowed again, to test his throat; the glands were distinctly swollen. He shot his cigarette into the dead grate; after a few moments, however, he lighted another. He said, "Damn this place for a tomb." A pause; then he continued, "When I stay very long in a place like this I always think, what if I were trapped in? . . . When I was a boy, I saw a crow early one spring standing bolt upright in a tree. I went closer, and he didn't fly. Then I saw that his foot had been caught in a fox trap. He flew to this tree, where the chain got caught in one of the branches. So he had been there during the winter, exposed to the cold and without food; and when he died, the trap weighted him so that he stood up as chestily as the healthiest crow you ever saw. . . . When I wait in a place like this, I can't help thinking of dying that way. Can't you imagine us all sitting here in this darkness, dead, you holding a pipe, and me like this, and him over there in the corner all hunched up!" At this point, the man in the Morris-chair arose, left the room, and could be heard immediately afterwards going down the stone stairs to the street.

The snow was falling now in thick wet gobs. Before he had gone fifty feet it was clinging to the fuzz of his woollen coat. Big banks of cleanliness had been stacked up. The lights of the store windows lay distinctly across the pavements. In that arc-light, in the carbon, in one molecule of the carbon, maybe, there was a little world, with planets and stars, and an infinite sky, and things living on some of the planets, and things living on those things. Some day some big hand would want our universe for an arc-light, and crunch, away it would go. "In one little corner beyond the stars, a world glowing up there all by itself, not crowded in the way ours is . . ." God, what a night! He listened unconsciously to the different scrapings of the shovels.

He started to turn into the subway, but did not do so, since an elation was on him. Instead, he went into the park, and stamped about in the heavy snow, even walked across one of the ponds, in fact. A gust of wind hit him strong enough for him to rise up against it, and yell into the teeth of it. Then he swung his arms, and charged an embankment. When he reached the top, he looked about him, a half mile across the park to the lights of the apartments along the edge. The wind dropped away; he was almost hot after his exertion. He opened his coat and laughed a stage laugh. Then he chanted, *"Sic erat in principio, et nunc, et semper, et in saecula saeculorum, amen.*

And the wind, appearing before me, spook, speek, spike, spuck, SPAKE, 'Behold the eleventh citee.' And I, answering unto the wind, spook, speek, spike, spuck, SPAY-ACHE, 'Verily, verily, do I behold the eleventh citee,' for there are ten others buried beneath it. Gloria!"

And then continuing to sing-song the *Sic erat*, his mind wandered off to elaborate the eleventh city. "It is in the bottom of the sea," he thought, "and lived in by extremely cultivated fishes." But I happen to know that it is not at the bottom of the sea; or that it is not even near the sea. But it stands, bulky and dead, in the middle of a plain, silhouetted against the sky, and cold.

It is granite. Even the beds on which the people sleep are granite slabs, built in square holes carved out of the walls. For people live in this eleventh city: quiet, grey-eyed people, who slip about the stone streets, and in and out of oblong holes which serve as doors. But the under cities are filled with corpses, lying in rows, perfectly preserved, and without smell. The streets are long straight lines, and other long straight lines drawn perpendicular to these; the same is consistently true of the architecture.

And there was a traveller in this city, by the name of Yul. Looking ahead at the end of the widest street, he saw a break in the two walls of granite, and went towards it. It was a stairway, he found. Broad stairs, the width of a palace in his own country, led down to a platform, and so on down and down to platforms. All this was lit with a uniform incandescence. While at the base of the stairs there stood two granite lamp-posts, of no great size, but which he could distinguish as clearly as though they were immediately in front of him.

But Yul did not descend these stairs.

PART TWO

YUL found the system of transit which had been evolved here of great ingenuity. It was composed of sixteen parallel tracks, or rather, endless platforms, which moved continually. These platforms were provided with benches, pavements, empty rooms, and the like. Now, as Yul stepped towards the south, he noticed that each platform moved slightly faster than the one to the north of it; and although the change from platform to platform was not abrupt, by the time Yul had reached the fifteenth platform to the south he was speeding enormously. The sixteenth platform, however, was entirely different from the fifteen preceding. To begin with, he found that it could not be boarded at any point, as with the other platforms. In front of him there moved a stone wall; occasionally, behind this he heard a roar, as of something which approached and retreated. And Yul, noticing that a group of grey-gowned figures had stopped near him on the fifteenth platform and seemed to be waiting, waited as well.

Within a short time he saw a tower approaching on the sixteenth platform. It advanced evenly, floated towards them, growing gradually above them as it came. When it was only a short ways off, he also noticed that there was a break in the stone wall at this point, and that some of the figures farther down the platform were already entering there. In due time it reached him, and he stepped under the square stone arch on to the sixteenth platform. Everything was quite different here. Instead of the stone benches, pavements, kiosks, there was nothing but this lonely tower and a straight steel track that blurred away to the east and west. Like the others, he entered the tower, and found it a sort of rest room or waiting room.

Finally, above the grinding of the platforms, a far-off whirr was heard. The grey-clad figures left the tower, Yul thinking it best to follow. A line of cars shot up to the tower and stopped. Yul followed his companions into one of the cars, and they sped along the sixteenth platform. Yul sank into a stupor from this accumulation of speeds, partaking of nothing but a bitter, burning liquid which was brought to him at intervals. After another two days, Yul tired of the cars, and descended at one of the towers. Then he crossed the fifteen other platforms to the north, and found, when he stepped off the last of them, that he had returned almost to the starting point.*

He came to the wide street again, and entered one of the oblong cuts in the stone which served as doorways. Inside, there were winding stairs, lit with the same unvarying incandescence that he had noticed on the stairs leading down to the buried cities. Yul wound slowly upwards, his steps slapping back at him in a confusion of echoes. The stairs curved into a room; a large, square room, empty except for a tablet on one of the walls and a bench placed before this tablet. Yul, who could not read the tablet, noticed the firmness of the characters, and passed on into the next room. This room, too, was large and square and empty. But there was a window hewn out in one wall, oblong like the doors in the street, except that it was lying on one of the longer sides. From this window Yul could see across the plain to the even, cold horizon. It was in still another room, the third, that Yul voided.

Yul then came from this place into the street, and walked along until he came to a larger granite entrance

---

*He had circled only once about the city in all this time, and that in spite of the enormous velocity with which he had been travelling; which facts, it is hoped, will tend to show the vastness of the eleventh city, and of the ten cities buried beneath it.

than was usual. He entered, finding himself beneath a balcony. He walked farther and saw a floor of white marble, dipping in a slow curve toward a stage or altar in the distance. Yul fell upon his knees and wept, this quiet curve was so soothing to him. Looking above him, he saw that here, too, there were curves; the walls reaching up thin arms of broken arches; a ceiling behind shadows, and vaulted; and thick wooden beams that worked among one another like a mass of human bodies. The church was nearly dark; while the altar, seen far off through a cylinder of darkness, glowed with a soft phosphorescence.

As he wept, Yul felt something like a purring of the floor, while an uncertain but penetrative odour filtered about him. The marble was warm, so that he lay flat on his back and sent his eyes into the shadows of the beams.

The odor increased, until Yul felt a restlessness come over him. He arose, and began putting aside his clothes, until finally he stood naked in the middle of the vast, empty church. Then, listening with great intensity, he thought he could distinguish footsteps. They were far away, but hurrying. They would increase, then nearly fall away completely, so that Yul began to despair. But finally they became firmer; they were advancing; they were upon him . . . and down to one side of the altar he saw a form coming toward him.

While it was still far off, Yul could already distinguish two eyes, which were like moist planets shined on by the sun. That is, they seemed to lie on the face, with an aggressive clearness; while they did not burn but had rather that quiet, steel-blue light of a planet. Of a moist planet, that is . . . not of some dry planets which are like a copper-red spark. Yul watched the eyes, as they came nearer to him, like magnets.

And as the form stood before him, Yul saw that it was the form of a woman; and at once he loved her clamorously. But she picked up the clothes which he had thrown off

and held them out to him, so that Yul put them all back
upon his body. When he had dressed, he stood in front of
her, and looked into her eyes. They were big and deep,
like lakes, for he could see down into the rich black pupils
as though they really were made of water. She took him by
the hand and led him toward the altar, until Yul threw
back his head and sang. But his notes began lingering and
grumbling to one another among the beams, so that he
quit singing. . . . He was led to the edge of the altar. Then
she let go his hand, and jumped. Looking where she had
jumped, Yul saw that she had leapt across a pit in the
centre of the altar. He looked down into this pit; it was
dark, but so far below that it made him shudder he could
see the incandescence of the lowest of the buried cities.
Then he jumped and followed his companion on the other
side of the altar.

For a time they laboured along together, down steps into
cold damp places; around sudden bends into rooms which
were warm and brilliant; through some narrow passage
with a rough, pebbly bottom; then across a little stone
bridge under which a spring flowed out of the rock and
back into it. But of a sudden she stopped and opened her
arms to him. Yul closed against her, looking into the roads
and caverns of her eyes. She stepped away, tore back her
garments with one fling of her hand . . . and Yul crumpled
on the ground under the impact of his disgust. For shin-
ing out upon the hairs of the *mons Veneris,* there was a
third eye, which beheld him steadily and without blink-
ing.

. . . When Yul awoke, the woman had gone. He began
working his way slowly back through the labyrinth of
rooms and passages. At last he came upon the pit, and
jumped across it. He saw as he went out of the church that
immediately in front of it was the broad stairway which
led down into the other cities. He looked along the nar-
rowing avenue of stairs, and at the end of them he could

make out something which moved. But a peculiar sickness was upon him; he longed for his own country, and dropping where he stood, he fell asleep on the first of the granite stairs.

PART THREE

LATER Yul returned to the stone church . . . and the assembled multitude, lifting its thin voices, chanted in unison the Litany of Error:

> We shall go into the tenth city
> Glory glory unto our woes
> And take the hands of our fathers
> Glory glory unto our woes
> And kiss the nail holes in their palms
> Glory glory unto our woes
> And in the palms of our mothers
> Glory glory unto our woes
> And touch the old shells of their skin
> Glory glory unto our woes

And rejoice that now they are alive oh unfolding of the revelation oh ecstasy of blossoming into a world of eternity oh
astonishment of opening their petals in the warm garden of
our Maker glory glory unto the woes of our fathers and our
fathers before them and whatever may befall us in our own
day

The multitude, and the priest . . . they had alternated, the
priest alone, standing in the glow of the altar, carrying the
"Glory glory unto our woes." But when the lob-end of the
prayer was reached, the priest and the kneeling multitude
rose up, while heavy music was suddenly sprayed into the
church. After the singing was ended, the music wound on
for a few bars in reminiscence . . . then it suddenly regained its vigour, and while the multitude knelt again

with bowed heads it repeated the entire form of the litany, growing at the last into a tangle of chromatics, with agitated notes crawling in among one another, and accumulating fugues, while the whole jumbled mass grew more voluminous and climbed slowly up the scale. Out of it all there burst one neat, soft chord, high in the treble. This chord hung, while the rest of the music dropped away, until finally it existed all by itself. Then it, too, gradually weakened. But for a long time after it was gone entirely, the multitude remained kneeling.

Now the ceremony seemed to drop more into the business of worship. At times the multitude would rise, kneel at times, while there were even times when it became prostrate on the white marble floor. Up from out of the altar, a long sermon was delivered by one of the priests. It was a well-wrought sermon: it showed the effects of a mind which had devoted long nights to working out the arabesques of its idea. "That which is created creates in turn that by which it was created." The voice from the glowing altar suffered its little elations, its momentary discoveries, its occasional felicities between the idea and the expression thereof . . . the words spread out over the quiet multitude, certain sounds lodging among the beams of the ceiling, others shooting straight to the ear, other floating up sluggishly . . . so that it all became slightly confused and mellow . . . in spite of the hard little stones of the priest's inexorable logic . . . and the voice rose and fell, went slower in places for the purpose of emphasis, hurried across parenthetical explanations, paused before launching on new developments of the idea, halted and retracted a statement to a degree, dropped into a steady trot of exposition . . . the multitude, far from being disturbed that the words of it all did not reach them with clarity, rested comfortably on the dips and fluxes of the priest's voice.

The sermon was followed by a prayer . . . in trailing sentences of unequal length . . . some short . . . some stretching out to the length of two breaths . . . and at the end the multitude joined with the priest in praying . . . the frail single line of words from the altar, then the confused growl of the multitude. After the prayer, the church lay lifeless for a few moments.

Then a flash of light shot across it. The priest climbed in leaps upon the altar, until he stood looking down upon the multitude. A chord was struck, and the priest, taking his pitch immediately as the chord vanished, chanted:

LET THE NINE CHOSEN BE BROUGHT INTO THE HOLY ARENA

And off somewhere, lost in the caverns of the church which led away to the right behind the altar, the chant was repeated in a little thread of voice:

Let the Nine Chosen be brought into the holy arena.

Then even fainter, away to the left behind the altar:

Holy . . . Holy . . . Holy . . .

LET THE NINE CHOSEN BE BOUND UPON THE BEAMS OF THEIR CROSSES

. .Let the Nine Chosen be bound upon the beams of their crosses.

Crosses . . . crosses . . . crosses of holiness . . .

LET THE NAILS BE DRIVEN INTO THE HANDS AND THE FEET OF THEM AND THEIR SIDES TRANSFIXED WITH SPEAR HEADS UNTIL BLOOD MIXES WITH THE SWEAT OF THE EXECUTIONERS AND REJOICE THAT NOW THEY ARE ALIVE OH UNFOLDING OF THE REVELATION OH ECSTASY OF BLOSSOMING INTO A WORLD OF ETERNITY OH ASTONISHMENT OF OPENING THEIR PETALS IN THE WARM GARDEN OF OUR MAKER GLORY GLORY UNTO THE

WOES OF OUR FATHERS AND OUR FATHERS
BEFORE THEM . . . AND LO! BEHOLD THEM
ENTER!

The voice stopped; the priest's arms were stretched out
in imitation of the agony of the cross; music broke out,
while at the same time a shrieking rose to the right of the
altar; silk streamers began dropping and twisting, played
upon by lights of all colours. The college of priests hurried
up before the altar, howling "Glory, glory!" leaning forward and bearing the crosses of the Nine Crucified like
banners. They stopped short before the pit; the music
dropped away; the streamers subsided into a lazy billow;
the lights became one penetrating reddish purple, which
lay in all corners of the church like a sunset. The bodies
of the Nine Crucified could be seen moving in silence on
their crosses. . . . The priest, from the summit of the altar,
gave a signal with his hand, and the crosses with their
burdens were dropped into the pit. For a time they could
be heard, scraping now and then against the sides, or
colliding with one another. Finally, as they reached the
bottom of the lowest city, faint thumps came up out of the
pit.

The multitude huddled together, closer about the altar.
It seemed to be listening. The thumps became heavier;
they recurred at set intervals, like a slow treading of feet.
Outside the church, beheld by no one in all this city, the
march of the armless giants . . . advancing down the broad
stairway which was the width of a palace in Yul's own
country . . . little ripples passing along their ranks and
being lost in the distance . . . armless giants, which rise up
boldly out of their legs, like towers.

A PROGRESSION

A PROGRESSION

So all these people are adding their mite to the fortune of Mr. Dougherty. That little bald-headed man, for instance, is head of the bookkeeping department; only last week he was publicly lauded by Mr. Dougherty himself for working out a system which would take care of the new factory in Hoboken. He is evidently worried, says something over-hasty to the treasurer, comes down the green plush carpet on the run; so that the treasurer winks at the filing clerk, who winks back, hoping thereby—in accordance with a vague enough logic—that he will get his five-dollar raise next Friday. As Miss Rosenberg's typewriter goes tink at the end of the line, Mrs. Murdock's typewriter is just being charged with a white sheet and two carbons, and the typewriter of the new girl in the corner leaps into the beginning of a new paragraph. A man from one of the departments upstairs passes the head of the bookkeeping department, while an office boy is crossing the room diagonally, steering among the desks.

Dougherty had evidently done right to wait for Griffiths to call him. "Never let 'm think you're too anxious, that's my philosophy," he said in the direction of his private secretary. Then he dismissed his desk completely, lighted a cigar, and went over to the window. He could see down twelve floors of the building opposite him before it dropped on out of sight; looking up, he could see five floors before the partly drawn blind cut him off.

But it was already after four; Mr. Dougherty would have to be starting home soon if he did not want to get caught in the rush hour. He slapped shut a few drawers, put some papers somewhere else, got his hat and coat out of the wardrobe, and left. As he stepped from his private office into the general offices, the ripple of prestige preceded him. An aisle was cleared through the comers and goers; the operator put her best into a "Good evening, Mr. Dougherty"; the elevator boy caught the door half-way as he was closing it, and held his car for Mr. Dougherty; downstairs, the starter saluted professionally; then Mr. Dougherty stepped out into the street.

Objects moved. Things passed irregularly, some slick and shiny, some looming up and approaching like a broadside, some wheezing. Others crossed, went down, went up, bunched, shot ahead. One peculiarly agitated division kept working in and out, crying. He moved himself among shapes, sizes and directions. The wind of an approaching storm writhed through a gulch, but he was firm in his resolution, and drew close the flappings of his mantle. He advanced, steering himself without question.

Suddenly he swerved, dipped behind two other figures that were moving to cross him, and plunged into a warm breathy chamber, descending into the thick smells. He reached a platform in time to catch the local which was just pulling in; he took it, changing for the express at Chambers street.

The first fifteen minutes or so of the ride was carried off without anything unusual occurring. In fact, the train had already pulled out of the station at 116th Street without the hint of a catastrophe. But there the tracks become temporarily exposed, running high in the open for a disturbingly long time before they would dive into the protecting earth again. Suddenly a swarm of airplanes descended on the train, buzzing about it, flying in among one another, dipping at the cars, and swooping up and over them. As one airplane drew up for a moment alongside the speeding cars, it became clearly evident that it was filled with Indians. And judging from the hideous expression on their faces, they were giving war-whoops, although nothing could be heard but the spitting of the airplane engines and the rolling of the car wheels. Then something shot out of the airplane, breaking the window directly in front of Mr. Dougherty. A second later he was lassoed firmly about the waist, jerked out of the window, and hauled rudely into the airplane, the swarm of them disappearing toward the south, flying all the way to one of the deserted islands in the South Seas, in fact, where they killed Mr. Dougherty and ate him, which recalls the somewhat similar case of Ellery Smith.

On returning home one night over a not particularly difficult road to his farm less than a mile out of town—further, there was even a full moon—Smith lowered the bars of the pasture gate and discovered that he was in an unknown country. He started back to town; but the town was gone. Between that and early morning when, crawling with open arms toward the broad, clean sun, he fell into the abandoned quarry south of Crow Hill, and broke his neck.

But there is this difference: that Ellery Smith suffered mishaps of an obviously superhuman or metaphysical import, whereas the loss of Mr. Dougherty bears heavily upon one of the most deplorable paradoxes in all the length and breadth of modern society. For in Heaven's name, how can we without blushing speak of Progress when we mean thereby the invention of a mechanism thanks to whose ingenuity not only can remote and seemingly inaccessible places be reached by methods which at one time would have appeared almost Divine, but also the unscrupulous can utilize as still another accessory to rapine and murder! This, I say, is nothing other than a vomit in the face of that Higher Idea of Progress, which takes into account, besides the increase in man's scope of mechanical effectiveness, also a concomitant chastening of the spirit; which, burning away through education all dross of savagery, leaves the greatest of God's creatures with a mental and moral equipment capable of putting to the complete—and undefiled — advantage of society those super-tools which our restless ingenuity has fashioned.

How, for instance, to take the problem up from yet another angle, can a society consider itself anything but ridiculous wherein the man of thorough and well-digested learning, the scholar and the philosopher, finds his liberties infringed upon by the meanest superstition-monger, the lowliest believer in ghosts? Pursuing the matter still more deeply, we see that scholarship itself cannot exclude those persons of a weaker mental muscle who, lifting the burden of much learning upon their shoulders, display thereby how miserably unfit their frame is for sustaining it. My mind runs at this point to the case of M. Henri Basle, a member of several learned organizations in France, and an excellent stylist as well, but whom I must quote as a muster of dark and crooked thinking:

"From behind thick smears of trees and the unevenness of the ground—which, in addition, was covered with a tall grass —you could see certain parts of the upper story of the house. Especially, if you had had courage enough to climb inside the wall. A gravel path wound toward the house, and a boy once took a stone from this path and threw it at one of the windows. When the hole was made in the glass, a butterfly fluttered away, the boy dying that same evening. . . . All this happened, it is true, before my time; but I did see the house and the gravel path which led up to it, and I have heard noises come from it with my own ears. . . . If I remember rightly, it was constructed of some dull grey stone, which had been made even duller by the soot coming from the mills along the river."

In the above quotation kindly notice first of all that the writer's honesty has proved even greater than his credulity. It is more than significant that in the very paragraph which aims to plead for ghosts the author's characteristic circumstantiality contains the germs of the rebuttal. If *this* man had seen the butterfly, I should be much more inclined to waver in my denouncement of the whole thing as either quackery or superstition.

Then again, if ghosts really do exist, how are we to dispose of the problem of their propagation? For if the ghost is the simulacrum of the human, by what logical step can it be denied the possession of male or female organs, whichever the case may be? Or, if the possession of these is granted, by what further logical step could it be maintained that the ghosts were barren? Yet there are no more so-called ghosts than there have been people to contain them. And if the body is rotted, and the soul is in Heaven, Hell, or Purgatory, what is there left whereof a ghost could be constructed? Nothing but the memory of a man, which is to say, *nothing*. For memory is a mere inclination of the worms of the brain, like the leaning of tall grass after a storm.

Therefore, *there are no ghosts*. The invention of the ghost is a mere northern aberration, with an origin that is easily felt when one considers the blunt mists rising from our bogs, or if one has happened to observe the broad blossoms of fog which frequently nose through our dark forests. And we will even grant that one could wish there were ghosts, to sift about the rooms of a deserted mansion, or blow down low corridors, serving, in short, to counteract the increasing blatancy of our customs. The truth is that these unearthly existences about us are not ghosts, but *ghouls*, or *demons*, devoid of all this austere, ghastly poetry. They are hard little pebbles of malice, and cancers of envy, and running sores of hatred, and like the Great Bent Master of them all, quick moving, keenly intelligent, and fiery-tongued.

"Fiery-tongued," I say, for at times when I consider the idiocy of those who maintain that the devil's tongue is rounded, I marvel that I could hold my peace even so ably as I have. For why, I ask, if the devil's tongue is rounded— or even has that soft amorphousness at the end which is the property of the tongues of humans and of cattle—should we associate the lascivious with those things which protrude in points? You have but to cast one glance upon the azalea when it is flourishing at the height of its lubricity to become convinced that the tongue of the devil is as dart-like as a flame, and as disastrous as that object—if we could call a flame such—when it penetrates into the vase of the ear. And ah, Christ! what ill-formed dreams come frequently of this copulation. But I am being led by passion to wander from the topic—for there are times when a passion will engross me much the way a blood-hunger will engross a gnat; the gnat (or in some parts of the country I should better speak of a black-fly and in others a punky, while I believe the sand-fly of the south-eastern beaches is also similar) when it has at last succeeded in alighting and penetrating the skin and the water under the skin, falls into such a rage of feasting that it seems to forget everything else, even the necessity of fleeing to preserve itself, so that the bitten party can approach his thumb with leisure and crush the life out of it without its so much as attempting to leave the well it has sunk into the flesh. But let me close this digression abruptly, and step forth now, once and for all, and declare myself as avowedly against the round-tonguers and the soft-tonguers as I am against the Black Angel himself.

Yet, almost without knowing it, I find that we are naturally prone to over-stress the darker phases of a subject; applying which to the present writing would mean that there was a constant danger of giving too much to the devil and his horde, and not enough to God. So I consider this decidedly more pleasant aspect of the child Argubot, whose father and mother always told the truth, told the truth so much, in fact, that while Argubot was still young the King came and had his mother's ears cut off, while his father was put to death. Thereafter the boy lived alone with his widowed mother, who still told the truth even though her husband was dead and her ears were cut off.

But Argubot never told the truth at all. Once when he was late for supper, his mother asked him where he had been, and he said that he had been out with the ghost of his father riding on the moon. His mother said that he was untrue, and that he had fallen asleep in the hay, and called him to be whipped. But Argubot said that his mother must not whip him, because his father told him he would be King some day. So that his mother had to put the whip back behind the stove unused, for the ghost of his father *might* have taken the little boy for a ride on the moon, and she had always felt that Argubot was going to be King some day. At other times he told similar perplexing falsehoods.

Until the poor woman didn't know what to do. She wanted her boy to be honest, like herself and her dead husband, whom the King had killed; for she didn't want him to become another untrue King. She puzzled for many days how that she could prove that her son was not true, so that she could whip him. Although she was very poor, she gave a candle to Mother Mary. Then a plan came to her; but she would have to tell a lie. She hesitated for a long time, finally deciding that she must do so for the sake of her son.

She went to a neighbour at the far end of the town, whose cat had kittens, and asked for one small black kitten. Then she came home again and called Argubot to her. "Little son, I have brought you three kittens, but that you may not get tired of them, you may have only one of them at a time. But as all the three kittens are nearly alike, it will be hard to tell them apart. But if you look into their eyes, you can tell them apart, for their eyes are different. One is called Big-Eyes, because the black of his eyes is always as big as the whole eye; I will let Big-Eyes come to bed with you; if you awake in the night, and are afraid, just move your toes under the blanket, and Big-Eyes will tumble and prance at them. The second is called Little-Eyes, because the black of his eyes is only a slit; he is a lazy fellow, and at noontime you will find him stretched in the sun on the back door-step. The third is called Medium-Sized Eyes, because the black of his eyes is neither big, nor is it just a slit; you can play with Medium-Sized Eyes in the mornings and afternoons, but be careful of him, for he is the liveliest of the three, and is liable to scratch you."

But Big-Eyes, Little-Eyes, and Medium-Sized Eyes were all one kitten, although Argubot did not know it. For at night a cat's eyes are big, and at noon they are very small, while in the morning and the afternoon they are neither big nor small. And the widow was sorry that she had been untrue, but she stood by her plan and waited to see what would come of it.

The next morning, when they were eating their porridge, she asked Argubot about the kittens, and he said he awoke and was afraid, but he didn't have to call her because Big-Eyes was there and played with his toes. And his mother said nothing. . . . The next morning after that, when they were eating their porridge again, she asked him about the kittens and he said that he awoke and was afraid, but he didn't have to call her because Big-Eyes was there and played with his toes. And again his mother said nothing. . . . But the third morning, when she asked him about the kittens, Argubot exclaimed, "Oh, mother, Big-Eyes and Little-Eyes and Medium-Sized Eyes were all three on my bed last night." And now his mother knew that he was untrue, and she went behind the stove to get her whip.

But Argubot ran out of the house and became King.

And when he was King, he despatched a messenger to the south, telling him to bring back a cat with big eyes, and one with little eyes, and one with medium-sized eyes. But the messenger returned cold and hungry, and fell before King Argubot, saying, "My Sire, I could not contain the cats, for some evil spirit changed them in the bag. . . . The first day, I caught a cat with medium-sized eyes, and put him in my hunting-bag, but when I rested that night and looked at him, there was another cat like him in his place, but his eyes were big. 'Very well,' said I, 'we will let

this be our big-eyed cat.' The next noon I caught a cat
with little eyes, but when I sat down to rest in the afternoon I looked at him and his eyes were medium-sized.
'Very well,' said I, 'we will let this be our cat with medium-
sized eyes.' And the third day at noon I caught another cat
with little eyes, and returned home, happy in that I had
fulfilled the commission of my Lord. But after trudging all
day I came upon the castle at nightfall, only to find that
all three cats had eyes as big as the full moon.''

King Argubot was displeased, and despatched the same
messenger to the north with the same mission, but the result was no better. Then he sent other messengers in other
directions, and they all returned with the same tale. Thereupon the King had all the messengers thrown into the
dungeon.

The King was sad, and went out into his garden. But
here a good fairy appeared before him and said that if he
would release all the messengers from the dungeon, the
three cats would be given him. He did so, and they were.

Then he sent the messengers out over the land again,
this time to find his old widowed mother, if she was still
alive. And they returned with his mother, bringing her
before the King, but she did not recognize that he was her
son.

"Old woman," he said to her severely, "do you see that
cat at my feet?" and he pointed to the three cats which the
fairy had given him. "Now I pick it up and its eyes are big.
I put it down and pick it up again and its eyes are little. I
put it down and pick it up a third time, and its eyes are
medium-sized. Is not that so?"

And the old woman began to weep, and said, "Please my
Lord, but it is not so. There are three cats at the feet of
my Lord."

The King Argubot roared out with anger, so that the
old woman began to tremble, "What! does this old woman
dare to gainsay the King!"

"Please, my Lord," she sighed, "but I lost my dear son,

once when I was untrue. And now, although I can not understand it, I must tell the truth, even though it cost me my head, even as it cost me the head of my husband many years ago." King Argubot was sure that this was his mother before him, and he told her who he was, and stepped down from his throne, and led her into a great banquet prepared for her.

Soon after this, King Argubot, hearing of a beautiful princess who was weaving a golden garment of a golden thread on a golden loom, but who lived in a country very far off, went in search of her to make her Queen. When at last he found her, she looked upon him and fainted with love, so that she broke the skein of gold with which she was weaving. But there was a curse upon this princess, whereby, if it should ever happen that this golden thread was broken, she was doomed to die nine months after that time.

The King and his Queen began wandering to fling off the curse; by royal decree, thousands of witches and ugly old women were burned; but the curse could not be flung off, so that at the predestined date the Queen died, after giving birth to a Prince, who lived on after her. King Argubot returned to his own country, and mourned for five years. Then, finding that his people were at the mercy of usurers, he had all money-lenders put to death, and devoted himself to the welfare of his kingdom, at the same time teaching the young Prince also to love and protect his subjects.*

---

*Not to be confused with a later Prince Argubot, of a different lineage, and of whom it is recorded: While walking on the seashore and thinking of the problems that beset his kingdom—most especially the pestilence which at that time was raging in the larger cities—Prince Argubot was suddenly conducted away on a carpet of zephyrs, and into an intensification of beauty which was beyond the endurance of mortal eye. When he was returned to earth, little children hid at the mention of his name, and old men marvelled that their Prince, once so kind to his people, should have grown more cruel than even his uncle before him.

So wisely did King Argubot pilot his kingdom that all who were good became favoured and happy, while the malicious and the scheming among them could not flourish nor take root, so that finally they crossed the border into other countries. And when at last it was time for the King to die, all his subjects threw down their tools and neglected their crops, allowing pests of all sorts to spring up among them; for, they said, they wanted to perish with their King. But when the King heard of this, he blessed his people, but asked that if they still heard his authority they should return to their tasks, so that his corpse might not be buried in a land of desolation. And the people, hearing of this, returned to the fields and the work-benches, that a thriving state might be maintained as a monument to their beloved monarch.

Soon after, King Argubot breathed his last, and as his soul rose out of the window, the voice of his Angel-Wife was heard calling him to her couch in Heaven. O glory of their re-union in that gentle land above the sky!

IN QUEST OF OLYMPUS

IN QUEST OF OLYMPUS

1

WITH an uncertain tide—or better, current, since I am
speaking of a little lake, or an enormous spring, or some
sort of underground river—I simply took all chances and
allowed myself to drift. For the most part it was black; me
lying in the bottom of the boat, conscious by means of
some complicated mechanism of sensation, or rather, some
peculiar centralization from divers termini, of a gentle motion; the boat scraping now and then against an unseen
rock that jutted up, or perhaps the sides of the cavern.
Once or twice I passed a little ball of pale bluish light,
however. A crunching sound. The boat had grounded on
pebbles. Feeling in the dark, I stepped out on a smooth
bank which began to ascend immediately. I said farewell
to my boat—perhaps forever!—and began climbing. It
was rough and jagged, like a sieve for grinding nutmeg;
then became almost as steep as a perpendicular cylinder;
and finally narrowed after the manner of an inverted funnel. I had to stop, for I had come upon a wall, a smooth,
flat surface; and further, I was exhausted. I dropped where
I lay, fell into a sort of stupor, and when I regained consciousness it was owing to faint irregular taps coming from
far beneath me and forcing themselves upon my notice. It
was my boat, broken from its moorings, starting easily on
its way!

I cursed the foolhardiness that had got me into this
thing. And I confess that I even wept, for the feeling of

desolation and loneliness which came over me was too powerful for resistance. Then I remembered my training, and putting away all fears, confided my problems to Him who sees even the slightest move we make, and who hears even the weakest little sigh from our uttermost within. A new courage poured into me like wine, and I recommenced examining the wall. At last I came upon a place where the smoothness of it was broken by cracks large enough for me to insert my fingers, and the ascent continued.

As I climbed, it began slowly to dawn in the cavern. (The noonday sun of the countryside above, that is, was penetrating through some cavity into these depths.) I came upon the first sickly weeds, a few beetles, worms and the like. And it was not long before I was in full daylight, struggling through a thick underbrush which was so luxuriant, so impenetrable, that I almost wished for the cool desolation of my cavern. Working among the briars, especially the insistent blackberries—insistent because they seemed to be actually reaching out to catch the wool of my coat—I came upon a cluster of sumac, and then an even thicker muddle of ferns and alders. As the ground was unusually rough, my feet would slip from the rocks, and lodging in some unnoticed cavity covered with dead leaves, they would be held there by a tangle of roots, while at the same time I was kept busy dodging beneath the low crooked branches, making detours, or creeping through chance holes in the foliage. And then of a sudden I broke through to a road, and looked across broad easy meadows . . . and why! there was the house where Treep used to live!

And that stump in front of Treep's house, that was where the oak used to be which Treep had loved so much and then his master had ordered him to cut it down. Treep used to go out and pat the shaggy bark of this oak while it was still standing. But his master said finally, "Treep, cut down that oak." Since it was decided that the oak was

needed for timber. Before that Treep had even felt that
long after he was dead the oak would stand there; but now
the oak had to be chopped down, and Treep went out with
his axe to chop it.

No one was near, however, so that Treep rubbed his
head against it, and explained how unhappy he would be
without it, and how he would hollow out the stump and
plant therein some of its own acorns. Then, after weeping,
he attacked the trunk with his axe.

But as he swung his axe, it caught in a low branch which
was sagging somewhat, Treep being knocked on his back
by the rebound of this branch. At first he was angry; but
he said that it was right for the oak to defend itself, and it
should not be rebuked. When he returned to chopping,
however, a rotten branch from high up in the tree became
dislodged, and cut a gash in the nape of Treep's neck.
"Thou ungrateful oak!" he shouted in anger; "Thou must
know that it is not my fault that I must kill thee, and thus
not place the burden of thine own disobedience upon a
heart which is already weighted down by the necessity of
fulfilling a loathsome command put upon it by my master!" And Treep resumed his task.

But as the axe sank into the trunk, a large chip of wood
flew up, striking Treep full on the forehead, so that the
blood poured down into his eyes. Treep arose at one leap,
regained his axe, and began brandishing it about his head.
"Oak!" he shrieked, "Oak! Thou art no longer the big
friendly thing that I rubbed my ears against and hugged
with my arms, but a monument of malice and spitefulness
rising between me and the commands of my master. And
the love I bore for thee now being completely vanished, I
swear by the blood dripping from my forehead that I shall
attack thee in all ferocity, not stopping until thou lyest a
corpse at my feet!"

And then Treep assailed the oak with bitterness, half
blinded by the blood from his forehead, his body aching
and tired, but sustained with such a vengeance against his

old friend that he hardly knew what he was doing. Indeed, blinded as he was by the flow of both his blood and his emotions, and although a practised woodsman, he was not felling the oak properly. And when at last it became so weakened that it began to topple, he saw that it was falling toward his master's garden. At this point he was plunged into an inordinate hate; he did not even take into account the enormous mass of his enemy, but as the oak began leaning with increasing rapidity, he hurled aside his axe, and heaved his shoulders against the falling trunk, trying in this way to change the direction of its fall!

But the oak continued on its descent, and as it stretched out along the ground it held Treep beneath it, crushing the life out of him almost instantly.

2

Treep was aware of no change whatsoever, except that he was growing. Soon his hand alone was as big as his whole body had been, with the rest of him increased in proportion; and soon after this his hand was as big as his new body had been . . . and so on, indeterminately. When he had ceased increasing, he looked about, stretched his arms which were as thick as a countryside; and opening his jaws, he yawned as wide as a gulf. But he was conscious of a pain beneath the nail of his right little toe; and reaching down he pulled out a splinter, the oak which had killed him. . . . This had been the magnification of Treep.

Noticing that the sky was only a few arm-lengths above him, he sprang into the air, caught hold, and hoisted himself on to the other side. The country was rough but comparatively level. Glistening in the distance there was something which looked very much like a palace. He made off in this direction.

As he came nearer he could distinguish figures moving about, all of them as big as he was himself. Then messen-

gers came ahead to meet him, small, the way he had been
before death, and they perched on his shoulders like doves.
They explained that they were the former poets of the
earth, and that this was Heaven, and that they were usually the only earthly existences admitted here. But Wawl
had seen Treep's struggle with the oak, and had decreed
that he should be magnified among the gods, and then
they all fell to singing their own compositions at once. He
walked ahead, not much disturbed by their twitter, until
one of them climbed into the shell of his ear and explained, shouting above the others, the dilemma which
Wawl had occasioned by his deification. For in magnifying
Treep it was not found possible to magnify his name, and
there were no more names nor offices left in Heaven. Wawl
had decided, however, that if Treep dared he might attack any god he so desired, and if he defeated this god
could usurp both his name and office. Treep asked the poet
what gods were disliked in Heaven, and the poet mentioned both Arjk and the Blizzard God. Arjk, it went on
to say, was undoubtedly a powerful and handsome divin-
ity, and would be a much worthier foe to unseat than the
Blizzard God, who relied mostly on cunning and harassing.
. . . Treep decided that it was Arjk whom he would battle;
and halting outside the castle, he sent word to Wawl that
his faithful servant Arjk was approaching.

Soon a distant tumult was heard, and the poets in a
panic scrambled down from Treep's shoulders. Then Arjk
appeared, growling and cursing, and demanding to know
if this was the liar who was adorning himself with the
name of a god. Treep answered him, "Step aside, Treep,
for I am Arjk, the faithful servant of Wawl, and I have
come to pay him homage." Thereupon the two of them
closed in upon each other, a battle following which lasted
for two years. At the end of this time Treep conquered
and threw Arjk out of Heaven. Then he sent word again
to Wawl that his faithful servant Arjk was approaching,
and entered the palace.

3

Some time after Treep—become Arjk—had established himself in Heaven, Wawl summoned him to the palace. Arjk entered and bowed before him. About the feet of Wawl adoring women sat, their breasts dripping at his glory, indeed, their entire bodies flowing with love of their Lord. Wawl dismissed his attendants and began speaking to Arjk immediately. But the castle was so large that it had its own internal weather. And as Wawl commenced to speak, a little storm descended about the august forehead, filling his hair with a silver moisture and pricking him with minute tongues of lightning. Wawl peered through the mist wavering before his eyes, and raised his voice above the small but distracting thunder.

"Arjk," Wawl addressed him, "thou art the most mighty of my warriors."

"Whatever strength I possess was granted me by Wawl."

"I trust that thou wilt remain faithful to me, for thy powers, if turned against me, could cause all manner of evil in Heaven."

And Arjk, bowing even lower, answered with emotion, "Before everything else comes my gratitude to Wawl. In the magnification of Treep there was also the magnification of Treep's devotion. And this devotion is mortgaged solely to Wawl." And then rising to his feet, Arjk gave way to his elation, and sang to Wawl of the glories which he, Arjk, had accomplished in Heaven, and of the might and splendour which belonged to him, Arjk. Saying among other things, "I, Treep become Arjk, can drink and carouse in Heaven and yet retain the most powerful arm among the gods." The elation continuing, Arjk took leave of Wawl, and went for a mad ride in his chariot, hurling bolts haphazard out of Heaven, and shouting to the rattle of his steeds' hoofs.

Then of a sudden Arjk spied the Blizzard God riding

in the distance. And looking closer, he distinguished Hyelva fleeing before him, her white robes fluttering back in confusion. Arjk wrenched his steeds until they were headed toward the Blizzard God, and his chariot went swaying and rocking back and forth across the clouds. The Blizzard God was shrieking as he pursued, "Hyelva! Hyelva, open the great gate of thy body! The great gate of thy body, that I may enter in!" while the hoofs of Arjk's horses set up a reverberation through Heaven, Hell and Earth. But Hyelva sped on in silence.

It became evident that Arjk would overtake the Blizzard God and rescue Hyelva from his fingers. But Littic, who was a kindly deity, though under the domination of the Blizzard God, released his lights through Heaven, so that both Arjk and his horses were blinded. Letting his reins slacken in his stupor, Arjk watched the lights play on all sides of him, saw the thick trunks of flame with tongues protruding, or semi-circles stretching across the whole sky, with balls of a bluish jelly sliding along them, or puffs of light waving like dust toward the zenith. And while Arjk relaxed, enchanted, the Blizzard God sent a broadside of tempest against him, blowing him out of the chariot and the bolts from his hands. Then the Blizzard God hurried again after Hyelva, falling among her garments like a hawk among the feathers of a dove. His appetites were so ravenous that he tore away everything which covered her body . . . and the little bits, whirling about in the tempest, spilled finally out of Heaven, and falling, covered whole states and provinces of the earth, so that some houses were sunk even up to their second stories in snow.

4

And one of the places where this snow fell was New York City; I am speaking particularly of West Sixteenth Street. Ah, how lovely it was before being shovelled away at a cost of some hundreds of thousands of dollars! The air was almost black with snow; it was so thick that at times stray flakes, falling down the particular air-shaft, swerved and sifted through the partly open window of the particular kitchen. This kitchen was dark, with dirty dishes showing up here and there, while the other rooms of the suite were lighted. All were empty, however, except the one in the extreme front, where James Hobbs was lying on Esther MacIntyre.

The point was this: Could Hobbes, or could he not, succeed, with only one hand, in capturing the object which Miss MacIntyre held in both of hers—if she held anything at all!—but would not willingly relinquish? Hobbes had maintained that he could; Miss MacIntyre had sassed back that he couldn't; thus, a protracted struggle had begun between them. Resulting in their tussling on the couch, and Hobbes groping resolutely — but awkwardly! — after the hot fists she held against her breast. Then of a sudden he made a dive of his hand, which silenced the giggly thing. And he continued the attack, disposing of garments rapidly. When Esther's bewilderment was startled away by the realization of a still greater boldness on his part, she began to resist . . . weakly, however . . . but he no longer cared . . . slipped off the couch . . . thumped against the floor . . . like a sack of potatoes.

Someone was knocking, jerking them out of their sloth. She went for her hat and coat, and as Hobbes returned to the front room with Harowitz, mumbled something about being in a hurry, and dashed out. Hobbes yanked a chair at Harowitz, pointed to a magazine, and went after Esther. As he came out into the blizzard, hatless and coatless, he could see nothing of her. Besides, he was not exceptionally interested. He returned to his apartment slowly, even stopped in the dark kitchen a few moments and leaned against the wall. Then he went to the front room where Harowitz was waiting for him.

Harowitz was moving about the room, from one island to another. Hobbes stretched out on the couch, giving a

slight grunt which was a mixture of many things—such as
self-comfort, the necessity of saying something, disapproval, nothing at all—but mainly composed of this: that
Hobbes had planned the next time he would see Harowitz, to look at him abruptly and say, "Harowitz, what
would you think of a man who walked into your house,
and when you weren't watching him went into your cupboard, and stole a drink of whiskey?" Harowitz wore a size
eight shoe, carried a cane, could speak both French and
German fluently. His left eye was weaker than his right,
but not enough to necessitate his wearing glasses. He was
not married, had graduated from a law school *magna cum
laude,* and also knew some Spanish. On his mother's side
he was not full Jew.

Or perhaps Hobbes would have waited until Harowitz
had begun to explain something, such as "The perfection
of machinery, and the consequent large quantity produc-
tion, has made war an absolute necessity for the first time
in the world's history." Then Hobbes would answer, "Yes,
Harowitz, quite right, but what would you think of a man
who walked into your house and when you weren't watching him went into your cupboard, and stole a drink of
whiskey?"

It was not the drink of whiskey that Hobbes had minded. It was the *principle* of the thing. But he said nothing
to Harowitz. The statement, after all, would be too blunt,
so blunt that even if Harowitz had not taken the whiskey
he would realize that he was being accused. But first of all,
he must make sure that Harowitz was guilty. It did no
good to mark the bottle, since a small amount could easily
be replaced with water. Perhaps there was some harmless,
colorless, tasteless substance which he could mix with
water in a decanter beside the whiskey bottle; but if this
mixture were poured into the whiskey it would make the
whiskey change colour. Hobbes imagined it turning a
brilliant green or blood-clot red immediately before Harowitz's eyes. Then Hobbes would come in and offer him a

drink, bring out the whiskey bottle, look at it, look silently at Harowitz, put the bottle back, glance at his watch,
and regret that he had an engagement.

Until he had something as definite as this, however . . .
so he had grunted merely, as he lay down on the couch.
Harowitz explained to him how war was inevitable at this
point in the world's history, and while he was talking
Hobbes brought out the whiskey. . . . After a time they
were not clear-headed; the mixture of whiskey, gas fumes
and old breath had taken the freshness out of them. They
watched each other now and then with tired eyes, trying
to become interested in some assertion. Harowitz left within an hour, while Hobbes continued to lie on the couch.

Hobbes listened to the soft pads of snow flattening
against the windows. Rising, he switched off the lights and
opened a window in the next room. The cold air began
circulating. . . . His mind was completely lax. So that the
form of this procedure began to impress itself upon him.
That is, he revolved it that he had been hot, and that now
a cold current was blowing across him. Later on that evening he wrote the following poem, which, after he had
finished it, sent him out for a long walk in the storm.

Here are the facts, given as I have known them:

Last night I slept with my shame bared to the ceiling;
The bed was hot against my back and buttocks;
My arms were swollen with the bites of black-flies.

And now the thunder-caps quit dropping below the horizon;
The thunder-caps are beginning to march above me;
I watch, with the salt stinging the rim of my eye-balls.

A breeze starts up, making the lake look blue-black;
The blue-black swallows fly even more click-jaggy;
The green trees in the distance become also blue-black.

I close the windows fronting on the southwest;

The thunder falls immediately on the lightning;
And the rush of rain in the trees upon the thunder.

The black-flies of Massachusetts are blown into New Hampshire;
And the black-flies of New Hampshire are blown into Maine, while
Those of Maine are blown, some into Canada and some into the ocean.

Water hits in bucket loads against the wood shed;
Water hurries beneath the dried-up shingles;
Water drips mysteriously in the pantry.

The rain settles now to a steady business;
It lays itself without violence over the pastures;
Night falls, with the rain now gently piddling.

A new wind falls upon us from the northwest;
Veering, it whips the fog along the hillsides;
And shoves the entire storm out of my knowledge.

A haze of light spreads in the north horizon;
Pale shafts of light waver on the north horizon.
And puffs of light like dust wave toward the zenith.

A calm lies on the face of the earth and waters;
It sits among the trees and in the valleys;
A frost is nosing against the wild cherry blossoms.

The sun comes up as clean as a brand-new dollar;
The pink sun edges flatly above the skyline;
As rash as a blast of unexpected music.

Praise to the Three-God, Father, Son and Spirit;
Who, as He found Himself at the begining;
So is He now, and so shall be forever!

5

Father, Son and Holy Ghost, so comfortable in Heaven.
(Oh merely that I might live in one of the back alleys of
Heaven, though my house fronted on some dump heap of
empty bottles and rusty tomato cans! Indeed, I conceive of
Their comfort as that of a royal family that never was. A
family, composed of king, and queen, and princes, and
princesses, living in a suite of rooms borne upon the
shoulders of their subjects. The palace marches across the
country, through rivers, up and over mountains, while the
populace, squirming beneath, hold it up with poles. Ten
thousand, say, labour simultaneously at these supports,
while others rest, others follow to take their places, others
have been relieved from duty and return to their families.
The palace moves in a straight line, and in the course of
this line there is a lake. The subjects disappear beneath
the water; others take a long breath, dive down, and replace them at the supports. Some are lost; many are content to suck the water into their lungs, thus ending their
unhappiness; but the palace moves on. At times music is
heard from above, or a platform is let down for food, or
filth is thrown out, falling on the populace. But otherwise,
it travels like a silent cloud above them.) So comfortable
in Heaven, and yet Jesus must go out into the night again,
leaving the warm fire of this sanctity.

Some people were sitting in a prominent café in the
theatre district, when lo! Christ was discovered sitting
among them. I can pay no greater tribute to my countrymen than to recite the tact and affability with which He
was received. A committee was organized on the spot to
show Mr. Jesus the more prominent sights of the town,
such as Riverside Drive, the Woolworth Building (from
where He could get a good bird's-eye view of the city) and
the Brooklyn Navy Yard. At this last named place He was
to be given a private demonstration of a new gas which
our chemists had invented and which promised to put us

far and away in advance of all other fighting units of the world. (The intention of this demonstration being to show that so long as Christianity possessed such weapons there need be no fear of the spreading of Asiatic paganism.)

It was suggested taking Him to one of our larger churches, but this was quickly hushed up, as it was realized that the situation would surely result in ill-feeling, since, even if the Catholics could be persuaded to sacrifice this honour to the Protestants—which was, of course, out of the question—at least twenty Protestant sects would have arisen to dispute the honour amongst themselves. So it was thought wisest of all to take Him to a theatre.

The play was by a very prominent American dramatist, and had been reviewed by the New York critics with such really gratifying and penetrating comments as "Every man, woman and child should see this play (*Times*) . . . really scrumptious (*World*) . . . Grips you from start to finish (*American*) . . . One of the best plays of this season and far better than anything of last season (*Tribune*) . . . An all around good play (*Sun*)." There was some skating on thin ice, but no one could fail to catch the moral tenor behind it all, and it was hoped that this moral tenor especially would appeal to Jesus. In one detail, however, the play had been amended, a short passage having been omitted from the first act which ran, "Why am I so crucified with poverty!" It had been unanimously decided that nothing unpleasant should be suggested to Him.

Jesus was interviewed between the second and third acts, but declared that he had nothing to say, refusing especially to compare conditions here and in Heaven. But in spite of his reticence, favourable comments appeared in all the evening papers, although one anti-Church labour organ queried mildly whether it would be the Star of Bethlehem this time or the Star of Bethlehem Steel.

During the play—which was a matinée—the city administration had been anything but idle, and it was decided to give Christ the freedom of the city regardless of what might happen to the Jewish vote. So He came out of the theatre and walked down Broadway to City Hall, and behind Him followed a long procession of scenario-writers, burlesque Amazons, fairies, lounge-lizards, Jew and Irish comedians, jazz-hounds, pimps, promoters, whores, travelling salesmen, confidence men, bookers, gamblers, kept women, millionaires' sons, publicity agents, sporting experts, dopes, land-sharks, connoisseurs, rum-sellers, holders of boxes at the opera, ammunition makers, specialists in men's diseases, whatever of the general populace, in short, happened to be passing through Times Square . . . and also angels. Not those Angels that sit at the feet of Jesus in Heaven, however. I mean those more immediate angels, angels from Wall Street, the backers for plays and movies . . . bald-headed angels, angels whose intentions are juicy in proportion as their groins are parched, angels who will dribble as much as twenty thousand, say, against some coozy's leg. Yes, there were a number of these sweaty, red-faced angels in the procession.

Christ suffered these honours, and many others, ultimately slinking away from His followers, down side-streets with warnings, "Commit no nuisance," through the smoke and slobber of the men's saloon of a Jersey ferry, and then, quite alone, as the sun was going down, He stood in a graveyard, on a hill, looking out over the Jersey swamps; kneeling—I know my readers will pardon the theatricality of the gesture—with His arms outstretched to Heaven, He prayed and wept. Then, growing calmer, He read the tombstone of Johann Bauer, geboren 1827, gestorben 1903, at present Mit Jesu. Weakened by a peculiar lassitude, He sat on one of the iron railings surrounding the grave. . . . Crickets began climbing upon His sandals, and Christ, noting their hunger, took a boo from His nose and dropped it for them to eat on. When this boo was consumed, he put another in its place . . . and so on, until all the crickets had been sated.

As Christ heard a faint noise now, He bent His ear to the ground, discovering that the noise came from one unusually minute cricket which was rubbing its wings across its back to produce a little whir of gratitude for the Divine Food it had received. A second later the entire swarm joined in, the graveyard trembling with their praise. Then, with a blare of Hosannahs, an Angelic Horde flew toward Him out of the sunset.

Other battalions answered from the West, as they likewise advanced steadily upon Jesus. And still others, from all corners of the compass. The sky was churned with song and Seraphic Manoeuvres. For these great fleets of God's Elect, multiplying egregiously, began winding in among one another, melting together, separating, deploying in the shape of V's like wild geese, or banked up like pyramids, or upside down, or advancing in columns . . . while miracles were scattered upon the earth like seed. The sun, the moon, the stars, the planets and all the wandering bodies shone together. Fountains burst forth; wild beasts lolled among the clouds.

All motion and song stopped . . . some thunder was climbing across the sky. Then, as it disappeared in the distance, things began revolving, a Sublime Vortex sucked up into Heaven. In the very centre, unmistakably wide open, stood the Gate, with squadron after squadron of Angels already hurrying within. Christ, too, began rising, while God called out to Him, smiling, AHRLOM AHRLOMMA MINNOR. And Christ answered, MAHN PAUNDA OLAMMETH. Thus had one spoken and the other answered. Then He entered Heaven, the rear armies of the Angels following Him rapidly.

> Olammeth! . . . the seed
> . . . This sudden certainty!
> Fulfillment, bursting through the mists
> Olammeth, His Breasts!
> Across night
> Projected . . . (latent) . . .
> when lo! the *Sun!*

Heaven's Gate swung shut.

FIRST PASTORAL

FIRST PASTORAL

1

Is the Divine present to a degree, so that one could speak of It as either more or less present? Or must this Divine be either present or absent? To the eye of an athlete the sun is gloriously brilliant, while an old man with failing sight may see it as a dull sullen glow behind a mist. Is it that way with the Divine? Or is the Divine like some figure of a flower or animal in the clouds, which one man sees and another does not see, while there are no possible gradations between the seeing and the non-seeing? The question is not at all impious; for to ask whether the Divine must be either present or absent does not imply a limitation of the Infinite Being, even though the word "must" has been used in the statement of the question. For this "must" refers not to the Divine, but to man, with his limited orifices of penetration. Obviously, God is universally present, and we can speak of His absence only from the standpoint of man's failure to distinguish Him.

Grant, first, that the Divine must be either present or absent, with no intermediate gradations. Which means that a man either lives with God, or does not. If he lives in the understanding of God, of what use to him are the mere functions of Churchly worship? Further, if the Divine must be either present or absent, then it follows inexorably that It can only be absent, for otherwise we should have an Infinite Being understood by a finite being, which is absurd.

Granting the antithetical proposition: The Divine can be either more or less present. In this way the world would become hieraticized after the manner of a pyramid, with the countless hordes of ignorant but faithful followers of the Church forming the broader, heavily weighted base, while as we went upwards with a decreasing proportion of mass the Christians corresponding to these higher positions would have a clearer understanding; and at the very top would cluster the body of martyrs, crowned by Jesus. The entire construction would be the glorious edifice of that combined πίστις and γνῶσις which marks all those who have remained untorn by schism; while the dry sands, swirling in the wind, tossed about without meaning and without incorporation into this stable structure . . . these sands, obviously, would be the pagans, the heretics, and the like.

A stirring tope. But the difficulty enters when we examine further just what this "greater or lesser presence" involves in the way of conduct. Would we not, for instance, be drawn dangerously near to some of the neo-Platonist errors? For if the Divine is present to a greater or lesser degree, the worshipper must serve in accordance with the abundance or meagreness of his light. This leads us towards a general synthesis of religions, for if God is present in degree, then He is present in the religion of the most impious pagan, but present so faintly that the entire system of worship is distorted from the true worship of the Church beyond recognition. It is far removed, but exists nevertheless, just as the echoes of the Words of God when He commanded "Let there be Light" are still trembling in the air, becoming fainter and fainter, even more faint as our thoughts are upon them, but bounding on eternally. That peculiar "rustle of silence" which we hear in a perfect calm is the accumulation of just such infinitely faint noises, piled up from the first crack of creation. But the point to be emphasized was that if we grant the greater or lesser presence of the Divine, we must recognize the

pagan as worshipping the True God, but in his own ignorant manner.

How, then, should we go about it to bring such people
into the Realm of Jesus? By letting them worship in their
own manner, once their provinces are under the temporal
jurisdiction of the Pope. They would thus be looked upon
not as pagans, but as the weakest members of the True
Church, and much nearer to the lowest Christian than this
lowest Christian is to a saint. But obviously, such a line of
reasoning would bring us close to the subversive teachings
of Plotinus and Porphyry. Yet as we have seen, the opposing doctrine leads to just as unholy an attitude towards
the Church. What then is the conclusion to be drawn? It
is: *Let man always distrust any ratiocination which does
not follow hand in hand with the Word of God at every
step.* That true understanding is not in γνῶσις but in
πίστις. Or rather, that πίστις is γνῶσις .

The greater the cogency with which the brain could
make the Church seem wrong, the greater was the proof
thereby that the soul had become infected. And Brother
Angelik's deep learning in theological subtleties made him
perfectly aware of what turpitudes logic without love
might involve. Still, he had indubitably been enthralled
for a time by the heavy bonds of his antitheses. And as he
lifted his head now to deliver a short prayer of thankful-
ness to his Maker—Who had guided him so securely out
of this intricacy of the Devil—he observed that in his anguish he had wandered far beyond the walls of the monastery!

Here was Hell's mockery. Angelik had thought that this
bejewelling of heresy marked out the nature of his struggle against Evil, while it had in reality been a mere sub-
terfuge, a lure to produce the breaking of his vows, since
he had stepped out into the world, beyond the pale of his
seclusion, beyond the point stipulated in his solemn oath.

While, further, Brother Angelik had come upon the
shepherd John and the shepherdess Jocasta. This John hav-

ing slipped his hands against Jocasta's flesh, the two of them were now lying earnestly interlocked upon the sod.

If prayers possessed the properties of mass and weight, and their density under ordinary temperatures were that of a thick, sluggish fluid, prayers then would have nosed quietly down the corridors of the monastery, oozed through the cracks of the massive, ill-fitting doors, and perhaps even set the statue of the Virgin to circulating on its side by the altar. Again, a blackness, obviously symbolic, of heavy clouds, had gathered over the sky; and having gathered, these clouds lay there like a threat. In the late afternoon the clouds were split to expose a sun which was already part eaten by the shadow of the moon, and which dropped below the horizon in full shadow. Thus, without twilight, midnight followed on the heels of day, while the storm broke, slashing and stumbling in the dark, and rocking the monastery like a ship.

The forces of sin silently multiplied, filling his brain with their progeny after the manner of vipers. When the she is in heat, her gaping, filthy maw is turned to the male. He inserts his three-tongued head into the jaws of his woman, buries it avidly even to the eyes, and projects into her, by the junction of their mouths, his procreative venom. Maddened by her pleasures, the wife then slays her lover by ripping open his throat with her teeth; while as he perishes, she drinks in his spittle. Thus, the father is consumed during the excesses, but the sperm of his spittle still remains to destroy the mother. For later, when the seed has aged, small objects begin wriggling in her warm insides, slashing and beating against the womb. She realizes now what her sex entails and bemoans her wretched husband's offspring, which are destined to murder in turn, and are already tearing at the barriers which enclose them. Until, since there is no channel whereby the young can be born, they split the agonized bowels with their struggles, and the belly is rent to provide an exit. The little snakes

lick the body which bore them, a generation of orphans
even at birth, since they had hardly seen the day before
their miserable mother was dead.*

Nocte surgentes, vigilemus omnes; let us all leap up in
the night, and wait! But not for a fleshy love. For some austere sign, rather, which will be found lying across the sky
like a comet. Charmed thesis and antithesis of love, of that
higher love. And in despair he prayed, loudly and disagreeably, complaining, defying, hemming and hawing with
his temptations, his moans echoing down the corridors,
and buzzing with the storm in the ears of his Brothers, who
listened in the darkness and understood that Angelik was
struggling for his Faith.

Let me hold in my arms Salvation.
Le me lie between the breasts of the True Church.
Let me speak and in turn be spoken unto.
Let the belly tremble at the touch of my hand on the door.

Dilectus meus mihi, et ego illi!
One unto the other, and that other unto the first.
Moving among the lilies, while the day dawns, and the
     shadows lean.
Thy dugs are richer than wine.

He crawled to the statue of the Virgin, and touched the
stiff marble folds of her garments. Another voice near him
piped up in prayer. Then his fingers fell away, and he was
ashamed. "*O gloriosa virginum, benedicat te Deus et sanc-
tum ventrem tuum.*" . . . He sneaked back to his cell.

"Lord, my God, help me, for I am weak. A sign, oh
Lord! Show me that I am not alone." Then Brother Angelik became peaceful. He was contracting business with
his Lord. "Tonight it is storming. Let it storm tomorrow,
and I shall remain with my Brothers. But if there is sun,

*Prudentius, Hamartigenia, lines 585-607.

I shall know that Thou has forsaken me." Now, as it had been written before the world was assembled out of Chaos, the sun shone unusually bright the following morning, and looking across the hills, Brother Angelik saw that everything was as calm and pure as a mirror.

2

It was dawn, although the sun had not yet risen . . . full day, without the sun, as though the world were lit by a calm but thorough Logic. The hills lay about with a dogmatic distinctness. Every pebble possessed its contour, every grass-blade its line of demarcation. Or, when some group was too far off to necessitate a definition of its individual components, it in turn formed a unit of itself; in just this way, for instance, a small patch of timber extended like a pronounced ellipse on the bias against one of the farther hills. Sky, cloud, earth, and the things on the earth . . . all this was differentiated categorically.

Brother Angelik wandered over the hills as the shepherd of John's sheep, John having been persuaded to visit a sister in Padua. And when Angelik had led his sheep to where Jocasta's were already grazing, he called out to her, "Hast thou an apple, shepherdess?"

"Ha, we maidens have many things, shepherd, but not an apple."

"That is an ill omen."

"And why, Shepherd, is it ill that I should not have an apple?"

"Because then thou shalt feel compelled to give me a kiss."

"And why, shepherd, must I give thee anything?"

"Because I am going to wager with thee that I can tell thee thy name, and I must win something for my wager."

"But my name is Jocasta; I need lose neither apples nor kisses to be told that."

"And I, Jocasta, am the appleless, unkissed Theodoce.

So now we know each other, and our sheep have already made friends without this banter, and if thou wilt sit here beside me I shall tell thee a story."

"Tell me, then, the story of how Theodoce comes to be tending John's sheep."

"Ho, that is a homely story. I should rather tell thee how Zeus gained entrance to Leda as a swan. Or perhaps thou hast already been told that story by some shepherd?"

"Where dost thou come from, Theodoce?"

"From Padua."

"Then I must believe that the shepherdesses of Padua love stories more than virtue."

"In truth! The girls of Padua do not put themselves above the gods. And if Zeus could invent such escapades, the shepherdesses of Padua are not too virtuous to hear of them."

"Well said, Theodoce. And I, as a reward, shall hear thy story. But first, thou must tell me why that story of all stories, has been chosen."

"Because I had hoped that perhaps I, by changing myself into a slave, just as Zeus changed himself into a swan, might gain admission to the bosom of some lovely shepherdess."

"Beware, Theodoce, lest thine incantations fall amiss, and thou turnest thyself into an ass."

"I have no fear, Jocasta. Indeed, I am quite willing to become an ass, if that is the surest way to charm a woman."

"Ah, thou hast a barbed tongue, and I shall leave thee."

"No, thou wilt pick them up and carry them away from me like precious baubles? Lips, breasts, shoulders, thighs, in short all those lovely parts of woman? Stay, Jocasta, and let me at least ravish thee with mine eyes."

"That is an undressing which all maidens must suffer; thine eyes attempt not my virtue but thine own; so I shall stay, and be looked upon."

"Such things are so much polish, that virtue may shine the better."

"Virtue! I think my hearing is better this morning, Jocasta, than it has been."

"And why is that, Theodoce?"

"Because yesterday, when I was by here, I heard thee say no such word to John. Ho! but we will dismiss that, Jocasta, if thou answerest me these questions. First, dost thou grant that we should strive after happiness?"

"Yes, Theodoce."

"And that, therefore, any moment which could be made happier, and is not, is a waste of that moment?"

"Yes, Theodoce."

"And dost thou further grant that there is more happiness in the marriage of a shepherd and shepherdess than when they remain unjoined?" (Brother Angelik was aware that here he was confusing the two ideas of happiness and pleasure, but that this ignorant girl would not perceive the sophism.)

"Yes, Theodoce. Since thine eyes yesterday were sharper than thine ears, yes."

"Then Jocasta, I have conquered thee, for here is a moment which could be made happier and is not!"

"Thou art very learned, Theodoce."

"Ah, but thou hast armed thy virtue with words, and even if I lay low the words, the virtue still remains to be stormed. But see, Jocasta, while we have been wrangling here, how easily our flocks have intermingled! Finding convenient pasturage in the same place, they have all gone there without question. Or note the slight jerk of the sheep's head, effected while the grass is firmly between the teeth, and serving to rip the blade and its stock asunder. If I should draw the picture of a sheep, I should draw its legs to establish the laws whereby, if one leg rests at a given point and forms a given angle with a line drawn horizontally to that point, the other three legs, by the reason of a sheep's balance, would be at three other predetermined points, the whole presenting a rigid relationship. But all this is foreign to the sheep, which, finding the grass of interest, grazes upon it. Ah, would that I could wander thus over Jocasta's knolls and hillocks!"

"Thou art a poet, Theodoce, and poets can sing just as well unto themselves."

Jocasta ran suddenly into the thicket, and would not appear even though Angelik threatened to kill himself. Finding a dagger on the ground, he plunged it into his breast, and fell with his heart against the sod. The blood from the heart soaked into the grass, trickling still warm through the cool pebbles beneath. What was it seeking, that it worked so swiftly among them? For it went with unmistakable haste. As it filtered, the impure red passed into the lonely pebbles; until as clear water it trickled between slabs of bedrock, and mingled with little pools that lay down there in the darkness. Then in elation, this pure water of Angelik leapt steadily towards the sunlight, and Jocasta, who had come there to drink, drank of him and murmured, "How thirsty I had been!"

As an interesting parallel it might be well to add that the day of Brother Angelik's death was the same as that on which Paulus Thessalonicus, then residing at Alexandria, wrote what was considered among his friends to be his most successful epigram. It runs:

Lamp, when there is a faint shuffling of sandals outside my
      door,
And the odour of unguents and perfumes
Calls me like a blare of trumpets, so that I
Arise hastily from my table . . . go out, lamp.
For tonight I shall be laying aside my text
To become the grammarian of sweet Amyctis' body.

PRINCE LLAN

PRINCE LLAN

*An Ethical Masque in Seven Parts, including a
Prologue and a Coda*

I—Prologue

Programme: In the beginning was the waters of Chaos, with their
horizons lost in blackness. This was unbeautiful, and without
history. Following the *fiat,* sprouts that long line of descent
ending in Prince Llan.

LoGos Verbum the Word — universal brew bubbling
and collapsing—then this wad of runny iron and rock settles into a steady elliptic jog—cools, crusts, that objects
wriggle in the slime, and box-like things bump against the
trees—heroic march of that one tender seed through groan-
ings and agues of the earth, through steaming fevers,
through chills slid down from the poles, hunger, fire, pestilence, war, despair, anguish of the conscience, lo! this
clean-blooded man, this unscrofulous unsyphilitic neat-
skinned gentleman, this ingenious isolated item, Prince
Llan.
But where was Gudruff?
Gudruff was gone.
Why should we care where Gudruff was?
Gudruff was Prince Llan's intimate and adviser.
Where were they last seen together?
At table, drinking grog, and talking of the future.
Prince Llan himself—his mind had moved elsewhere—

and when the auctioneer had shouted Who buys these women? Llan answered I buy these w— and flung down the
money inasmuch as they were dear girls they were lovely
girls nor were they afraid by God of him. Their breasts
were tight up beneath their shoulders. Their breasts, they
stood out firm like pegs. When they walked, one could
note their sitters, how they undulated. And taking each
girl by an arm, so that his thumbs were pressed carefully
into their armpits, Prince Llan started with them out into
life.

II

Programme: The Prince, his life and character. He has undergone
    hazards and ingenuities which, though varied and of long dura-
    tion, telescope into a single enlightenment. Then he falls into
    one period of focus, of anchorage, and this is like years of
    vicissitude. The Prince, being an earnest man, becomes uneasy,
    attempts vaguely to formulate some principle of living. He
    would find some one exhortation or admonition to simplify
    human conduct.

Lost in a forest of Siberia, cold, destitute, and rained on,
the Prince found three leaves blown under a rock, and dry.
With these, by rubbing sticks, he builded them a fire, and
they became so warm that in time the two girls sang.
Caught in an avalanche on some far-off peak, they rode
laughing into the valley on a ledge of ice. He tugged them
through shaking sands by the arm. He dragged them from
flopping seas by the hair. Together they cooked with disease. Together they bowed down to Siamese gods. They ate
yellow dogs together. When beset by Arabs, he suddenly
leapt with these girls to one side, leaving the Arabs crushed
by a falling star.

"Let us have a garden," he said to them, so they grew a
garden of flowers, mostly depraved. When it was trumpet-
ing with colours and pleasant stinks, the three of them
withdrew. For days he martyrized himself, draining his
poor body of its very marrow. Long after his groins were

appeased, the itch, the erotic erethism, continued in the mind. If he had lain on his back, and made an idle half-turn, burying his nose perhaps in the rancid grease of their hair, at the odour, the odour of rotting apples, he would become alert again. If he but saw a fountain innocently playing, or a steaming kettle, it derailed him. His garden, rained on by bees, was calmly impregnated. The blossoms withered, to bear fruit; the Prince crashed a rock through their little house, and the three moved on across the face of the earth, across its nose. mouth, cheeks, and hair.

Shortly after this the Prince went alone up into a mountain with a burning bush on it—and standing, his arms Napoleon-fashion, he took stock:

"If I incline to a certain dish, it is that I like it, even before I have first tasted it, the vacuum of this as yet untasted dish pre-existing in the mind. There are vacuums of millions of combinations of organic substances pre-existing in my mind, and I shall die without quieting their pressure.

"Love, the love of one object to the exclusion of all others, enables us to thrive despite this famine. Love is a process of individualization: there is the general vacuum Love, and it is filled when one finds a specific object to adequately symbolize this general. The poet loves his material when he must have that material and none other. There are poets who may choose this or that, being interested primarily in the arrangement, and to this extent they are not filled. Similarly, these girls for me may particularize, but they do not symbolize, the general. Which is to say that I do not love them, because I ask only that they be delicate and smell right. They cannot end the famine, and I am the most forsaken of men, loveless, tossed without anchor.

"Thou shalt not commit adulteration."

III

Programme: "If we cannot yet be wise, let us be passionate." But this is a *spring* of human conduct rather than a *maxim,* and the

Prince is, therefore, in mid-career, engrossed quite simply in the keenness of his sensations. The poet adopts his protagonist's viewpoint, and portrays life as a mad-house wherein even logic would be a kind of derangement, of bias. Yet the Prince, with Grailism in his blood (and by Grailism would be meant precisely that search for a rule of human conduct) hurries on, if not towards something future, then away from all things present.

On a screen the projection of a beating heart, the size of an elephant, convulsing irregularly. Its owner suffering some spiritual or physical torment. As they watched, a large drop of blood collected on a valve, sidled across the slope of the meat—like a tear rolling down a cheek. The drop detached itself, and they shouted, with hell an eternity of having the finger-nails pulled out, the walls crooked. The chairs tire one's elbow, or the muscles of our necks. The lights will go out, come on again, flicker. Lewd pictures were hung, the lewdest portions obscured by splotches of ink. The floor slants, occasionally a door would open, so that a chill passed through, with the lyric cook stumbling across the room, skinny and starved. The Pontificers fought their way among the ruins of chairs and people; carried banners: Let each man build a bridge, if every man builds a bridge the world will have no time for vice, build bridges, signed, The Pontificers, the lyric cook gnawing at his knuckles. He was mumbling recipes, describing the setting of tables, rehearsing an ideal course of dishes, and in the midst of a peculiarly dull catalogue of ingredients, he will burst out with songs in praise of food.

Mine enemy was strong. He possessed the good things of this world. I was a coward, timid and lugubrious. I slunk. I slunk on my belly. I slunk with terror into her bed, taking the wife of mine enemy. When he returns, she will spew upon me, and he will beat me with a horsewhip. Ampersand placing the germs into the blood through the sucking of lice not affable skulls whom the madam lay with

the man so aloof from us as he stood on stilts that passing
dogs stopped to befoul them.

Euonymism holds our salvation to lie in the use of the
left side. It points out that past civilizations decayed, and
that they held the left side unlucky. Yes, the founder of
Euonymism was here: a tailor, descended from twenty-
seven generations of tailors, and they all had lifted the
pressing iron with their right hands, until his race was
puny on the left side of its body. He had plugged up his
right nostril, and cast out his right eye, and was standing
on his left leg, shouting his doctrines at the parade of
Pontificers, *out of the left corner of his mouth, wiggling
his left ear. That is why it is called EUONYMISM.*

(Sitting down, the chair collapsed. Stepping across to
pull a lever, he was soused with water. Falling, he arose.
Rising, he fell. Sighing, he threw off his clothes, finding
them distressing.)

Now:

The Thirty-Three Systems strive after a synthesis. As
they watch, the synthesis is attained, and the Thirty-Fourth
System joins the ranks. Regardless, Euonymists and Pontificers rushed at each other, trampled down a convention of
three thousand specialists on the mating habits of the female Polar dung beetle. Prince Llan leaped up, and ran
with his two girls for the shore. The ship was waiting. The
mob threatened. No time could be spared. He threw them
across the gang-plank as the ship commenced a yaw toward
the South. SLIP THE CABLE, SET THE FORE-STAY
SAIL and the FORE-TOP-MAST STAY-SAIL. These filled with a groan, as the first of the pursuers began stringing
over the hill. CUT THE SPRING; SET THE SPANKER
VANGS, the MIZZEN-TRY-SAILS, the MAIN-TOP-
GALLANT STUDDING SAILS—the ship now moving
confidently out into the water. They cast off the club-haul;
next, gammoning, they gybed the boom taut with a grummet, gave a sharp bowse to the bolt-ropes, and luffed the
halyards to the fag-ends of the davits. The ship scudded

into a vicious head-sea, simultaneously with the clewing up of the spun-yards, while several men under the second mate went madly to work keckling the parbuckle, and marling the lazy-guy with gudgeons. The captain's voice rang out thwart ships above the gale, giving orders to loosen the crupper till it squared the jibboom — and Prince Llan knew that he was advancing into another world.

IV

Programme: Through the conversation of two well-formed but ignorant women, we learn of a new curve in the Prince's emotions. The Prince himself, by his speech and behaviour, corrobo-
rates this.

(Scene: A dense grove in the midst of a rolling barren plain, rather like the pubes on a white body. The Prince's two girls sit observing the horizon. The Prince sleeps. Tableau. Music. Finally one of the girls begins talking softly.)

One of the girls: He calls us Alpha Nomega. So you, dear, be Alpha; I'll be Nomega. Or if you prefer, I shall be Alpha.

Alpha: Back on the farm; home and mother; thought-less; happy; brute made me woman; thirteenth year; knew no better; driven away; city; loved; at times didn't love; I hate men, Nomega.

Nomega: Drunken father; invalid mother; nice man; took to room; gave candy; tickled; happened; fourteenth year; had to pay; but it died; now I am a big empty place, Nomega.

Alpha: Bring carpet slippers; sits reading by fire.

Nomega: Lean over back of chair and kiss; smile; pat cheek; both tiptoe across room; pull back curtains; smile to each other at what see there asleep.

Alpha: Tiptoe back to fire; lay head on his knees.

Nomega: Look up into eyes.

(They fall silent, observing the horizon. The Prince sleeps. Tableau. Music.)

Alpha: But the Prince is good to us, Nomega.

Nomega: Too good. How can we be assured of a future with such a strange man? Look what he wrote, just before falling asleep. I watched the words forming. *(She slips a paper gently from under the Prince's right arm.)* "Taken in the absolute sense, taking old age, that is, divorced from the example of some specific old man, the loveliest life and the loveliest thoughts should be produced after the sperm is silenced. I imagine a life as broad and deep and quiet as a mountain lake, and it seems to be solely the property of old age. I am speaking, however, absolutely, without concern for examples."

Alpha *(taking up the notebook):* "Metaphysics is the yearning to see one's own eye, when there are no reflections, and when one eye cannot be taken from the head to be examined by its fellows." And he, Nomega, is the man who has crawled with us into secret places.

Nomega *(receiving back the notebook):* "True love is specific; but mine is more generalized, like that of the housefly, or the philosopher."

Alpha: Thank God he can still talk of love.

Nomega: We should have run off and hidden among the Horrors. Have sneaked behind the big screen with the heart going on it. We could have hired servants had we stayed there, and had others to tie our shoes for us.

Alpha: The hungry man would have cooked for us.

Nomega: But now we must make the best of things. We must use technique with the Prince.

Alpha: Yes, but he is becoming too forgetful. He is interested in other things. Yet such an earnest man should still be grateful for any display of science.

(Silence. They observe, not the horizon, but the Prince. He moves in his sleep, and mutters, "Gall in the blood. The passions are like gall in the blood." He smiles, becomes quiet, and a flute bleats tenderly as they turn their eyes

again to the horizon.)

Alpha *(sadly):* But let us put this worry aside, Nomega.
Let us recite.

Nomega: Yes, what should it be? Why, let us recite the
First Litany of our Profession.

Alpha: Yes, let us recite the Office of the Enormous, the
Mis-shapen, and the Ill-formed.

Nomega: No, dear, let us recite of that rarer movement,
the Natural and the Divine.

Alpha: I shall try, although I remember the other better.

(They recite. And their unhappiness seems to vanish as
they become engrossed in their connoisseurship. The recitation is half lyrical, half shop talk; it involves both the
philosophy and the procedure of coupling, and becomes
at times somewhat clinical. It seems to clear the air like a
discharge from the clouds. When it is finished, their interests change. They glance appraisingly at the Prince, to
gauge his slumber.)*

Alpha: Nomega, the cat is asleep.

Nomega: The cat is asleep, little mouse.

*(They crawl into each other's arms. But the Prince stirs
and awakes.)*

Prince Llan: Pathetic little girls. I have doubtless inserted many barbs into your tender minds. These barbs
will rankle, until some day, when you are older, you will
understand. At that time it might aid you to remember
that man possesses a species of seed which, if properly laid
within the soil of woman, can frequently result in her
drinking poison, or falling from a bridge. . . . Now, go,
little sealed things, little unplumbed possibilities, little
fields unplowed. Ride off in a carriage tight shut, where no
ray of sunlight can enter.

*Their recitation, which appeared in the *Broom* version of "Prince
Llan," is omitted here, as it is thought to have caused the suppression
of that issue of *Broom*.

(They go, after each has received a kiss and a gift of money from the Prince.)

Prince Llan *(to himself):* There, how gently he sent them off. And he might just as readily have driven them with clubs. He bowed them away as virgins, instead of beating them as bitches. That is better, since more proper to a parting.

(They went, and the Prince watched them mould together into a spot on the horizon.)

V

Programme: The Prince in harbour. The Prince as sage. The Prince at rest. An equilibrium, however, which was gained by too ready a simplification, too hasty a survey of the territory, the Prince's defence of reason being simply a more remote aspect of his passion.

THE universal brew had bubbled and collapsed; boxlike things had bumped against the trees; there had been, you will remember, war, pestilence, and anguish of the conscience; the Prince had bought those girls; he had ridden avalanches with them; he had rushed them away during scramble of Euonymists and Pontificers; gammoning, the spanker vangs were gybed taut with a grummet; and he had become a new man; sent them away as virgins, though he might have beaten them as bitches; and he now walked with a slow tread, after all these years, thoughtfully, to himself, saying:

"A reality encompassed by intelligence falls outside the realm of a complete experience, outside the realm of an organic understanding. There is described to me, in every detail, every elbow of height and breadth, every vibration of smell, every grade of colour, some place—but this place does not live for me as an immediate possession until I, too, have been there, and experienced it through the orchestration of the senses. Yet a reality so encompassed by the intelligent cannot be mistaken for any other—and when I do come upon this place I can apply my tests, and make sure whether or not it is the place intended. Or even going beyond this, I could say that the glory of philosophy lies in just such an act of intellection; in the stating by intelligence of what can never be immediately, *organically*, experienced."

Was this the man who had martyrized himself? It was. Speak, that the younger may be edified. Let them hear what they already knew in their minds, but shall not know in their bodies until they, too, are tottering.

"A man, suffering from untold miseries, can go out and plunge his knife into a wild beast, or his axe into a tree, and by so much resolve his discomfiture. An act is unmistakable: this man has acted. But he cannot plunge his knife into an odour on the wind, or a sudden memory of childhood, or a vague forewarning of death. Vicariously, he has tried to slay the wild beast instead of the sudden memory of childhood. He stoops over his kill, spies a single leaf detached, on the ground, contrived ingeniously, and his misfortunes are suddenly situated elsewhere. . . . To obviate this, let him divorce himself from organic experience, and translate these vaguenesses into the certainties of the intellect. Life, established by the poets as a fever, remains a problem of distress which cannot be solved in terms of positive happiness, but may in terms of pains absent."

The Prince transcribed carefully.

"The intellect is the most advisable narcotic, since it enables us to live a waking deep-sleep, to get the completeness of the facts, but without the poignancy. By the word I create, I act—which means, I slay. Man by nature a slayer. Having become too subtle to dispose of his maladjustments by the slaying of wild beasts, he turns to the slaying of his emotions. The intellect unites living with death, perception with immunity. Let us admit only as much emotion as will serve to add zest to our perceptions. Let emotion be gall in the blood.

"To find that method whereby life, pressed into firm little bricks, is handled at leisure. For life to tear at our chimneys and howl faintly outside the windows. Or even better, life as a tinkling of far-off cow-bells, coming up irregularly over the low hills. This we mean by the consolation of our philosophies. We must search, not for experience, but for the symbols of experience; reason and art each aiming at a formula in accord with its particular properties, its own potentialities. Idea cuts through a tangle of emotion; emotion cuts through a tangle of ideas— and each, expressed by the formulas of art and thought, are remedies against the complexities of existing. I bare my teeth at the yapping of the senses; I devote myself, rather, to seeing how, if a given thing is so, other things follow. Yet how strange that at this point, rising in thought above my own uneasiness, having found this rock on which to enforce myself, I should receive word from Gudruff. From Gudruff, and I once sat at table and drank grog with him. Has he, too, found fierce temperance? He writes, Gudruff writes: 'Sweetly tired body' . . . 'muscles of my throat' . . . 'hay, cow's breath, urine, manure, and old sundried timber' . . . *'temptationi inguinum'* . . . 'beyond the reach of duties' . . . 'blessings from Gudruff.' "

VI

Programme: The Counter-Prince, and Conclusion. Gudruff offers the rebuttal which the Prince had unconsciously determined to ignore. The Prince, deprived of both the anchorage of his wisdom and the impetus of his passion, moves on haltingly and irresolutely, the poet now comparing life to a troubled half-sleep.

To his good Prince Llan, greetings from Gudruff, or perhaps greetings from Gudruff's skull, or more accurately, greetings from that much of Gudruff as may still lie in the Prince's own heart, for the rest of him may have been thrown to the winds by the time Llan receives this letter.

This sweetly tired body may have been laid aside, stopped even by its own hand.

After they parted, Prince, he walked for days, eventually passing through a parched country and finding no water. His spittle was a dry pulp, a cotton wad in the mouth. He came to a stream, pushed his face against it horse-like, and suddenly the muscles of his throat began sucking in the water with a passion which astonished him. It was not Gudruff, it was his throat that was drinking, while he leaned back and watched. He threw off his clothes, he lolled in the stream. He let the sun dry him, and moved into the shade to sleep. But a change had come over him. He had learned, Prince, that one can observe with deliberation what is usually taken without thinking, that one might go through life holding a minute ear to the body.

He found that he was close to a village. It is somewhere adjoining, but beyond, the territory of the dear Prince's father. There is wealth, but not the kind to tempt a restless and grasping people. He entered, and forthwith five women and nine boys were brought to him in recognition of his station. He felt it advisable to send some of the women away, but perhaps this was due to the fatigue of his long journey. Since then, Prince, he has remained in this village, where, in his own fashion, he has become wealthy.

To witness: The heavy sirupy smell of over-ripe strawberries; cool mint; the worminess of rich loam soaked with water; the bitter-sweet of a barn, its mixture of hay, cow's breath, urine, manure, and old sun-dried timber. This ensemble of growth and decomposition, freshened with morning. . . . He lay there in peace. And suddenly, suddenly, *plena recognitio facultatum corporis latuit subito ei; se relaxabat, est molliter lapsus contra terram, deinde se debat suorum temptationi inguinum.* The remainder of the morning he spent in reading.

Patiently and earnestly, his dear Prince, he has gone about it since then to enlarge his knowledge. Each day, perhaps, some new pore has been opened, some new nerve

stroked. As he grows old he feels creeping over him the haze
of venerability. He is now a veteran, dear Prince, and he
feels that he has used his intelligence nobly to heighten
every channel of sensation. He is at least fortified with the
feel of moral victory, of having done what *he* could to ex-
tend beauty further into the realm of ugliness. This body
has not strained and fed and given off unheeded.

But now an illness is on him, and perhaps the roots are
numbing. Perhaps when the Prince receives this he shall
have passed beyond the reach of duties and obligations.

Good Prince, blessings from
     Gudruff.

Prince Llan cried, "I am coming, Gudruff, I am coming." He stumbled forward, throwing himself heavily
against the door in front of him. It was an oblong door,
encrusted with minute carvings. There were houses, mountains, three peasants sitting at a table, women washing
clothes, lovers kissing by a well—tiny dramas were carved
upon this door, and Prince Llan shoved it open. His eyes
were partly closed, glued with a heavy sleep. An ear sat between a filtering kidney and an intestine with its lugubrious burden. Parts of himself, reduplicate, lay about him.
He climbed over a twitching leg. He pushed aside a piece
of throbbing brain tissue to keep from crushing it under
his heel. Other parts sauntered through the air like fishes.
Peering, he saw a door; it wavered beyond a film of mucus,
an oval door with a heavy brass knocker. "I am coming,
Gudruff," he murmured, as his body, dragged by unseen
weights, spread over the ground like molasses. He shifted
his bulk, forcing it to slope against this door, and the door
budged reluctantly, allowing him, down a corridor beyond, the glimpse of a door. . . .

VII—Coda

Programme: Might Joseph be the marriage of Prince Llan and
     Gudruff? Might these two unstable types be somehow joined,
     producing in Joseph a dualism at one with itself, a dualism not
     of strife but of mutual completions, a dualism of systole and

diastole, a synthesis? For a moment the poet so feels, and in the firmness of his certainty attempts to crystallize this enthusiasm into dogma. Whereat the cosmic burden overcomes him; and in killing himself he does no more than what for most of us is adequately symbolized in the abuse of alcohol, the listening to a symphony, or the turning out of a light and crawling into bed.

JOSEPH, singing with the birds in the morning, busying his carcass in physical toil before the heat of noon, next eats, and snoozes dog-like while the sun is most intense. When the splendour is diminished he appears again, and returns to the fields. In time the shadows lengthen; Joseph takes food and drink which, the body having been depleted with activity, is drawn in like water poured on a desert. At dusk the muscles have been appeased; the brain speculates contentedly. Joseph lies in wait for a better understanding. We are nearing the completion of the cycle; what has gone before has sweetened the twilight. The eye flows calmly over the silhouette of the black hills. The moment has come to shut himself away. Going indoors, the hero turns to his books, confining himself within the sharply restricted funnel of his lamp's light. Ultimately, laying aside the books, he goes to his woman, and the cycle closes.

Si hortum in bibliotheca habes, nihil deerit. If, says Cicero, you have a garden and a library, you have all. If you have life (*hortus,* garden) and the contemplation of that life (*bibliotheca,* library, books). Above the molten flow of emotion, a rigid and well-knit crust of ideas, said that great platitudinarian, Cicero, that unfortunate, knowing the laws of good fortune. But you will pardon the author, dear reader, if at this point he interrupts himself. For your author is dying. I, Morducaya Ivn, the respected chronicler of these meditations and events, rose from my desk but a few moments past, laid back my head, and cast a mortal potion into the belly. Already, there is a drowsiness mounting my legs. Between me and death there are less than my fingers full of people.

There is an old Chinese woman, exhausted of a dropsy. A baby in London, deformed by its mother's corsets. Three of five drunken sailors in a brawl at Singapore. Then me.

When I am dead the boats will still sail down the river . . . people will eat supper with their windows open . . . and doubtless take walks across the country during weekends. I will be dead. Dead in a coffin carried through the street, and my beard growing silently.

They say the baby won't cry when it's slapped. . . . Down, you bastard! and one of the sailors is gone. . . . Now that Chinese woman is staring: pingee, pongee, pungee, pung, yes, grandmother died of a dropsy.

I am demanded back to be remoulded. This borrowed ego returns to the great Warehouse. My collection will be scattered: this much of beef, swine, mutton, herbs, rum which, taken into the blood, became me. I could situate my elements thus, roughly, in pre-history. Twelve portions of this nose once floated in a tepid sea, the liver of a dinosaur. This mouth, or rather this eye-tooth of this mouth, was belched up in part during the ejaculation of the Himalayas; it is a relic of the earth's earlier enthusiasm. And ah! this little strip of thumb-nail, immediately within the border of the moon, who would believe that it was once included in a germ which gnawed at the brain of Jesus?

And so I am reclaimed metaphysically. Strictly to observe relationships, in the light of Jupiter, I do not matter. As I was slung together, so shall I fall apart, an aggregate of casual units, subject to the chemistry of the Law. And when the earth, the black cold earth drives on through space, drives on through force of habit I suppose, and there is left nothing but a dead worm sticking to the collected works of Shakespeare, what will it signify that Ivn perished of the nature of things, and of poison cast into the belly?

Ivn, you are dying! Not an aggregate of units, not a relative trifle in the light of Jupiter, but you, I—I—

Out of the big black hole
into my own awareness out of nothing
thus from the grinding womb of the Mother
    Nebula
I
my heart, *my* fingertips,
I, the affirmation, the solely significant. . . .

Facts, tiny facts, the patient ministering to our daily
needs, the balancing of hungers with appeasements. But
what—that tingling in the ears; it is music, or death. I fail.
I struggle once more to my feet, choking. Of a sudden I
am elated with futurity. I bellow:

I have suffered the prologue. I have heard the orches-
tra strike up, the curtain rises, and God! I am called
to go elsewhere. I saw their fat happy faces, caught a
glimpse of them dining, and the door slammed shut
in my face. To live among those beeves of art. And
here and there little cries come up out of the earth,
like flowers. When the world rises and sings—but I
am dead.

(Dies.)

METAMORPHOSES OF VENUS

METAMORPHOSES OF VENUS

I

ALL those goodly people came together and voted to live in peace. They made pacts, mutual checks and surrenders, and thus the better filled their bellies, and slept the sounder, and in time developed that pleasant convulsion of the muscles, that baring of the teeth, which is known as laughter. Thanks to their cunning and virtue, we could move in the assurance that three lines writ on a piece of pulp would designate one person among hordes, carrying our message across the errors and rumours of great rivers, across the coughing of the seas, and the heaviness of plains. This we shall call an edifice, a structure of rock and iron; and the flames overtopping this edifice, we shall call love.

No, I lay no snarls, oaths, or venom against the grinners and the smirkers, for they bear their own distress inseparably, like a hump. Their curse is in their solitude, which is a shadow stalking them in silence. Their curse, hear me, is in the way they eye their women. Their curse is in the meanness of life, the paleness of art, the dullness of their fellows.

I met a man who had met another man, and from one to the other, and from that second to me, was handed down this: There was a rich country where the grapes were fat and the cows oily, and people had learned to make all living things diseased, that when eaten they might be daintier to the palette. So their foods were pungent, and rancid, and bitter, and rotten-ripe, their cheeses gamey and their meats of a syrupy sweetness. These people died with abscesses in the heart, or foreign growths sapping the bowels, or great flower-like ebullitions of ebony blood beneath the armpits — and this was the life of even the sturdier and grosser among them, the peasants.

While the court had moved still further into artifice. When the Queen was rutting, she found even her engineers of value, who had for instance contrived to direct warm currents of air and musk across her and her associates. There were more inventions, serving some of them to frustrate and others to point her desires, but they are not within the focus of this parable. The stranger came simply to tell me how once the Queen, when supposedly nearing the height of her sufferance, had suddenly pushed aside her three labouring courtiers and complained that she was surfeited. Her face twitched and became withered. Then just as quickly, the witheredness vanished, she smiled at some new thing, and murmured "Paul." Now, the courtier who had been named Paul was in reality Hozzidac; and the Queen was Queen Muin, but he answered, he also with a new smile, "Virginia."

Cast on the island as a child, kept alive with turtle eggs and bananas, Paul had lost his one companion, a sailor who smoked dried ferns in calabashes, when he was hardly more than twelve. Since then he had sat daily, as the sailor had taught him, on a rock overlooking the sea. He had learned the quiet procedure of sunsets; unknowingly, his body had absorbed the march of colours, from yellows, through pinks, to velvet lavenders. But one evening, as the sun was half cut by the horizon, with the rest spilled out in a copper rope across twelve flat miles of new pennies, prodigally a star fell sizzling into the sea. Immediately after, he heard for the first time a female voice, and he knew that he had not sat waiting all these years for a ship, but for Virginia.

Leaping from his rock, Paul ran to the shore, and dragged her out of the ocean like a fishing net. She had fainted.

With one hand on her hair and the other on the firm mound covering her heart, Paul sat quietly and waited for Virginia to awaken. Her eyes opened slowly, then started, and she moved herself frailly away from him. She asked for food, and Paul brought her a necklace he had made of coloured stones. She smiled sadly, and made the sign of biting with her teeth. Paul, meek and distressed, held out his finger for her to avenge this mysterious wrath. But she pushed it away, and made signs of swallowing—so that Paul brought her turtle eggs and bananas, and also some dried ferns stuffed into a calabash. Later he led her to his hut and gave her a warm soup. Then she pushed him out the door, made signs that he must not enter—and Paul sat through the night, ready to rip apart with his hands whatever prowling thing he might hear clumping about in the blackness.

With that first impromptu evening corroding like a slow patient acid in the recesses of their memory, these two hastened to erect barriers of daintiness between them. They fought restlessly against everything in this scheme of living which pushed them too undeviatingly, too unsubtly, towards each other. From Virginia Paul learned again to speak, and with words came a new awkwardness. Language itself was a deflection of their purpose; even the simplest words were circumlocutions, while these simple words in turn must be circumlocuted. They developed comforts and amenities, and by so much the more they had placed a hard safe crust above the volcano of their desires. Unknowingly, they determined to forget the slow patient acid in the recesses of their memory; they would live and die, with that the last direct caress between them.

Here was an experience which no humans ever before had known. Their care for each other, their aloof delight in each other, was unique. The polarization of precisely these two egos could happen once, and only once, in eternity. Was it finally those very barriers, so unquestioningly erected between desire and fulfilment, which became tentacles drawing them closer together? At moments their words became a song; and All That They Had Done became All That They Had Done Together. Something arose which I shall call a warm glow—and this glow radiated from them across the world of objects so that, looking upon these objects, they saw things in a strange and astounding light.

Then, cutting across these complexities of evasion, came a storm. While the island shook from the blunt broadsides of thunder, and giant trees spun about and toppled to the earth, Paul and Virginia sat crouching in a tiny cave. Paul's eyes glistened; Virginia's hair was tousled, she laughed-with-the-wind. As Paul grasped her by the shoulders, she glanced at him with a shudder, then with something even roguish; finally she became limber, and here on the rough ground they bedded.

Later the ululations of the storm subsided; rain fell only when a casual gust of wind blew drippings from the trees. The storm had bundled off to some other portion of the globe; somewhere else the storm was stumbling across the waters; it was no longer their storm.

II

Returning from the war (a bullet had flattened against her picture worn over his heart) he sang his way back through France and sunny Spain, tossing to the mendicants small coins and curios plundered from the enemy, and carousing in the night with heavy-booted brigadeers, telling them, to the plunk of tankards on the oaken boards, how a girl (golden-haired) sat humming frail songs in a tower and waiting for his return. Arrived at last, he swam the moat, and scaled the walls with grappling hooks, and with a curt whisper turned the growling of the dogs into a whimper of welcome, and suddenly appeared in the tower kneeling beside his cousin. But she paled slightly at the sight of him, and her eyes faltered, so that he understood more than if she had spoken whole volumes, and with one stroke he despatched the head from its body, he himself stepping without hesitation along the parapets and free into the air. "The Warrior Returns."

An elderly couple, grown silently too old for the ravages of desire, live alone at the end of a winding lane off the main road, tending their gardens of flowers and vegetables, keeping one cow and a family of cats, and living in the letters they receive weekly from their daughter at college. She returns for the summer vacation, so that a man is brought from the county seat twenty-four miles off to tune the piano. The daughter plays strange music; also, without malice, every Sunday morning she plays old-favourite hymns to the accompaniment of their thin voices. She is receiving letters, this daughter; and by her exuberance they know that these letters are from a lover. The mother finds accidently where they are kept. Then every night the old couple read them over together in secret. They also sneak down to the rural mail box and take out their daughter's letter, steam it open, make a copy of it, and replace it in the post box. Finally the daughter expresses a wish to "visit a girl friend." But the parents know that a rendezvous rather has been arranged between their daughter and her lover, and that she is to spend the night with him at a hotel in the county seat. She returns; the old couple welcome her, and do not question her too much about her girl friend. That evening, after dinner, she retires to her room, and the old couple sit on the front porch, waiting for their daughter to post her letter, and for night to fall. "The Homestead Among the Lilacs."

They had first met at a sculptor's studio, where he was interested in the peculiarity of her figure. Milton exclaimed with vigour that she was built like a peasant, and thereafter called her *ma paysanne*. Aline discovered that she could be happy with this man. He taught her the luxury of big beers after an hour of tennis. They would go on long walks together, and returning on the train she usually fell asleep on his shoulder. But one evening in the early spring, when he was to meet her, he came two hours late, breathing heavily, with his eyes over-bright and unfocussed. "I tried not to come," he sighed hopelessly, dropping into a chair. The idyll was over. He burst out that he was in love with her. His good humour had been a deceit, and he could bear it no longer. While she, she was an unconscious vampire who demanded that men just be "nice" to her. She cried a bit, after which they "made up." He avowed that he was a fool for having been so tragic, and was hilarious the rest of the evening. He insisted on calling himself a victim, however, and when he was about to leave her for the night, he grew sullen again. Hereafter Milton was seen notoriously with other women. When he met Aline in a group, he would overlook her entirely, or else greet her with a boisterous, aimless familiarity. He "forgot" his engagements with her, then clamoured for a reconciliation, until she held out her lips to him, whereat he brushed them cheerfully and absent-mindedly with his own, and began talking of other things. Or again, with the sweetness of a benediction, he assured her that for woman to pride herself on being desired by man was like a cabbage priding itself on being eaten. About this time it happened that Aline met with a series of misfortunes entirely exterior to Milton. Yet he somehow "rode" upon them. Busying himself elsewhere, he secretly voted himself a victory: he was manipulating an indeterminate but efficacious vendetta. "Imponderables."

Miriam was unusually conscientious in her devotion to her husband and her three children, which may be accounted for by the fact that not only was she an earnest and well-meaning woman, but also she had a lover. Gradually, as the husband and lover came to know each other more intimately, the relationship was tacitly avowed and agreed to. Miriam remained delicate in her difficult position, and each man respected the other for his share in the possession of her. With this deep channel of emotion in common, the two became close friends, so that when Miriam fell ill they took turns watching at her bedside. After her death a hostility arose between them. "Death Us Do Part."

For twenty years he has lived alone in New York, going every evening to the burlesque shows; and for twenty years he has stood at the stage door each night after the show, hoping that to-night (to-night!) he will at last muster the courage to pinch a chorus girl as she passes. Finally one girl drops a package as she is hurrying home from the theatre. He snatches it up, takes it to his room, opens it, and finds that it is a slice of beef-steak. With gritted teeth he plunges his fingers into the flesh and pinches it unmercifully. The next morning his landlady finds him dead of apoplexy. "The Seduction."

Although it meant the loss of a fortune if she married him, Florence never hesitated. She stood up staunchly before her father, faced the old man's mouthings against popery, and then the two lovers set out for the station in the dark, through a howling blizzard. Their hardships during the next months, while she was furthermore being gnawed at by a child in the womb. He could seldom find work, so that hunger and deprivation were added to her miseries. The child was born dead, and she nearly succumbed to puerperile fever. Several times the parents wrote, offering to care for her if she would leave her husband; but she always answered, boasting of their prosperity and happiness. And though he himself begged her to go back for her own good, she would not: a life with him, even in destitution, was preferable to a life without him. Finally the husband gets a steady job as a clerk, and their hardships are over. In time they furnish a home. The household duties become irksome to her; she complains that he cannot afford a maid. She sees him now under steadier light: he is honest, kindly, but without brilliance—and now for the first time she resents her past sufferings. The flatness of her life becoming too unbearable, she deserts him. "Built for Speed."

The professor of physics in a small-town college lived quietly and contentedly with his wife and child in a duplex house not far from the campus. This child had come only after five years of waiting, when he and his wife had already begun to lose faith in her ability to have children. After school hours he goes on long walks with the child, or else spends his time in the basement making it mechanical toys. At night he sings to it:

> "By o baby Bunting,
> Papa's gone a hunting;
> He'll bring home a rabbit skin
> To wrap his baby Bunting in."

One of his colleagues in the biology department, who is collecting certain vital statistics, requests him to submit to a physical examination—as an outcome of which he learns that he is sterile. He takes the news quietly, but later complains of being ill, and asks that someone else teach his classes for the day. He goes on a long walk in the woods; at first he groans aloud, and then, shamelessly, he sings "By o baby Bunting." A kind of peace descends upon him: he is reconciled. After all, the child has made his life richer, even though he is not its father. He will steady himself, will struggle to preserve his old attitude towards both child and wife. He returns home, almost in elation, his victory has been so thorough. His wife meets him at the door, open-armed, smiling. She whispers to him the news: he is again to be a father. "The Rabbit Skin."

It was not as an old man that Faust first laid down his book to hear the choir of angels, and the young men returning from the harvest, and the First Citizen inviting the Second Citizen to go with him where the beer was best and the girls prettiest. During a strenuous adolescence, knowledge had meant to him precisely the one channel of escape from these discomforts. With that richness, or sensitiveness, of character which made him find things appalling which others took for granted (seeing one specific beautiful woman as beauty, or one specific white shoulder as woman, and thus finding terror where others found a purpose) he turned from life to the relics of life. For here, after all, were the same factors, but under a simpler, or kindlier, aspect. With young Faust, then, the humanities were not the crowning of the human, but a substitute for the human; he was becoming gnarled when he should have been made mellow. And Faust would have already been a monster, except that he was young. As he aged, Faust deepened his knowledge, until as an elderly man he realized that this very substitute which he had sought for living led back in turn to the obligations of living. To be wise, even on his own terms, Faust saw that he should have to travel man's normal orbit, man's proper cycle. Thus, at a time when he should have relaxed, looking upon the world with the twinkle of a well-fed mind and belly, Faust saw that the structure of his years should rest upon the foundation of a different youth. In complaining of knowledge as vain, Faust was too wise to apply this universally; it was meant simply as the diagnosis of his own diseases— and Faust suffered remorse, was without dignity. With the help of artifice, Faust *purchased* his youth: Faust was now a monster. In purchasing Gretchen, in having to purchase Gretchen, Faust understood exactly the extent of his poverty, and was consumed in his own bafflement. "The Tragedie of the Doctor Faustus, Done Into Words of Four Syllables for the Children of This Country."

If a virgin among the Maroans dies, and she is under the

age of ten, she is buried lightly, with one foot exposed, that her body may be digged up and devoured by wolves. If between the ages of ten and twelve, she is similarly buried, her shame having first been removed and mummified and hung in the Sepulchre of Hope. But if she is twelve or more, and is nubile, yet has died a virgin, then the body is warmed over a slow fire, and given to the young men, themselves warmed with a brew of bay leaves, to exact their pleasure. "The Tribe of Maroans, Their Virgin-Worship."

III

Of fish, the male exudes a cloud of sperm which, by encompassing the female, leaves her fertile. Was there, on a subtler plane, some similar interrelationship of human minds and emotions? As he sat here now, unprisoned (unprisoned! for erratically enough he thought of convicts, turning in their cells, in a life without the imminence of transgression) sitting here, he recalled a kind of flush which had seemed to pass from his vertebra and arms and shoulders, and to be projected like a cloud about the clothed figure of this woman. Those silent spasms — he wondered if she too had been aware of them, or if they had filtered somehow into her subconscious, if some sperm might now be basking in the cells of her brain, thriving and growing sturdy, until, with apparent suddenness she became amenable to him, or pliant rather, or mentally supine: a seeded field, waiting to be sunned and rained upon.

Where she deliberately blinded herself, he was trying to see more keenly. Obscuring the basic facts, she would spend her time rather going beyond those facts. She might, for instance, be thinking of some trip with him in Italy, or her making clothes for a four-year-old child, or even deciding what kind of flowers grow best in window-boxes. He, on the other hand, was stepping, or eyeing—or sparring even.

At times he would drop some little root into her, some tentacle; or he would crouch back, wounded with apprehension like a snail.

He had sat and nodded with her, and held out his cup to be refilled; and the excitement of their dialogue, mounting into the abstract and will-less, into the pure inutile, had made him overlook the slinkings and sneak-thieveries of his profounder business. After such moments he returned with something like freshness and guiltlessness to their vague, indecisive dalliance, their warfare without visible objectives.

"I remember," he wrote her, smiling with a mixture of beatitude at the sudden clean memory, and amusement at his own unconscious trick of making love to her by recalling an affection for another, an affection which she could not dismiss, as it had values, and which she could not resent, as it had innocence, and thus which should pique her most in that it both provided an object for jealousy and made jealousy unjustified, came, you might say, fully armed, but bearing palm branches of inoffensiveness, "I remember" [nor was this something social, something which could be exchanged, smiling, at the club for something else] "that I was sitting in front of a humming stove, and the door opened, and a girl broke into the room, her clothes smelling of the crisp snowy air, her smile stiff-muscled from the wind. We had not known each other intimately at all, but I leaped up suddenly and embraced her. I kissed her, almost without knowing it—so had the act preceded the emotion."

Those were the simple words: she could take them as such. Everything behind them, that unique combination of declivities and purposes which had contributed to their genesis, could be caught by him alone; even now, immediately after the event, they were scattering and fading off into one another. After all, that memory, remembered here, was not a fact but a *symbol*. He had been weary with his own bandyings and wanted something simple, some smooth rails to glide upon. Perhaps, then, he had not written those sentences in accord with any vague technique of seductiveness; perhaps she had not even been within the focus of his aims. And all that was involved here was the curve of his emotions from complexity to simplicity, a curve which had been materialized, or symbolized, by his choice of two corresponding specific factors. His complexity, that is, had taken form as the stiffness and purposelessness of him sitting before the fire. And the desire for the sudden smooth rails of simplicity had attracted this other memory of the time when the soft, cold-nosed girl had appeared and "the act had preceded the emotion." While this woman had been simply the gravitational element; that is, since he was writing *her* a letter, and a *love* letter, he had made the unconscious selection of this particular symbol rather than some other.

Oh, it didn't matter, it didn't matter, it didn't matter. "I believe that at bottom man expects to find in woman a haven, yet this is precisely what she is not." Woman as the prostitute type, woman as racially a vendor of love. When she yields, she yields not to a man, but to some social distinction. She must take a car conductor because he is the *best* conductor. With a young man of promise (are destitution and promise identical here?) she is prompted by the potency of his youth, but yields after the imaginings of a problematical future. In the course of years, as his merely physical, or technical gifts decrease, he retains her or loses her in proportion as wealth (or reputation if she is subtler) is won or lost. Where then is the haven, since one gains it the more only by needing it the less?

Back in those Dark Ages of adolescence, when every train ride he took or every time the whistles blew at New Year's, or when vacations began or vacations ended, or on his birthday, he had decided that from now on it would be a closed book. Each day was to be a fresh day. In despair he resolved to drop each time a quarter into his bank as penance; and soon he had enough to buy his little cousin

Ethel a Christmas present. Then came the startling birth
of a *philosophy*. For how, he reasoned, could he be mag-
netic, so long as the surcharge was being led away through
inappropriate channels? How could he set another in tune
with him, unless he himself were vibrating enormously?
Circulus vitiosus—for if he could not acquire the proper
recipient of his energies until he had turned from himself,
no more could he turn from himself until he had acquired
the proper recipient of those energies. A ghastly pessimism,
which he solved strangely enough by simply waiting until
the manna fell from heaven, until a woman came and jok-
ingly asked where she should hang her toothbrush, and
then—praise God—really did hang it there.

Occasionally with real warmth, with a willingness and
pliancy, he pursued his letter. He wrote of a certain song
which they had heard once without thinking, and how,
when he had heard it again recently while alone, it recalled this time they had been together. He requested that
she return to her usual mode of hair-dress. And he hoped
that she would go to the concert with him.

CODA

His friend Jim, an older man, had told him: When undressing beneath the eyes of a mistress strip first to the
waist, then remove shoes and socks, and last, drop the remaining garments at one stroke, so as to pass from attire to
disattire without suffering the indignity of intermediate
stages.

She had been borne for this; in blind accuracy her body
had been fashioned and steered towards this one thing.

If he smiled upon her, her whole body smiled back—by
his frown she was left hopeless—she looked at him silently,
with moist dog-eyes—he spat.

A record of sheer concupiscence; a mass of lewd and
lascivious imaginings; things obscene, indecent, and lu-
bricitous.

Appreciating the abstract syllables beyond the actual content, noting the growth of a dead up-rooted flower, forgetting the heart, finding sufficient excitement in the lips, yet broken suddenly with pure anguish.

THE ANAESTHETIC REVELATION
OF HERONE LIDDELL

THE ANAESTHETIC
REVELATION OF
HERONE LIDDELL

I.

"IN THAT MOST BODILY HOUSE"

THE first thing of importance that had happened to Herone Liddell following the accident of his birth was a near-fatal tumble he had taken, about the age of three. Spitting meditatively from the height of a second story, he lost his balance, and fell at an angle on his head. Subsequently, he tended to assume that he had hit the ground before his own spit.

Had he been older, his neck might have been broken. But the bones were still soft enough for the dislocation to be rather like a bend than a break, leaving him, as a quirk, a tilt of the head slightly to one side, the way some dogs intently listen.

Yet in one notable respect this fall, this accident, had become part of his essence. For it had marked his early years by their own peculiar kind of "falling sickness," sudden spells which the family called "fits," when he felt himself sinking, and would create a great clamour in the belief that he was about to die. Similarly, night after night, he re-enacted his "traumatic experience" by dreaming exactly the same dream—a dream of walking down stairs that vanished into a pit of nothingness, at which point he would awake in terror.

Nowadays, Herone would probably have been diagnosed as having the amount of neurosis "normal" to his injury, and perhaps would have been treated by a child psychologist, had his parents been able to get one cheap. But as it was, he was left to improvise his own cures, which were along the lines of religious piety (a "natural" compromise, since such reverence is a species of fear, yet also has strong connotations of solace) .

So young Herone lived much with thoughts of God the Father and Christ the Son, often trying to be exceptionally good. And when, sometimes at sunset, shafts of golden sunlight shot down from turbulent black and golden clouds, he saw them not as the physical things they were, but as paths one might traverse in the other direction, by spiritual ascension such as he had seen depicted in his books of piety.

However, in the course of living, his earlier attitudes gradually became submerged beneath successive deposits of secular realism, the accumulation of experiences with people in the everyday world. And by the time he was ready for college, his religious interests had become so transformed into sheerly aesthetic analogues, if he thought of "grace" at all, it was neither the theologian's kind, nor even in general the social graces, but the possibilities of stylistic grace, to match the possibilities of stylistic grandeur.

So much, for the present, regarding the first thing of importance that had happened to Herone Liddell, following the accident of his birth.

The last thing of importance (we omit intermediate hirings and firings, marriage, divorce, remarriage, and other incidental steps along his way as a Word-man) was a surgical operation, which was now to be performed on him, at the age of sixty. It was the sort of operation usually classed as "minor." In fact, beforehand the surgeon had proffered with a laugh, "For cases like this, there's no need to make out your will," whereat Herone, who had not thought of making out his will, promptly began wondering whether he should make out his will. Also, something had happened (if it had happened!) which was to make Herone think of his operation as decidedly "major."

Either the hour for which the operation was originally scheduled had been set ahead without the surgeon's being notified, or the surgeon had been notified, but had forgot. Or there had been some other hitch. Or Herone, already drugged to the stage of near-dementia, was reading the signs wrong (under conditions certainly not favourable to his reading them right). In any case, while he lay in a semi-maniacal state, fighting helplessly to be listened to, and hearing the words he tried to form become vexingly dissolved into inarticulate tongue-waggling, he heard, or thought he heard, snatches of conversation.

They seemed to be about the surgeon: Where was the surgeon? . . . Had he been notified? . . . Someone should phone him. . . . Yes, he was still at home, having breakfast. . . . He'd hurry right down.

Did Herone really hear these remarks? And if so, by how long were they separated from one another? Meanwhile, the situation contained an ingenious kink of this sort:

Somehow, since early childhood, there had lodged in Herone's imagination a strong misgiving as regards anaesthesia. He had feared with a fear almost magical a possible point at which, partially anaesthetized, he might still be conscious, yet wholly within the power of another, unable to call a halt in the proceedings, despite his rights as customer. Somewhat, he said, as a suicide might feel who, after having leapt, wanted to retract his decision, but was powerless to do so. In his imagination, this moment of helpless resistance, when others could do with him as they chose regardless of his struggles, had seemed somewhat like the sickened sense of falling he had experienced, in the recurrent nightmare of his childhood. Related to it was a horror of being confined. Thus, even under the most trivial of conditions, as were his arm to be so caught in his sleeve that a few moments' patience would be required to extricate it, his spontaneous tendency would be, rather, to attempt tearing himself loose in a frenzy. And his present condition was a perfect instance of such a situation—for as he lay half-conscious in the operating room, he felt several expert tugs, and lo! both arms and both legs were clamped tight. So now he lay there, raging helplessly, with no more rights than a carcass, bound in the very way he had most greatly dreaded.

It was a Poesque situation, as with the story of the man who, having all his life dreaded the thought of being buried alive, awoke to find himself confined in what, in stony horror, he took to be a coffin.

However, in his imaginings, Herone had overlooked one notable motivational distinction. The Philosopher admonishes that anger drives out fear—and true to the book, Herone's fright turned to rage, almost rage in the absolute. For he was so confined that the only mode of fighting possible to him under the circumstances was limited to whatever kind of surgings could take place within his own guts. At least the physiological processes that might load his blood with his own adrenalin were not strapped down, so he freely seethed within. Outwardly, the resources of hating were reduced to mere cursing—but even that outlet in turn was reduced, by the aphasic conditions resulting from the amount of anaesthetics already in his system, to ineffectual words that somehow refused to come out right. Things were so set up that, if wanting to call someone a filthy bastard, he would at most hear himself, as though from within himself, shouting as though from outside himself, "oo lya snar!" This was especially vexing for a Wordman, in his ferocious but futile struggles against the "indifferent Powers" that bound him.

There was one other surprise: For many years, in his

bouts with insomnia, Liddell had slept with a red bandanna kerchief over his eyes, to keep out the faint rays of the early dawn. But now, during the delay (if there was a delay!) while waiting for the surgeon (if they were waiting for the surgeon!) his eyes were exposed to the glare of strong lights immediately above him (presumably floodlights to be used for illumination during the operation?). In his befuddlement, they had upon him the effect of the blinding glare used by police officers when questioning criminals or attempting to break the spirit of political prisoners. He felt not merely assailed, but invaded.

So there he lay, suspended in a state of helplessness and rage, just on the edge of extinction, while vaguely around him were persons whom he could remotely hear in snatches but could not see, and who seemed to be waiting. He heard himself almost as though he were an observer from without. But no, it was something very much inside him he was hearing. And he would go on hearing it for some days after the operation was over. In its purity, it was not him; but it was an aspect of him, and it would try to make all of him over in its image.

"Bruised bleeding maniac," he reconstructed afterwards, heroically; "made powerless by straps and pain and drugs," though he had of course lapsed into total oblivion before undergoing any of the processes to do with the actual incision. "Cursing whoever from outside attends him, him there inside his own seething—his will to live made pure revilement."

Or otherwise put: "The little man with the great big bad unconscious; the timid man with a roar somewhere within, emerging as out of a chasm." Somehow, apparently, his sheerly vegetating body had received as an outrage the very service that his citizen self was paying to have performed.

"The groins divided, a mind divided," he wrote in bed, using pencil and clipboard. (He had quickly come to the conclusion that the operation had produced a "psychic shock," that its nearness to the genitals made it psychologically equivalent to castration.)

One almost comically unstable symptom made him swing back and forth as between two wholly different personalities. Certain ideas that occurred to him (or came to ride him, rather) turned his diaphragm into a band of steel, stopped all unfoldings, transformed the churning gases of his bowels into stony immobility. But other ideas, equally beyond his willpower, brought with them relaxation, and a corresponding flow of blessed flatulencies, until in the course of events things shifted again to associations of the rigidifying sort—and in a flash, the muscles of his stomach became hard knots, as clenched as a fist. In brief, he could shift (or, more accurately, he was shifted) between tense associations and relaxed ones, with the muscles of his bowels and stomach making a burlesqued behaviouristic replica of the difference between the two attitudes.

Had he started under bad auspices? The morning he was to leave for the hospital, being awakened early by the sputtering of a car down the road, he had made up these lines (he had numbered the stanzas, to accentuate their development as stages) :

STAGES

(1) Ducks quacking, dogs barking,
     A kitten scurrying for cover—
     And there he was.

(2) All day
     The songs, the games,
     The friendly altercations.
     "My compliments! My compliments!"

(3) A dim shape
     Borne away by shadows
     In the dead of night.

Bad auspices, unless you interpret such things after the manner of counter-boasting (saying the worst, to "prevent" the worst) .

Now, lying with distended bowels, a loathsome tube inserted through one nostril into his stomach, he tried to wince ("in that most bodily house, where there was no place to wince to") —and all the while he kept wondering whether it was a good sign or a bad one that he could not stifle a refrain :"pity for each wincing thing / pity, and thanks for the eventual / kindliness of cure-all death."

Herone was impressed first of all by the extreme *physicality* of his condition. He thought of himself as an item in the process, to be poked or jabbed, at set stages along the way, in accordance with a pre-arranged schedule—and things would proceed as per schedule despite the fact (if it was a fact!) that something had gone radically wrong with the schedule at the very start—if he could trust the naggingly unforgettable though muddled memory of his impotent rage while lying strapped and waiting (a maniac in a straight-jacket) , under the inquisitorial glare of the floodlights, or whatever they were.

Had he fought even while wholly anaesthetized? Could the body, even in sheer mindless physicality, hate the instruments that prodded at its tissues; and might it thereby load the blood with the juices of sheerly physical strife?

When, all full of his experiences, though still somewhat in a fog, he had started to discuss them volubly with his room-mate, an intern who happened to be present made a sign indicating that Herone should shut up — and then severely murmured to himself for Herone's benefit, "Writers talk too much."

Even in his befuddlement, Herone had to admit that the intern's point was well taken. In fact, Herone had often made the same point himself, and about himself, particularly during recent years when, the country having swung far to the right politically for a spell, Herone found many of his earlier liberal attitudes and utterances in danger of being made to look absurdly suspect. Yes, for some years Herone had been ruefully proclaiming that it was, alas, a writer's business to talk too much, though he finally had had to abandon this line when he heard some damned newsman on the radio say the same thing about newsmen.

In any case, now at a time when Herone felt a great desire to verbalize about the bepuzzlements of anaesthesia, and would gladly have enlisted the whole hospital in the task of speculating about his symptoms in particular, and about the symptoms of the anaesthetized in general, he found himself abruptly put Under the Sign of the Quietus. Thus, the degree of persecution-mania "normal" to his profession was greatly increased by the Kafka-like quality that pervades the disrelation between the immediate physical ministrance of the nurses and the Hidden Authoritative Essence somehow brooding invisibly above and beyond all this particularity — the great Godlike Routine that loves us all equally and impersonally, and decrees what is best for us, while we need but surrender ourselves, in full confidence, to its judgments.

Since he could not surrender himself psychologically (subjectively), while at the same time his physiological (objective) surrender was necessarily almost absolute, Herone in his role as impatient patient came to think of himself as a prisoner, perhaps even a "lifer."

Add this angle: Quite as a person pursued cannot sleep, so a person who cannot sleep is like one pursued. And for the week following his operation, Herone's insomnia, which had always been a major topic of conversation with him (as of an attainment), had acquired proportions nearly of grandeur. As he lay listening, round the clock, to the muddle of sounds (some clearly interpretable, others vaguely so) that mark the cycle of a hospital's routine, his mind felt tense as a steel trap, set but never sprung. Thus, he *was* a prisoner, almost literally, to the extent that The Routine would not or could not or simple did not prescribe sedation sufficient to release him from the dreariness of his stony vigil.

He wrote:

PRAYER FOR INSOMNIACS

Great God, thy wondrous world is full of aches,
Of which a goodly share of them are mine.
On every side are proddings to mistakes
And most straight things get twisted serpentine.

Great God, the mass of miseries is deep,
And many are the wounds that will not heal.
But all I ask for me is: Let me sleep—
And Great my Lord my God, it is a deal.

Yes, maybe his psychologer friend was right, when contending (in a case not unrelated to his, though Herone had protested violently) that operations of this sort often aroused a "castration anxiety." Maybe our hero had got himself into a jam.

Lying awake as stony as a statue, he began trying to get things straight.

How look for origins? Herone thought it possible that his experience managed somehow to link up with a "primal scene" as early as his fall at the age of three. Both were, you might say, species of the same genus, or even particulars of the same species—and thus, as regards the logic of the emotions, it was as though he had recently had his childhood all over again.

But what of the malice? The early experience, so far as he could remember, had been wholly without warfare. It had simply happened. But apparently his new experience had involved almost an orgy of hating. Apparently (as he gathered from a passing remark by the surgeon) even when completely unconscious, on two different occasions his muscles had knotted while being sewed—he had been fighting at the very roots of himself. Was that merely physiological, the sheer will-to-live manifesting itself fundamentally as meanness? Or had it also owed something to "conditioned" kinds of reflex?

How deeply might an idea-motivated body hate surgery? Enough even for the ideas to do their work when the mind had lost all track of them, like a kind of "pre-hypnotic" suggestion?

At least there was the fact that at the height of his adolescent religiosity, he had joined a sect of faith-healers, and had been a most devout believer. True, the sect's stress upon the healing properties of "love" left no place, overtly at least, for endrocrinally stimulated hatred as a mode of survival. Yet religion goes deep, and the depths are full of paradoxes—so he had to consider this possibility. And at the very least it was a simple realistic fact that he was on principle as dubious about "medical progress" as he was about "progress" generally. There might, then, be this strong "doctrinal" resistance, capable of God only knows what ultimate corresponding response in the tissues—and attested by the fact that, on the surface, he tended to associate hospitals much more readily with death than with cure.

Similarly, he resented the ways in which the modern hospital had restored the ancient art of blood-letting, though the New Phlebotomy was contrived indirectly, by the resources of finance. He had quickly become so cantankerously resentful of the present procedures, with their arrant gadgetry, that he was fairly let alone. For he loudly protested his distrust of the very thing that most people seemed to associate with the greatest glories of modern medicine, and he had always contended that medicine should be pills or nothing. But he watched his room-mate being assailed by an endless procession of pretty girls who entered at regular intervals, to stick that elderly, longsuffering gentleman abruptly in the behind, as per the doctor's orders. Herone held that someone should invent a combination walkie-talkie, hypodermic needle, and cash register so that, each time the patient got another shot, a bell might ring, while the charge for the deposit of rare metals and pedigreed bugs would be recorded grandly in the accountancy department, and thus could show on the patient's bill even before it began to work on his body.

But attitudinizing of that sort had come later. It could not have accounted for any battles directly connected with the operation itself.

Second, how deeply might he resent his surgeon? He had originally intended to have the operation performed by a different knifeman, or seamster—but delay and distance were involved, and he chose his present practitioner instead. Such initial indecision as to the choice of surgeon could lie there as a fertile source of resistance, insofar as anything went wrong—and is there not a sense in which even the "best" of surgical operations could be said to go wrong? At any discomfiture, the patient might be tempted to resent his choice—and all the more so if one were an old liberal, his politics much the worse for wear, and had lain helplessly bound beneath the "politically inquisitorial" glare of a long narrow searching light that he remembered vaguely as the visual equivalent of a piercing shriek.

Then again (and this was along the lines of Herone's psychologer friend's ideas), there is something somewhat "outrageous" about an operation on the groins. The repairing of Herone's hernia involved a radical "invasion of his privacy." True, he knew that he had paid to have it done—but doubtless his tissues didn't. And once his identity as a customer had been put to sleep, maybe a more conservative self took over.

Ultimately, however, as always with a Word-man, the problem had developed into a problem of the Quietus. The ideal patient was expected simply to *believe in* the Routines, and no questions asked, whereas nothing was normal with Herone until it was talked about, if even then. But the surgeon had become so evanescent, Herone almost had to scheme to see him—and for quite understandable reasons, nurses and interns avoided all discussion like the plague. Everybody going about his or her business —and from the standpoint of a Word-man, it was as though some Dirty Deed had been done, with no one returning to the scene of the crime.

Directly from this situation came his sense, or conviction, of the Ultimate Trap. Another name for the Ultimate Trap was Writer's Guilt—and he had built up his data on Writer's Guilt thus:

On many occasions in the past, in his younger days, when he was walking the city streets working things out, he would stop by a store-window or hallway or lamp-post, to take down a note that he thought might be usable—and almost immediately, someone would come out (the store-keeper? the janitor? a plainclothesman?) , and would edge towards him, to spot what might be going on, just in case. . . . Or, at least, it seemed that way! And now, he suddenly thought, that's how his note-taking might seem, to all these people expertly going about their business.

For Writer's Guilt derives ultimately from the writer's sense of The Guilt of the Written-About, which can be avoided only if the subjects have strong reasons to believe they are about to be praised.

Still, without even thinking of it in these terms, Herone seemed to have hit upon a kind of solution, in connection with a local priest whose company he had recently come to enjoy.

Though essentially an agnostic, Herone roundabout resembled a believer—for his distrust of pronouncements about the supernatural extended also to a distrust of the naturalistic critique of supernaturalism. Sensitive above all to the ingenuities of dialectic, he knew that one need not believe in God to love theology. He relished the sheer stylistics of piety—and he thought it gallant of monastics willingly to put their wills at the disposal of the wills of others (as one does in effect, when taking the vows of obedience to a monastic order). He was troubled in particular by the religionists' talk of "humility," while attributing to human kind so arrogantly high a place in the cosmic order (though he had to admit that often such "arrogance" did seem to manifest itself as considerateness, whereas his own tendency to belittle mankind's role in the universal scheme often went along with a tendency towards "pigheaded mulishness").

In any case, Herone asked that his monastic friend come visit him—and improvising, in a kind of "secular confession" whereby the non-believer's sheer utterance would have to be its own absolution, Herone discussed his quandaries almost hilariously. When it came time for his friend to leave, Herone felt purged of all Kinks. And when his wife came to see him that same afternoon, he bobbed like a cork on the waves.

Accordingly, all the more surprising was the development a few hours later.

Once again, it seems, Herone had been the victim of circumstances, responding with over-promptness to a certain telling convergence of events:

His room-mate, who had undergone an "exploratory operation" (cystoscopy) with the aid of spinal anaesthesia, and who had been consistently the very soul of good-humour, surprisingly took it upon himself to become a howling demon of pain. For several hours, without let-up, at each exhalation he groaned, a groan that sank into Herone's weary wakefulness until he felt as though his own guts were being torn apart.

Let us call it The Night When Room XQ-27 Went Crazy. The closing routines before bedtime were over. Herone had been given his pathetically ineffectual sleeping pill. The lights in the hall had been dimmed. The mixture of clearly and vaguely interpretable sounds in the distance had dropped to a minimum. But here, within a few feet of him, was a formerly good-natured man darting about the room, groaning aggressively, and ceasing to groan only during the intervals needed to draw in the breath needed for the next groan when breathing out.

Herone began to twitch. Whereas he had been quite weak, he got out of bed, and (along with his groaning room-mate) started to wander up and down the corridors, ignoring the pleas and imprecations of the disgruntled night-shift. Of a sudden, he felt so strong, he could have dressed and walked out of the hospital, speedily and without assistance.

In fact, he tried to figure out how he might scheme to do just that. For as he found his body jerking, rigid and strong, he decided that he had been given, not a sleeping pill, but strychnine. He wrote notes, hiding them about his clothes, in case, when he was dead, "the evidence" would be destroyed. There could even be a "motive." They had misunderstood his note-taking!

Finally, having burnt himself out, he crawled back into bed to await his end. His room-mate, in time, ceased groaning. Herone became aware that the muscular jerks were diminishing rather than increasing. He would live!

The next morning, attempting to read, Herone made a discovery. He noted that he was affected by a kind of aphasia whereby, when he got to the end of a sentence, he had already forgotten the beginning of it. He could follow an idea consecutively when writing it, but he could not maintain the sense of continuity when reading.

Now, of a sudden he realized: He had been taking as "reality" a kind of world that had come to him through the partial distortion of drugs (probably the original anaesthetics) not yet eliminated from his system. His *crise de conscience* had been primarily a matter of unaccustomed chemicals.

He was glad to get back!

The next day he was almost infantile in his sense of con-
trition. He apologized profusely to any and all — and
though no one seemed overtly resentful of his antics, the
Quietus popped up again, as soon as he touched on the
subject of "symptoms," possible responses to drugs, and
the like.

One especial absurdity resulted from his over-eager desire to make amends. It involved his Two Gigantic Aides,
the one More Gigantic, the other Only Slightly Less Gigantic, one on the day shift, the other on the night shift—
and the two of them together would have made at least five
of our hero.

He liked them both, but particularly the More Gigantic,
who had inducted him into the routines the first night he
came to the hospital, in preparation for the operation the
next morning.

The day after his brain-storm, when he was sheepishly
telling his wife about the turmoil of the night before, the
More Gigantic Aide happened to be in the room at the
time—and she said, "I'll bet you wouldn't have acted like
that if I had been on duty last night."

To Herone, who was to this Giantess "like a cat at the
feet of a queen," this notion seemed quite correct—and he
exclaimed spontaneously, "I believe you're right!"

But later, he began worrying about his remark. It im-
plied an adverse criticism of the other Aide, he felt, the
Less Gigantic One, who had been on duty that night—and
he was trying to make up with everyone. Yet the More
Gigantic One might pass on his remark to the other Aide,
without wholly explaining how he happened to say it.
(This had become a major matter!) And he felt all the
surer that some such misunderstanding had come about
when the Slightly Less Gigantic Aide, while arranging his
bed, began (in what seemed to him exploratory tones)
praising the Aide who was his favourite.

So he wanted to explain to her that, in saying he would
have acted differently had the More Gigantic Aide been on

duty, he did not mean to imply any criticism of the author-
itativeness of her, the Less Gigantic One.

It was a difficult matter. So he took her hand, and
started to explain. Whereupon, before he could say a
word, she wrenched her hand loose and rushed from the
room.

And Herone saw himself in the role of an old goat who,
the moment he began to get the least bit better, made a
pass at a nurse! Also, he had no illusions as to how long it
would take for that story, in the Less Gigantic Aide's interpretation, to filter through the staff.

II.

"WE MUST TENTATIVELY READ THE SIGNS"

But what of the "Revelation"? It happened thus:

Mostly, his sleep was too scant and shallow for dreaming. Only in flashes, at best, could he get beyond a kind of
half-awake dozing, a semi-stupor while conscious of the
nearly constant hospital processes. (In all hours of the day
and night, a hospital suggested to him the hustle and bustle
of a grammar school at recess.) But there was one notable
"epistemological" dream, and he clung to it for hints of
something; though it had the evanescence of a fever dream.
The main difficulty is: A fever-dream is far from providing
the best example for making clear the precise logical difference between the realists' notion of intuitions that grasp
reality as it really is, and the idealists' notion of intuitions
that, in their role as appearances, are essentially different
from the ultimate things ("things-in-themselves") they
represent.

In this dream he saw several rods of glowing white light.
These rods were symmetrically arranged somewhat like the
blades on a lawn-mower, except that lawn-mower blades
are somewhat curved whereas these glowing rods were
straight. There could have been five, six, or seven of these

—and one of them might have been central, like an axle.

The important matter was their relation to one another. In one sense, each was distinct; in another sense, they were all one (the kind of dialectical ambiguity one meets in the relation among the persons of the Christian Trinity). Almost immediately on coming out of the dream, Herone thought of a possible explanation for the ambiguity. At one stage in the progress of the anaesthesia, the patient's eyes might have become so unfocussed that the long rod of glaring light above the operating table (if there had been such!) was seen as several. In this respect there really would be a sense in which the different rods of light could be simultaneously one and many.

Along with his perception of these glowing rods, there was a voice speaking (a kind of Voice in the Absolute, proceeding not exactly either *ab intra* or *ab extra*, since it was too remote or impersonal to be his, yet too much in tune with his own thoughts for it to be someone else's). In any case, it was giving a *rock-bottom explanation* of things, and with regard to the effects of "proprio-nyl," Herone's dream-name for his anaesthetic.

However, in the solemn pontificating of the Absolute Voice, "proprio-nyl" was being praised not for its value as an anaesthetic, but for its contribution to the understanding of "reality." The design of the glowing rods (in their ambiguous shift between oneness and plurality) purported to reveal the structure of the universe in a wholly *realistic* way (a point that must be stressed, because of what came later). It was intended to teach *exactly how* the universe is constructed. And though it was an invention made for pedagogic purposes, it was intended not as a "model," not as a "suggestive illustration," but as a revelation of the literal basic fact.

Yet that pedagogic note must have introduced a principle of instability into the "vision." Or rather, it must have provided a transitional bridge whereby the Absolute Voice could pass from a *realistic* to an *idealistic* position.

For the Voice explained how, on one occasion, something went wrong with the working of this fundamental educative device—and in the course of repairing it, an important new discovery was made. It was found that the rods could be seen from different angles of approach (that objects could be seen from many sides), so that the interpretation of reality became more complicated (we might say more "perspectival," though this word did not present itself during the dream).

The dream ended just as the turn had been made from the wholly realistic view of the design (the notion that its appearance was identical with the way things really are) to the kind of thinking that is essentially idealistic (because of its "perspectival" emphasis, its suggestion that the true vision is to be approached through the obscuring yet revealing fragmentation of many different local standpoints).

In the last analysis, Herone thought on wholly awaking, the first version of the design would be scholastic, the revised view Kantian. And the best way to possess the first position is to begin with it, since it cannot be reached from the position of the second. For anything perceived must be an appearance; by definition an appearance is to be distinguished from a reality; and thus, the appearance must be what reality is not.

A world of appearances could be known as a set of usable signs; but no matter how well a system of signs was made to serve in the pragmatic business of survival, you could not get around the purely formal consideration that a thing can be an appearance only insofar as it is not the reality behind its appearance. For if it were an out-and-out reality, then to that extent it would not be an appearance.

A painting can be an imitation of a tree only because it is not a tree. And a real tree, by reason of its realness, cannot be a mere painting, or imitation, of a tree.

Anyhow, rightly or wrongly, Herone had the conviction that he had watched the very essence of realism, through the very essence of criticism, become the very essence of idealism. (Later, he decided to define idealism somewhat punningly as: "A philosophy that, confronting the distinction between mind and matter, asserts that only mind really matters.")

But speculation on his dream quickly moved from questions of "aesthesis" and "anaesthesia" to problems of an ethical, or even sociological, order. In fact, he was not averse to wondering whether the sort of considerations he came to next had in reality been prior to his "vision." In that case, the "vision" would have been in effect the reduction to a corresponding but simplified design, somewhat as when complicated attitudes are duplicated by absent-minded "doodles" that somehow stand for them (the attitudes leading to a kind of act that translates the attitudes into graphological terms quite different though essentially analogous).

From the realistic point of view, the design had been intuited to be as purely and simply and immediately real as the taste of an orange, or as the thought that, if A is bigger than B and B is bigger than C, then A is bigger than C. But once the Absolute Voice had noted that, in the "repairing" of the design, a way had been found to see around the corner of its immediacy (and thus, in effect, to change its status as immediate into a status as mediatory), then forthwith the simplicity was gone. The intuiting of reality would now be idealistically indirect and complicated, with the medium of observation itself prejudicing or distorting the observation (though one might hope to approximate the state of simple, immediate, absolute, "intuitive" knowledge to the extent that one could by critical analysis make allowances for the distorting effects of the medium, including the medium's nature as "informative").

The social-minded parallel of Herone's Radiant Quincunx (and it had been radiant though he was not sure it was a quincunx) involved two views on the nature of hierarchy, as it applies to our views on human relations. Certain relationships are simple, he thought, and thus allow for the direct "realistic" awareness that something is as it is. But certain other relationships intrinsically involve a contradiction, which must be idealistically discounted (the discount usually being guided by materialistic notions of "interest" as the primary motive behind the given social transaction).

To illustrate the case of a simple, realistic relationship (though aware that his example was rife with possibilities of interpretation in the spirit of idealistic symbolism), Herone told himself:

"A, let us say, is a ferryman. B wants to be ferried across the stream, and is willing to pay A for this service. Here, obviously, observable at a glance, *uno intuitu,* is a direct and simple relationship such as fits perfectly with a realistic philosophy. A has an immediate service to sell; B wants the service and is willing to pay immediately for it." The example was not quite perfect, Herone felt, since a purely barter deal would be much more realistic than one involving money, which already had a highly "idealistic" element in it.

Or, more accurately still, realism must begin even farther back than barter, prior to any "justice" of the *quid pro quo* sort. Realism would be naturally tribal, grounded in services of sheer familiarity, like those binding parents and offspring. It centers in such sense of purpose as results spontaneously from the combination of agent and scene (motives reflecting the needs proper to a given natural species in a given natural situation). Realistic services would be basically incommensurable with one another, like the variously interacting functions of the organs in a living body.

Herone even wondered glancingly whether talk of the "incommensurable" relation between "eternity" and "time" could have its sociological beginnings in a wholly "pre-talionic" sense of community, before the thought of scales had furnished the material for conceiving the idea of justice in over-simplified terms, at the very start, as reduction to the image of the balance. Might speculations on the "absurdity" of the "incommensurable" relation between God and man arise as a late-idealistic, "post-talionic" attempt to recover the principle of this primal realistic order? And thus might "ancestor worship" begin philosophically in the "incommensurable" relation between the power of the adult, as compared with the pathetic limitations of the infant, the powers of adulthood corresponding to the "infinite" or "eternal," and the limitations of infancy corresponding to the "temporal"? And surely a "pre-talionic" idea of justice is needed, if we are to think of God as "just" in sentencing all men to natural death because the "first" man had fallen into disobedience.

In any case, nothing could be farther from realism, in its essence, than the kind of thinking now called Realpolitik (which is a materialistically toughened brand of idealism, idealistic sentimentality in reverse). The problem of co-operation that Herone's tentatively imagined Ur-Realismus could not solve, and that accordingly called for the death of realism in its purity, was signalized perfectly in the Spanish proverb, "When two share the same purse, one laughs and the other weeps." True realism can't long survive the ability of language to observe that, when the cream has settled, one can "by sheer oversight" grandly pour himself the thick and leave the thin for others, in their role as mean, justice-mongering grumblers.

One might become more exacting still, and contend that realism could not prevail in its Simon Pure state except prior not only to all taliation but even to all speech. Thus, the "truly" realistic vision of the Design was impaired as soon as the Absolute Voice entered the situation (which it did almost at the very start of the dream as he remembered it). Implicit in the Voice would be the *dialogue;* and implicit in the dialogue would be the *dramatis personae* of different points of view, the "perspectival" element.

But at least, the nature of the transaction between A, who would transport for a consideration, and B, who would be transported for a consideration, was clear and direct. And in this sense, it could serve as an example of the intrinsically realistic, particularly when contrasted with another kind of service, which Herone thought of as necessarily involving a contradiction. For instance, it is a doctor's job to cure us of our ills. But insofar as he succeeds, he does himself out of a job. Or, less drastically, if he cures us in one visit, he'll earn much less than if he cures us in ten. To an extent, then, we must take his goodwill "on faith." We cannot directly know. We must tentatively read the signs. The situation itself contains this contradiction, as an intrinsic part of its nature. And in this sense it is a relation intrinsically "idealistic."

By the same token, there would be intermediate cases (most of the world's relationships would probably be in this class) where quasi-realistic claims may be affirmed despite the intrinsically idealistic nature of the case (a situation that contains the maximum opportunity for an essential deception).

Herone did not flatly assume that "contradictory" relationships (like that between hospital and patient) led necessarily to deception. On the contrary, he assumed that the principle of good faith was generally predominant, and sometimes complete. He merely had in mind the fact that the situation was intrinsically "contradictory," hence not the kind that could properly be treated in terms of simple realism.

(He had heard tell of a time in old China when the relation between physician and patient did have the kind of directness that would naturally allow for simple realism. Then a man paid a physician to keep him well, but stopped payment whenever he got sick. However, Herone reflected, such an arrangement might set the conditions for an opposite kind of twist, as a pinch-penny person might become chronically ailing, if only to do his physician out

of his wages. Herone further noted that there was a sense
in which modern medical insurance did operate along the
lines of the old Chinese custom, with corresponding tendencies on the patient's part.)

In any case, the dream's two views of the Design suggested to Herone how a philosophy of realism might fit
(and thereby be a misfit) with the conditions of a medical
bureaucracy built atop a "kinked" or contradictory kind
of relationship. Or, going farther, he glimpsed the possibility that all bureaucracies, in their double role as servants of the community and perpetuators of themselves,
called for "realism" while needing the check of idealism,
in turn checked by materialism.

Where there is bureaucracy, "realism" combines with
absoluteness and authority, to suppress inspection. It re-
quires, first of all, an act of *faith*. One must put himself
trustingly in the hands of those who "know best." He must
take things at face value. Whatever is done to him, or
whatever he is told to do, is purely and simply for the
purpose of cure—and that's that.

"Perspectively," discounting with the aid of an idealistic dialectic that contains at least one strongly materialistic
strand, he may see, or think he sees, an essentially contradictory situation that calls for a more complicated terminology of explanation. He may see, or think he sees, situations whereby "medical ethics," supposedly designed to
protect the patient from mistreatment, could function
rather to protect the profession from inspection (much as
military men use "reasons of security" to avoid civilian inspection of their policies and expenditures) .

But insofar as the physician's professional manner (with
all the corresponding hierarchy of attendance by interns
and nurses) is accepted realistically, *simpliciter, uno intuitu,* as equatable with the poise, authority, competence,
dignity, and professional goodwill that it proclaims on its
face, then the patient is enfolded in a Grand Mystique of
Absoluteness, calling for silence and obedience, and readi-

ness to pay. Something untoward may have happened? Try and find it! Indeed, try by questioning even to prove to yourself that it did *not* happen—and the wall of the Grand Mystique was just as impenetrable.

Thus, in sum, Herone, by profession one who "talked too much," and above all a lover of the "comic discount," confronted a mighty, awesome monument, built out of little things that went unanswered—a great chasm of tiny silences—just when he had been all set to chatter like a jay.

Though Herone had been greatly relieved on finding that the worst of his over-responsiveness had been due to the drugs themselves which were still vestigially with him, leading him to interpret physiological symptoms in terms of sociological causes, he still did somehow greatly want to mourn the loss of something. "I feel," he wrote in the style of *Galgenhumor* to his psychologer friend, "as though I had had my connotations cut out"—to which the psychologer friend subsequently answered: "You're lucky. In many such cases I have read about, the patient feels rather as though he had had his denotations cut out." And he told of one poor luckless devil whose wife had decided to have their second baby, just about the time when he went for his operation. She had her baby, all right; but by the time he had recovered sufficiently to make it, she had decided to have it by a different father—so the operation was closely followed by a divorce.

Herone kept trying to remember a poem in Catallus he hadn't read since his adolescent days at college, on lamentations by one of the priests of Cybele, just after the operation that vowed him permanently to the deprived physical condition required of those ministrants (the *Galli*, in ribald jest called *Gallae*) .

In particular, he worried about some lines of his own he had written only a few months ago. For he felt that, from the symptomatic point of view, they lent themselves to two completely different interpretations:

SEASON SONG

O when will the snow melt on the mountain?
The valley is now in heat.
And when will the heat of the valley go
The mountain snows to meet?

O once I went to the mountain
A feverish one to meet,
That we might go
As quick through the snow
As though to be in heat.

O I fear the time in the valley
When heat and cold have met
And the sun has set.

Actually, there had been no snow on the mountain, that hot day when the lines occurred to him, just at the turn from spring to summer. The valley had been unusually hot, but some bare rocks on the mountain had happened to glisten in a way that suggested snow. The second stanza grew, not out of an actual experience, but out of the first stanza. (The "one" didn't seem quite right, though the inversion of the words "to meet" somehow seemed passable in this instance.) And at least, he had been through the second stanza "in principle."

It was the burden of the third that worried him. One can never be quite sure when such imagery is prophetic, creative, eager to hasten the day, and when it is an attempt, by counter-boasting, to forestall the dread time prophesied. At the moment, he inclined to fear that the "creative" possibility was uppermost. "Oh, that something fortunate had ever happened to me or my brothers!" Keats wrote just before the end; "—and then I might hope,—but despair is forced upon me as a habit." But alas! it was more than a habit, or even a premonition. Events only a few weeks later proved that Herone would have been justified in taking his attitude as a certainty.

Still, Herone told himself for solace, between the futuristic symptomatics of the "Season Song" and his post-operational symptoms of the present, he had dipped into another kind of scheming; and he asked himself just how far the stylistics of gallantry might legitimately be carried. Here had been gestures that, borrowed from a long tradition of poetic posturing, seemed to him somehow to build up — or "imitate" — a world cunning enough to keep a metaphysical body engrossed with the proprieties of thanksgiving and leavetaking, since Man (in his role as Word-man) is sentenced to the sentence:

SOMA AND PSYCHE:

A Body's Platonic Converse With Its Soul

Soma, pleading:
        Inbeing,
        Flask without fault,
        Give, give,
        Until we melt.

        Now, beyond all thinking,
        Give towards an ultimate drinking.

        Give me unearned
        Thy chaliced selfhood towards me turned.

Psyche stirs. . . . Pause. . . . Then Soma resumes,
    more excitedly:

        What flower is this
        Unfolds in darkness as furtherance
        Of my mute ministering utterance?
        O—I would mount to depths,
        To drain full cups

At near-collapse,
To kiss
A silken secret's lips.

Psyche, to herself, musing:

Move,
Be led,
Let wings be spread
To give,
That he may love
And dying live.

How far carry this sort of thing, the Kantian (hence, idealistic!) principle of *As if?* There he had written *as if* snow were on the mountain top. And here he had written *as if* he believed in body's being related to soul like masculine to feminine (the flat opposite of the classic equations, yet using a classic idiom, though perversely).

Might his "anaesthetic revelation" (or, more accurately, his "post-anaesthetic revelation") be reducible ultimately to but the more pressing realization of a condition that he had realized long before he ever took his somewhat expensive punishment? Were there certain resources of language, driving us towards a purely linguistic fulfilment, as though towards the origin of everything? A terminology had certain logical conclusions implicit in it, certain possibilities of completion, or "perfection"—and for a symbol-using species maybe these can form as real a kind of ultimate purpose as any congeries of material things and physical sensations. The Kantian "as if" would be a variant of such a notion.

For instance, we might say that a poet writes "as if" certain perfections "really" existed, or that a person could act gallantly in real life itself "as if" the poet's imaginings "really" existed. But an "as if," so conceived, would not quite hit the mark. Rather, one should approach the matter roundabout, thus:

First, there would be the sheer physicality of life, the human organism as simply one more species of alimentary canal with accessories.

Second, there would be the miracle, or accident, or perhaps even morbidity, of language, in various ways helping this particular species of alimentary canal to guide and protect itself in its tasks of growth, temporary individual survival, and reproduction.

Third, there would be the motives intrinsic to this special property, this miracle, or accident, or morbidity, of language—a plane of symbolism capable of pointing towards "perfections" intrinsic to itself. To live by these, in the sign of their sheer formality, would be to live by "real" ultimates, ultimates proper to the medium.

However, in the light of sheer physicality, from the standpoint of the human species as digestive tract with trimmings, such a way of life would be but an "as if."

Herone could not honestly say that this notion made him any richer. But he did know that, when he left the hospital, he would be several hundred dollars poorer.

What Liddell resented most was not the impossible slip-up as regards his operation (if there had been such a slip-up, and if he had not merely got things crooked as interpreted through the confusions of his drugs). He resented most the fact (and he could not fathom the reasons though the fact itself was brutally clear) that, whereas this institution must have had more soporifics per square inch than a poppy field, he was allowed to go so many times round the clock, burning brightly awake like a Blakean tiger in the forest of his quandaries. For beyond the nag of the insomnia, there was also the fact that such constant wakefulness denied him the guidance of his dreams.

How could our hero hope to see around the corner of himself, if he could not catch himself dreaming? What could he learn by simply trying to figure out where a particular flushing of a toilet or tinkle of ice water was coming from, or whose steps those were in the hallway? Herone had been kicked in the teeth—and at the very least, he felt, he was entitled to discover what the more primitive aspects of his personality, or personalities, thought about it. But to his knowledge, there was only one other occasion when he got far enough asleep to go beyond a kind of half-blinded observation of his surroundings into the *bona fide* realm of dream—and he was grateful for it, even though it resulted in a nightmare from which he awoke abruptly, in exceptional terror.

This dream seemed to involve a kind of counting game, that was played with bones shaped somewhat like wrenches, thus:

These bones were ambiguously motivated. In one sense, there were players who were somehow making them hop about; but in another sense, they seemed to be moving of themselves. There were at least two players, one of whom was Herone, though in an "absolute" sense—for no person was actually visible, nor were there any visible means by which the bones were caused to move. The "game" consisted mainly of pressing one or another of the four prongs against the ground.

At the same time, a kind of Absolute Voice (or Voices?) kept reciting pairs of numbers, such as "three-four," or "seven-eight," or "eleven-twelve." Then of a sudden a transformation took place. One of the wrench-like bones became Herone himself—and he awoke in terror when the pressure on one of the prongs became instead like a "full Nelson" in wrestling, a grip that was about to break his neck.

At this point, instead of paired numbers, the Voice had shifted to a group of three: "two-three-four"—and as Her-one lay awake, still fresh from the nightmare and trying to fathom it, each time he repeated to himself the numbers "two-three-four," shivers of dread would go through his body. The ability to re-induce this shivering effect by repeating the number persisted a surprisingly long time.

In trying to locate the implications of this dream, Her-one could not turn up one single possibility to work on. But after the shiver-effect had been worn out by several experimental repetitions, he found himself as it were changing the direction of his thinking. He thought of a literary conceit, along these lines:

Recalling the old Mother Goose jingle, "One, two, buckle my shoe, Three, four, knock at the door," etc., he thought of a possible trick whereby the numbers could be treated in a way to make them pointedly "meaningful."

By the time he was two,
He had learned to buckle his shoe.

At the age of four,
He found something oddly revealing in the response he got
When he had knocked at a strange door.

Between the ages of five and six
He became a useful participant in the mysteries of fire-
    making
And often went forth to pick up sticks.

And by seven or eight
He was actually building usable things with them,
Laying them straight.

And so on. But by the time the pattern had got thus far under way, Herone began to suspect that this dream might be quite close to the thing he was looking for. For it might cut all the way back to the "first fall," when his neck was

injured. (He kept clinging to the notion that his experience on the operating table had somehow harked back to
his "original sin" in falling on his head.) The counting
game might figure because, most likely, at the age when
the accident occurred, little Liddell was being taught to
count, and by such devices as the Mother Goose rhyme he
had now been making "meaningful." His spontaneous description of the bones as "wrenches" seemed to fit with the
same possibility. (It was also an unexplained fact that after
the operation he had a sore neck—though he had not the
slightest idea how he got it or what to make of it.)

However, even hypothetically granting that there was
some emotional connection between the operation and the
fall, he could not account for the tremendous change in
motivation that seemed to take place when his dream
shifted from the playful pairs of numbers to the shivery
group of three.

Did it all perhaps involve an ultimate magical difference
between even numbers and odd? In any case, there was
one other numerological moment that occurred to him one
morning when, in contrast with his usual depression and
disgruntlement, he unexplainably felt perky as a puppy. It
concerned a design that apparently contained elements of
"rebirth," since it concerned an idea for a cartoon-like
cover to be published on the Christmas issue of some
"smart" magazine. The scene was the little town of Bethlehem, on the first Christmas Eve. The Three Wise Men
could be seen coming down a lane that crossed a little
bridge and led to the Stable. Above the Stable there
glowed a large, five-pointed star. There were many other
stars in the sky; but they were all smaller, and six-pointed.

Ostensibly, Herone's contrast between the one large five-
pointed star and the many smaller stars of David referred
slyly to the historic turn from Judaism to Christianity,
from the "Old Law" to the "New Law." But Herone never
for one moment thought that in its nature as a "doodle"
it should be interpreted simply thus. Herone wondered

whether, numerologically, it could be another variant of the hidden distinction, in his psychic economy, between even numbers and odd.

Other connections suggested themselves as possibilities. Years previously, during a time of great distress, he had had the sense of an eye, staring at him from the heavens. The bright star of Bethlehem now seemed to him a benign variant of this same fancy. Next, he asked himself, might "stare," in his psychic economy, be the verb form of the noun "star"? He next recalled that his nonsense syllables for "you filthy bastard" had originally been "oo lya star." But later he changed the "star" to "snar," on the assumption that if, when he lay waiting half-drugged before the operation, a mouthpiece had already been inserted to keep him from biting his tongue, this obstruction could have been partly responsible for his difficulty in speaking. If it was there, he certainly hadn't noticed it; for he had been aware only of the vexing way in which the words he tried to form turned out wrong. But if it had been there, he thought, then a "t" would more likely sound like an "n." Hence he changed "star" to "snar." He next noticed, to his bepuzzlement, that the light of "star" also hides itself under the bushel of "ba*star*d."

Omnia exeunt in mysterium.

When he hit upon his rebirth symbol, Herone was moving towards the day when the "prisoner" would "escape." But there was still one further ill-starred moment to develop, before he was formally wheeled down the hall to the elevator, to descend to the street level, and there be wheeled to the waiting car, whereat — praise God! — the Rule of his Better Half would again take over. We cite the incident for reasons of symmetry, to round out the design:

Herone's room-mate, who entered the hospital later than he did, "graduated" before him. After one night when he had the whole room to himself, a new patient was brought in, a laborer who had fallen from a scaffold. Herone watched the badly wounded man's clothes being removed and heaped in a pile. Later, relatives came and took these away. But before they left, they remarked that his purse was missing.

Herone promptly imagined an ironic situation: (a) workman falls from scaffold; (b) others rush to his aid; (c) some expert scoundrel, under the guise of caring for him, frisks him and steals his purse; (d) and thus, when the hospital attendants arrive, while they think they are carrying away the victim of an accident, they are also carrying away the victim of a robbery. Whereupon Herone confided sympathetically to a nurse: "The poor devil, he gets a bad bump, and gets robbed besides."

Shortly afterwards, an intern entered, glanced at Herone severely, and muttered loudly to himself: "His purse is probably being held for him at the office." In brief, Herone's remark had been interpreted as a suggestion that the patient had been robbed by one of the hospital attendants. One more bad mark for Herone.

Slink away, Herone. Make your exit, as Keats of the letters might say, "like a frog in a frost." You didn't show up so well in this episode. Yes, you had been somehow knocked crooked — might it even be true, as you feared, that one eye seemed inclined to stare, and to be bigger than the other? Yes, you had been trampled on, worked over, kicked in the teeth. Now you were almost ludicrously limp. And the punishment you took was particularly humiliating, since the operation was rated decidedly as "minor." What if you had been processed in a "major" way?

Slink back to freedom.

III.

"HAUNTED BY ECOLOGY"

Convalescing, if we could call it that (perhaps "being slowed down" would be more accurate), Herone continued to ruminate about his recent quandaries. A man with paranoid tendencies, he thought, might be successfully transformed into an educator—but only insofar as things are not under the sign of the Quietus. (Further, he tended to assume that everyone is paranoid, since we are all pursued by the discords of the social order.)

He thought of that sanguine fellow, Benjamin Paul Blood, a protégé of William James, with avidity proclaiming the "anaesthetic revelation" he had experienced in a dentist's chair. Surely at the bottom of him there was a happy simpleton that took delight in the sheer affinities of sound (along the lines of his thesis that "icicle" is not a fit name for a "tub"). Here was the symbol-using genius reduced to one perfect strand.

Herone had this happy strand, too. He loved the sheer jingle of words. Even in his anguish, Keats had it, as when he wrote, just before the end: "Yet I ride the little horse, and, at my worst, even in quarantine, summoned up more puns, in a sort of desperation, in one week than in any year of my life." Whatever fragment of a damned outraged monster there may be, howling deep down in a chasm, there is the possibility of this pure exercising whereby essences are suggested by an engrossment with the sheer accidents of words.

Eager for a summary, he slowly put some things together (remembering his imprisonment, but now from the side of freedom, though a freedom vexingly frail). As Herone figured things out, they might be summed up thus:

"First," there is man the "economic animal," in the strictly biological sense, such a creature of ecological balance and geophysical necessities as he would be even without his "reason" (that is, without his ability to find words for things and non-things, though frequently, by misuse of his "reason," he puts himself geophysically and ecologically in jeopardy, at the same time victimizing many humble "lower organisms" that don't quite know what happened to them; but somehow, as the result of human improvising, they ceased to find life lovable, or even livable). Here would prevail, basically, the aims and behaviours that make for growth, self-protection, and reproduction.

Now add *language* (the "grace" that "perfects" nature). Henceforth, every "natural" movement must be complicated by a *linguistic* (or *symbolic*) motive—symbolic not just in the general sense that an animal's posture may be symbolic of its condition, but also in the more specific sense that the word "tree" is symbolic of the thing it names, and this word can undergo developments, such as declensions, syntactic location, grammatical and phonetic changes, that are quite independent of the nature of tree as a thing.

There may even be a sense in which we might say that, for the symbol-using animal, there never had been a wholly "natural" motive (in the sense of a motive wholly alien to the principle of language). From the very start, the human infant's sheer *potentiality* as a symbol-using animal must differentiate its responses from those of a species that does not possess the inborn ability to learn language. For a non-linguistic species would presumably not suffer the kind of "pre-privation" that must mark the linguistically helpless human infant.

Though Herone did so fearsomely, since one contradicts Aristotle in such matters at one's peril, he wondered whether his position somewhat invalidated the scholastic principle: *nihil in intellectu quod non prius in sensu.* For the forms and principles of a language are never present as sheer sensation, though they are at the very core of our intellects (as when we conceive of natural relationships after the analogy and grammatical structure, such as subject and predicate, essence and accidents, active, passive, and middle or reflexive).

In any case, once language has become re-enforced by a complex socio-political order (with its corresponding codes of "reason" and "imagination"), the *material* reality of the human body in physical association with other bodies human and non-human becomes submerged beneath the *ideality* of socio-political communities (which are saturated with the genius of language) .

We probably think by only a few basic terms, though their paucity is obscured from us by the ways in which the many synonyms are not quite synonymous; for instance, "proceed" or "advance" don't quite make the same cuts as "go" or "move."

Poetically, philosophically, the ideal world of the pun becomes at this stage available in all its reaches. Thus, if we speak of light as a stream, of ideas as part of a historical current, and of urine as flowing, then urine, light, and ideas can be secretly one (one with blood, with rivers, with the stream of consciousness and the flux of time) . For underlying such similarities of usage, there are affinities linking the human body, the world's body, and the body politic.

Also, an *attitude* towards a body of topics has a unifying force. In effect its unitary nature as a response "sums up" the conglomerate of particulars towards which the attitude is directed. See a letter of Keats (March 17, 1817) , modifying a passage in Act II, Scene iv, of first part of *Henry IV*: "Banish money — Banish sofas — Banish Wine — Banish Music; but right Jack Health, honest Jack Health, true Jack Health—Banish Health and banish all the world." Here, he is saying in effect: The feeling infuses all things with the unity of the feeling.

Attitudes, in this respect, are a kind of censorial entitling, reduced to terms of behaviour. They are an implicit charade, a way of "acting out" a situation. Or they are like a highly generalized term of classification, a broad logical category—for in effect they classify under one head all the many different particular situations that call forth the same attitude.

When an attitude towards the world is developed in a moment of poetic or philosophic fusion (epitomized in some over-all title of titles, for "Everything") , it probably embodies some such implicit puns as were already considered, in connection with the range of things that "flow." But such unifying verbalizing, or.entitlement, is in effect a step beyond human body, world's body, and body politic, though it draws upon analogies from all three of these realms. It is a kind of "transcendent" entitlement, since its unifying function is in effect an addition to the elements it unifies. And in this technical sense it could be called "cosmic," or "supernatural," or "religious" (being technically "religious" in the sense that, like religion, it infuses all things with the essence of the Word, the Logos, the personality of the "first" creative fiat).

Suppose you are a musician—and of a sudden, a likely theme occurs to you. You awaken—and there it is. And somehow it is like an unopened bundle of possibilities.

Maybe this theme appeals to you because of its hidden relations to some other theme—a theme that you may have actually heard, or all-but-heard, many years ago, in some situation then that seemed to you vaguely laden with some such futurity as you now experience clearly. The theme thus looks back to an earlier time when you were vaguely looking forward (in effect fumbling with the beginnings of a word, a class name which you would need later, when you came to classify this later actualizing experience under the same head as the earlier potential experience).

Next, you proceed to develop variations on your theme. Successively, you make it brisk, playful, plaintive, pensive, solemn, grandiose, nostalgic, muscularly ingenious, and the like.

On the surface, at the very least you have produced a form by carrying a principle of consistency into an area that threatened it with disintegration (disintegration insofar as the principle of consistency risked becoming lost in the variety). But insofar as you have succeeded, you have unified this variety.

And have you not done still more? For insofar as your theme originally welled up from a secret personal relationship to situations that, however tinged by symbolism, were themselves largely outside the realm of symbolism (as the *thing* tree is outside the realm of the *word* "tree"), you have saturated this whole range of the symbolic and the non-symbolic with a single personal motive, summed up in the attitude-of-attitudes that was implicit in your theme (which would be the musical equivalent of a title-of-titles).

Thereby you have had, in effect, an immediate vision of an ultimate oneness (thanks to symbolic manipulations that have brought many disparate things together). You have had the direct feeling of this principle. You have "got the idea."

Can you, then, ever rest unless this perfection is actually attained? Furthermore, the search is made especially uncomfortable, and on many occasions undesirable, by the fact that, in the course of your efforts after the perfection or simplicity of unity, you find so many reasons to be glad that the world is in pieces. For if it were really all one, where could you turn, at times when again you must make a break for it?

Man's symbolistic genius first exiles him, by putting a symbolic veil between him and the non-symbolic. Next, it aggravates this state of alienation by making possible the complicated world of social status, the ladder or pyramid or hierarchy of offices, with their various "unnatural" kinds of livelihood. Next, symbolism acts to make amends by dialectical devices — of poetry, philosophy, politics — whereby things otherwise thought disjunct can be said to partake of a single unifying essence that transcends their separateness.

Either the memory of such unities, or the feeling for the possibilities in such a unifying principle (a feeling sharpened by at least partial attainment of such unification) acts in a way whereby the momentary experience of unification becomes a motive, a desire to have perfect consistency always.

Here would be the realm of "gallantry," of purely ideal

gesturing, the realm where, for instance, a masculine alimentary canal pays a deft compliment to a feminine alimentary canal, using to this end all the resources of symbolistic finesse necessary for acting "as if" these were not *au fond* two animal organisms dredged up from the seabottom.

"Love" begins as a sheerly natural emotion (animal, non-symbolic). Call it simply appetite, seasonal desire. So likewise with "duty," insofar as we mean by duty the kind of loyalty that marks the relation between parents and offspring. Both emotions, in this sense, would be "positive," as positive as hunger or toothache.

But once the symbol-using animal has developed complex ideas of property, with their corresponding notions of propriety, these two sheerly natural kinds of love and duty "transcend" their positive condition, becoming profoundly inspirited by the negative (as in the thou-shalt-not's essential to the formulation of all moral and social codes: justice, etiquette, "protocol"). Primitive seasonal sexual desire becomes *amor, eros;* the kind of familiar loyalty that begins in the relation between parents and offspring becomes *charitas, agape.* Both "love" and "duty" are now best studied as variants of the "imperial" motive—for they derive their personality from their nature as responses to the conditions of status, ownership, governance that develop historically through the aid of symbolism and that are, above all, infused with the genius of the negative (the thou-shalt-not's, and their corresponding quasi-positive forms in the case of moral precepts expressed in an affirmative style).

A set of consistent sentences about "everything," with appropriate summarizing title (or "god-term") and symmetrically distributed sub-categories, would be the ultimate perfection of language. Metaphysics reveals this drive most obviously, but it prevails *mutatis mutandis* as the principle of all substance (which Leibniz defined as "unity in plurality," and which later theorists claimed more specifically for the role of the "imagination").

Here begins the drive towards a logic of completion, a cult of perfection, which shows up drastically alas! as a goad towards empire-building, while the ways of empire serve in turn to localize the terminologies of gallantry, with their increasingly minuscule codes of courtliness.

The issue will finally be settled by the extent to which the purely symbolic genius of perfection is allowed to fall out of line with the needs of the body as sheer body. For the world of gallantry (when science has been carried into industry by the applications of politics and commerce) threatens at every point to disrupt the "ecological balance" of the purely physical world. Man's "dominion" over the "lowlier" species that are put here for his "use" threatens at every point to become manifest in a way whereby he destroys what he needs directly or indirectly for his own survival. The great "as if" can be like a very delicate dance, at a gorgeous festival, atop a volcano that is about ready to blow. And often the dance isn't so delicate, or the festival so gorgeous, either.

Thinking along these lines, Herone began to feel "haunted by ecology." The very thoroughness of his concern with man's symbol-using genius forced him to think with new intensity of man as sheer animal. He must go south, and to the sea—he must stand "on the brink of the drink." On the shore, thinking of the sea as scooped out, he would be as though on a high mountain overlooking an abyss.

IV.

"WATCHING YOUNG KEATS DIE"

(In Conclusion: Herone Liddell's Letter
to a member of what Keats has called
"that most vulgar of all crowds, the literary")

Dear —,

What hit me? I had been trampled on, worked over,
kicked in the dentures. It was doubly humiliating, to be so
beaten by so minor an operation. Still, maybe there had
been a kind of "cleansing," too. For even an impatient patient necessarily has patience of some sort.

Gradually there emerged The Resolve: To the South.
To the South it must be, though the fall and early winter
following my punishment were mild, and even beautiful.
To the South. Yet never did a beckoning beacon arouse
less sense of expectancy. (Each year I come more to loathe
and fear the traffic of the highways.)

So, we have improvised again—and it may turn out not
badly. We're on a kind of key, not skeleton, I hope, though
the first live thing we encountered, on our first walk on
the beach, at sundown, was a dying black duck that mutely
begged us to respect its privacy, and we did. The next day
we found it again, now partly buried in the sand by the
tide.

Ironically, we got our place through the *ex officio* offices
of a kindly real estate man who, living palatially, had only
a palace to rent, but gave us a tip, presumably from sheer
pity. (May he not also need a dash of terror, to complete
his cleansing for the day.)

Barring car trouble on the way back (we had almost
none on the way down) we should be able to manage the
whole trip for surprisingly little beyond the amt. we shall
save on what our bills for heating would have been, had

we stayed north. Yet on the third day of the idiot drive south south south, I had begun digging into the new areas of self-doubt, and even thought compulsively of a U-turn in the grand style, north north north, straight back into the winter we had fled from. (Travelling even at our moderate speed is as crazy as snow; one falls into a kind of trance, a near loss of personal identity — only to be wrenched out of it, now and then, by suddenly discovering that one had been masochistically imagining oneself in a wreck.) I guess that by now the clock in the dining room has stopped.

Since we did not know where we were going (except for the general direction: south), lack of destination makes the trip seem more like a destiny. Here, on the beach, one is encouraged to mistake outlook for insight. And there is the doubtless anally motivated business of searching for the remains of things that died before we did. Insofar as one is Puritanical, shell-gathering can further gratify his moralistic compulsions by giving his walks the selectivity of an acquisitive purpose. And formally, the minuteness of such a concern is forced upon one, perhaps, by sheer contrast with the sweep of the horizon.

I greatly admire the coquinas, that live so dangerously in the unstable sand where the waves wash. The valiant little fellows make good broth.

Consider me a fairly well-stocked dictionary standing on the edge of the abyss, confronting the biological fatalities under the grim signs of geophysics and ecology, in a mood Ultimate and Beyondish. End of formula. (The fishermen, I suppose, are as though bringing up live truths from dark depths.) The shell-gatherer, let us say, is forever hoping to find a perfect specimen of Convoluta Rigidiformis Oblongata, and thereby solve the secret of all life.

We have a little house, only 100 yards from Old Restless —and I can hear him tossing throughout the night, an insomniac even more sleepless than I, though much less unsleeping than God. (Since God is by definition wakeful always, even to the most trivial details of His Creation, I guess it follows that my insomnia is my nearest approach to godliness, though at times it leaves me awfully glum. I envy those earnest fellows of earlier ages who, where we say "insomnia," would doubtless have spoken of "watching and waiting." They could have welcomed as a call, as a promise, what is now but a damned nuisance.) Yes, we are on a sheer slither, between Gulf and Bay. So we go scrunching our way on sand and shells along the Edge of the Ultimate, selecting from among the forms of things that conched off before we did, things dredged up from that profusely life-giving charnel-house, the sea. The good wife is so much more expert at "shelling" than I, whenever I do turn up something, I suspect her of making a special fuss about my find, to heal my ailing ego.

I have been doing my exercises. For instance, as regards the multiple personalities of pelicans, I have figured things out thus: Standing, these birds are as solemn as deacons; when they swim, they nestle in the water like sitting hens; they fly in formation like a band of witches; and they plunge after their prey like a suicide jumping from a bridge.

I'm not quite sure just why—but I have found this a fitting time in which to see re-enacted the poignant death of Keats. I have been re-reading his letters, particularly his last ones, with a mixture of professionalism and tearfulness. I have been watching young Keats die.

In August of 1818, his walking trip through the Lake Country, Scotland, and Ireland had been suddenly interrupted because of the "sore throat" that was the first symptom of his fatal illness. About two years later Shelley, when inviting him to Italy in hopes of aiding his recovery, would write: "This consumption is a disease particularly fond of people who write such good verses as you have done, and with the assistance of an English winter it can often indulge its selection." The word for the disease appears seldom, though near the end, when still in quarantine at Naples, Keats writes to the mother of Fanny Brawne: "It has been unfortunate for me that one of the Passengers is a young Lady in a Consumption—her imprudence has vexed me very much—the knowledge of her complaint— the flushings in her face, all her bad symptoms have preyed upon me—they would have done so had I been in good health."

During the time when Keats was nursing his brother, "poor Tom," the reference was usually to Tom's "nervousness." And it is almost gruesome to see this same word gradually coming to take over, prophetically, in Keats's references to his own condition.

But if "nervousness" is what we might call the passive word for a necessary involvement with the sensations of his body (and "sensation" is as lively a word with Keats as "passion" and "imagination"), the active one is "fever." You can get almost the whole scope of his quandaries by reviewing the variety of contexts, with corresponding range in attitude, that serve as setting for this many-faceted word.

In August, 1819, he writes to Fanny of his engrossment in his work: "I encourage it, and strive not to think of you —but when I have succeeded in doing so all day and as far as midnight, you return as soon as this artificial excitement goes off more severely from the fever I am left in." Later in the same month, he writes her applying the same word to his work: "I am in complete cue—in the fever." (This was about a year after the interruption of his walking trip. "Cue" seems a slightly strange word here. And I wonder whether, as incentive in the background, there could have lurked the word "cure.") There is another reference, written while Tom was still alive, to "the feverous relief of Poetry," followed a few lines later by an expression that, viewed in retrospect, was portentous: "There is an awful warmth about my heart like a load of Immortality." (I admit, I generally incline to consider the word "immortality" a simple euphemism for "death.") The passage was in connection with "the shape of a Woman" who had fascinated him. He writes, in a wholly accurate synthesis: "Poor Tom—that woman—and Poetry were ringing changes in my senses." (A few days later she would be described as "an imperial woman," with the "Beauty of a Leopardess." He had not yet met Fanny. For his first impression of her, he would be "forced . . . to make use of the term *Minx*.") On another occasion, when he refers to "seeing now and then some beautiful woman," he describes the experience as a "fever."

There can be an "idle fever," too, of months "without any fruit." And on the subject of money troubles he can lament, "I cannot write while my spirit is fevered in a contrary direction." Claret is praised because it fills the mouth "with a gushing freshness—then goes down cool and feverless." Near the end, his tragic "passion" for Fanny is referred to as "this fever" ("Through the whole of my illness . . . this fever has never ceased wearing me out.") And one passage, in a letter to Fanny, suggested to me some notions in the direction of a universal irony. He writes: "I had a slight return of the fever last night, which terminated favourably ["fever" into "favour"?], and I am now tolerably well, though weak from the small quantity of food to which I am obliged to confine myself: I am sure a mouse would starve upon it." The medical practice of the times, in reducing the sufferer from tuberculosis to a minimum diet, suggests the ironic possibility that, unless one has precisely the right remedy for a disease, or the right solution for a problem, one might tend to hit upon the *very opposite* of the right way. For, from the standpoint of sheer dialectic, there is a sense in which the "closest approximate" to the right way would be its diametrical opposite, the wrongest way conceivable. From the standpoint of dialectic, as Coleridge was assiduous in pointing out, "extremes meet." Thus, in this purely formal sense, the wrongest way would be next in line with the right way.

Fever or no fever, the tendency has been quite transformed into gallantry when, writing to Fanny of his fear
lest love burn him up, he dance-steps: "But if you will
fully love me, though there may be some fire, 'twill not be
more than we can bear when moistened and bedewed with
Pleasures." When his illness, we might say, has "pro-
gressed," the theme gets a variation: "There is a great difference between going off in warm blood like Romeo, and
making one's exit like a frog in a frost." (The choice here
is between fever and chill, I take it.) But the final form, a
few months later, is in a letter to his friend Brown: "I
shall endeavour to write to Miss Brawne if possible today.
A sudden stop to my life in the middle of one of these
Letters would be no bad thing for it keeps one in a sort of
fever awhile."

Going farther afield, but still interpreting in the light of
these passages, I'd say that the bodily sufferance and the
poetic activity are interwoven in Keats's formula, written
about two months after the interruption of his trip: "The
faint conceptions I have of Poems to come brings the blood
frequently into my forehead." And a statement written
about the same time shows how his often mentioned "indolence," by merging with his cult of sensation, lets the
paths of poetry and disease temporarily run along together:
"I melt into the air with a voluptuousness so delicate that
I am content to be alone." Symptomatic, in the sheerly
bodily sense, would be this sentence written in the spring
of 1819: "The weather in town yesterday was so stifling
that I could not remain there." But the symptom joins
with the motive of woman when, the autumn of that same
year, he writes to Fanny, who had "dazzled" him: "I cannot breathe without you."

Several months before the first gong had struck (the
hemorrhage of the lungs was the second), he had written
on the joys of being "passive and receptive" like a flower,
of "budding patiently under the eyes of Apollo," thoughts
to which he was led "by the beauty of the morning operat-

ing on a sense of Idleness." And still earlier, when talking of Imagination, he had struck his slogan, "O for a Life of Sensations rather than of Thoughts!" Later he describes "a sort of temper indolent and supremely careless," a "state of effeminacy," a "langour" (sic), a "Laziness," a "delightful sensation about three degrees on the side of faintness," which he called "a rare instance of advantage in the body overpowering the Mind." And about this same time the condition is described as "a sensation at the present moment as though I was dissolving." On this subject, I have corrected a memory that had played me false. At odd times, I had gone about, saying, "as prompt as the bee to the blossom," but it should have been "as punctual as the Bee to the Clover."

"I did not know whether to say purple or blue so in the mixture of the thought wrote purplue." As regards the parables of Paronomasia, I'd consider this statement, in its role as a "doodle," the perfect instance of the Word-man's method, when building up a world. To me this "portmanteau" construction is saying in effect, if we apply its lesson to the considerable range of things loosely brought together under the heading of his fever: I did not know where sheer healthy indolence stopped and a morbid kind took over; I did not know where such sensations were expanded into an abstract cult of sensation that would be in turn capable of serving well the cause of imagination generally; I did not know where the cause of imagination generally merged into its specific use for poetry; I did not know where my love of poetry in turn merged into my love of woman, and where that more general interest became narrowed to an almost insane engrossment with one woman, as I lay on my sickbed, imagining her in full health free of me, my powers of concentration now fixed upon her only, since their employment in my craft was now denied me by the mounting exigencies of my disease ("My imagination is horribly vivid about her—I see her—I hear her. There is nothing in the world of sufficient in-

terest to direct me from her for a moment") —so I somehow put them all together, in my "vale of Soul-making,"
quite as romantic and bodily fevers had merged in me,
until I could not know where one left off and the other
began.

For though he had earlier said that "A Poet is the most
unpoetical of any thing in existence; because he has no
identity" (at a time when, writing to his brother and sister-
in-law in America, he said somewhat belittlingly of his sister: "Her character is not formed, her identity does not
press upon me as yours does"), later he was to propose a
"system of Spirit-creation" that he considered "a grander
system of salvation than the chrystiain religion." And he
went on to explain: "This is effected by three grand materials acting the one upon the other for a series of years.
These three Materials are the *Intelligence*—the *human
heart* (as distinguished from intelligence or Mind) and the
World or *Elemental Space* suited for the proper action of
Mind and Heart on each other for the purpose of forming
the *Soul* or *Intelligence destined to possess the sense of
Identity*." (Incidentally note that, however roundabout,
Keats has made his scheme closely analogous to the Christian Trinity after all. For "World or Elemental Space"
would correspond to Power, "Intelligence" to Wisdom,
"Human Heart" to Love—so in his recipe for "Identity"
would be implicit the internal bearing of the three "persons" upon one another.)

One major strand, I'd say, was still to be supplied: the
motive of empire. Poetry, "the Imagination," is not complete until it also somehow links with the norms of governance. Though the connection was definitely touched
upon when Keats gave his recipe for the "imperial woman," and though Keats's discussions of ambition, and of
doing "good" with his poems, also bore upon this motive,
I think that the clearest reference to this strand in the
motivational recipe came in a long passage Keats quoted
from a statement by Hazlitt, in connection with an earlier

essay on *Coriolanus,* in which Hazlitt had written: "The language of Poetry naturally falls in with the language of power."

Writing to his brother and sister-in-law in America, Keats quotes Hazlitt as saying, in altercation with an opponent:

> I affirm, Sir, that Poetry, that the imagination, generally speaking, delights in power, in strong excitement, as well as in truth, in good, in right, whereas pure reason and the moral sense approve only of the true and the good. . . . we do read with pleasure of the ravages of a beast of prey, and we do so on the principle I have stated, namely from the sense of power abstracted from the sense of good. . . . Do you mean to deny that there is any thing imposing to the imagination in power, in grandeur, in outward shew, in the accumulation of individual wealth and luxury, at the expense of equal justice and the common weal? Do you deny that there is anything in the "Pride, Pomp, and Circumstance of glorious war, that makes ambition virtue!" in the eyes of admiring multitudes? . . . Is it a paradox of my creating that "one murder makes a villain, millions a Hero!" or is it not true that here, as in other cases, the enormity of the evil overpowers and makes a convert of the imagination by its very magnitude? . . .

Keats's comment on this passage (in all a very long one) had been: "The manner in which this is managed: the force and innate power with which it yeasts and works up itself—the feeling for the costume of society; is in a style of genius—He hath a demon, as he himself says of Lord Byron."

These pages were no mere retailing of literary gossip. Keats was quoting a writer to whose position he obviously subscribed. Twice he explicitly says that to him Hazlitt meant "depth of Taste."

I was particularly happy to observe how, in contrast with critical stupidities now current, the cult of passion, sensation, and imagination never led Keats to forget the notable element of *abstraction* in his calling: "This morning Poetry has conquered me—I have relapsed into those abstractions which are my only life." . . . A reference to himself as having "love of Beauty in the abstract." . . . "The mighty abstract Idea I have of Beauty in all things." . . . A reference to his "abstract careless and restless life." . . . He tells a friend that "any thing cold" in him should be attributed not to "heartlessness" but to "abstraction." . . . He writes amatively to Fanny Brawne: "Forgive me if I wander a little this evening, for I have been all day employ'd in a very abstr[a]ct Poem." . . . And when distinguishing between "imaginary woes" and "real ones," he observes that the imaginary ones are "conjured up by our passions," whereas the real ones "come of themselves, and are opposed by an abstract exertion of mind." . . . And among the lines quoted from Hazlitt is the passage: "We do read with pleasure of the ravages of a beast of prey, and we do so on the principle I have stated, namely from the sense of power abstracted from the sense of good."

Some months after the sore throats had set in, Keats writes: "My Thoughts are very frequently in a foreign Country—I live more out of England than in it." One might take these words purely as an expression of his romantic imagination. But near the end, this same Elsewhere Attitude has picked up an additional grim dimension. Thus, while still in quarantine, referring to the Port of Naples, he says: "it looks like a dream—every man who can row his boat and walk and talk seems a different being from myself. I do not feel in the world." And a month later: "I have an habitual feeling of my real life having passed, and that I am leading a posthumous existence."

Still speculating under the sign of "purple" (or rather, of the synthesizing principle embodied there), I next think of a letter (July 25, 1819) where, in connection with his "swooning admiration" of Fanny Brawne's beauty, he makes a somewhat Wagnerian reference to the love-death pair: "I have two luxuries to brood over in my walks, your Loveliness and the hour of my death. O that I could have possession of them both in the same minute." The sentence gives me reason to believe that in the "Bright Star" sonnet, written during his trip to Italy, where he was soon to die, the disjunction of the closing line ("And so live ever—or else swoon to death") should be interpreted not on its face, but as two apparently quite different ways of saying the same thing, the moment of Keatsian languor conceived as permanently prolonged.

Previously, in fact, he had given what amounts to a poetic definition of his word "swoon":

> The fifth canto of Dante pleases me more and more—it is that one in which he meets with Paolo and Franchesca— I had passed many days in rather a low state of mind, and in the midst of them I dreamt of being in that region of Hell. The dream was one of the most delightful enjoyments I ever had in my life—I floated about the whirling atmosphere as it is described with a beautiful figure to whose lips mine were joined at [read: as] it seem'd for an age—and in the midst of all this cold and darkness I was warm—even flowery tree tops sprung up and we rested on them sometimes with the lightness of a cloud till the wind blew us away again—I tried a Sonnet upon it—there are fourteen lines but nothing of what I felt in it—O that I could dream it every night—
>
> As Hermes once took to his feathers light
> When lulled Argus, baffled, swoon'd and slept. . . .

And so on. The makings of the "Bright Star" sonnet had figured further, in that same letter of July, 1819. "I will imagine you Venus to-night," he wrote, "and pray, pray, pray to your star like a He[a]then." And when, in closing, he calls her "fair Star," I suddenly seem to glimpse in the sonnet, and particularly in the opening line, "Bright Star, would I were steadfast as thou art," a motivational strand that may have been intensely there for the poet, though present only in the offing for his readers. In his transcendent way of getting union with a loved woman whose body his disease had denied him (a union got in spirit by prayer-like communion with a star that stood for her), does he not also make Fanny transcendently steadfast whereas, in his tortured, ineffectual imaginings as an invalid, when forbidden to concentrate upon his poetry, he could not keep himself from concentrating instead on the possibility of Fanny Brawne's levity, beyond the powers of his jurisdiction?

And may he have succeeded, too, despite the illness that kept them apart, in circuitously carving his mark upon her? For I take the words "prie*st*like *ta*sk" to contain a pathetic enigma, the building blocks of his own name, "Keats"—the consonants acrostically scrambled (*st-k* and *t-sk*), the vowel-sound preserved in "priest"—and even the silent *a*, if you will, that is sounded in "task."

When, quoting Ford's *'Tis Pity She's a Whore*, he writes, "I have endeavoured often 'to reason against the reasons of my Love,' " I think of a line (on the "reasoning" of love) I happen to have been reading recently in Dante on purgation: "*Amor che nella mente mi ragiona.*" And I would think of both these places when he says, "A Man's life of any worth is a continual allegory. . . . Shakespeare led a life of Allegory: his works are the comments on it." For I am coming to believe, more and more firmly, in the possibility that our lives cannot escape being "allegorical."

Think how readily, for instance, the materials of science can conceal the "allegory" of our motives behind pragmatic problems. A poet, let us say, writes of some icy region, and immediately we are warned: "Ha! Here is the imagery of frigidity. Let us look more closely, to see just how the discourse or 'reasoning' of self-willed castration figures here." But let that same man be an engineer who conceives of a practical device for improving the methods

of preserving foods by refrigeration—whereat the symbolism retreats behind the obvious materiality of the practical
problems to be solved here, and behind the publicly recognized utility of the results.

Or let a poet write of the moon, and by his very choice
of subject he forewarns us that he may be lunatic. Yet the
scientist, speculating on the conditions necessary for a
lunar voyage by "space ship," may be so accurately involved in his planning that the "realism" of his solution
deflects our attention from the essential "allegory" that
prods him to the project in the first place.

Implicit in all mechanism there lies an enigmatic image
—and its meaning is doubly hidden by the obvious materiality of the devices (with their material problems and
correspondingly material solutions) in which the ultimate
dream-like purpose is embodied. Thus we are trapped by
our contraptions.

And in this sense, quite as Dante's view of ultimate motives, in the last canto of the *Paradiso*, terminates in such
kind of folding-back-upon-the-self as can be figured (here
where the idea of Faithful Love is *generalized* as highly as
possible within the strict limits of *personalization*) in
terms of the Virgin Mary as the Daughter of her own Son
(*figlia del tuo figlio*—a realm where causes final and ef-
ficient merge), so man's worldly speculations about his
worldly destiny must come to center in the self-entangling
problems of Words About Words, which I would name re-
flexively as LOGOLOGY.

For there are things that on their face are symbols. And
there are things that, though intrinsically non-symbolic,
are by the human, symbol-using species infused as thoroughly with symbolism as all Creation is said by the re-
ligionist to be inspirited with the Word of Heaven. And
the sheer dialectics of the case is such that there can be
nothing else.

We could dialectically dramatize it all by setting it up as
a battle of Gallantry vs. Ecology, involving the nearly con-

tradictory attempt by the use of symbols to see around the corner of symbols, into a reality purely and simply extra-symbolic. Out of this arise the shifting lines of battle between business and government, the aesthetic and the practical, commissars and engineers, priests and prophets —of Pope St. Guelph grievously at odds with Emperor Ghibelline the Great (the issue being further complicated by the fact that even our most "down to earth" ways of living are as inexorably ruled by "spellbinders" as are the realms of poetry—and the man of "hard, cold facts" differs from the speculative man mainly in having less occasion to realize how ridden by the "gallantry"—and corresponding meannesses—of speech he is) . Do not the laws of "gallantry" inevitably make for a tragically prideful neglect of sheerly material motives, even while acting to make up for the insufficiency of sheerly material motives, which would literally bore the symbol-using animal to death?

As regards our first swim (in the Far South, with a light wind from the Farther South) : The sea was as mellow as an over-ripe cantaloupe, which is my ideal of culture. The sea was so mild, I got scared. For just when I was prepared to battle, not the waves (for it was calm) but the cold, lo! I found myself feeling as though about to dissolve in luxury. It was less like swimming than like Death and Transfiguration. And I have become so demoralized, as regards my attempts to understand the purport of my symptoms, I found the relaxation frightening.

Where were we? "Gallantry" vs. "Ecology." Might not the principles of "Gallantry" make for a tragically prideful inability to live a life modestly befitting a human animal, which is to say, a life that would permit us to be truly gallant with regard to the "lowlier" species, too?

To think words by the seaside is like hearing music from a distance. (Even a trivial tune, floating at night across waters, seems a bit fate-laden.) It is to be reminded that, though we think by symbols, we live or die by the demands

imposed upon us physiologically, ecologically, geophysically. Yet one goes avidly in quest of the question best designed to make his assertions look like an answer. We are
a dismal breed, needing our glasses to find our glasses.

Put me, motivationally, under the sign of Ailments,
Ecology, Geophysics, and Symbolism. Watching young
Keats die, I join him in the name of Royal Purplue, even
as I wonder what might be the special etiology of my particular ills. I live by dodges, and so do my symptoms.
Watching sunsets when shafts of golden sunlight shoot
down from turbulent black and golden clouds, I would
school the self to see these shafts as sheerly physically as
possible.

I dote on thoughts of verse that would have but frag-
ments of meaning, like shells the sea has pounded into bits.
The nearness to nonsense might help accentuate the lines
in their formality:

ENTRANCE, WITH FANFARE

Hornswoggle thus, you and all others of like ilk—
Hear now the words of Silkentine, and be
Content with golden laudability.
Whom should we stand at, whom against, and whom?
Braving their selves throughout all Christen-doom,
Gulp down hard liquor with their mother's milk.
Start stopping—spot like any run-down rebel
The eighty-seven ways of sitting at a table.
    (Bah! if the sea is restless, why in God's fair name
    Should *they* feel justified to petition for sound
        slumber?
    Consider me elsewhere . . .)
                    exit, trampling

The portion in parentheses would be spoken in an
abrupt change of rhythm, like a burst into petulant prose.
This next should canter:

They're scattered 'cross the countryside
A long ways from the house.
So gather round the gadgets, girls,
And we'll all have tea.

The absence of a final rhyme in a quatrain so much like a jingle should be experienced as outrageous. One critic suggests that Mother Goose, in her archetypal perfection, may be as near as poets *qua* poets ever get to Heaven. Poetry could not say something, while remaining pure. Poetry can be pure only when it attains to the sheer gestures and tonalities of itself, being statement but "in principle," Utterance in the Absolute, signifying sound and fury, full of nothing. At the farthest reaches of the mind, there can be but the undirected feel of language, going beyond doctrine to grammar, beyond verbs to the paradigms of verbs, loving verse most for its bare prosody, needing meaning only because by shades of meaning we increase the subtlety and range of accents.

Meanwhile, I comb the beach for a wrench-like shape such as I dreamed of in the hospital. If I could dream it, the sea can make it—and having made it, the sea can toss it up.

Sincerely,
Herone L.

P.S. One night, our two cots pushed as snugly close as could be, I lay awake listening to the bluster of the climate. The rain slapped loudly, as it fell from the roof to the cement floor of the porch. Farther off, the thrashing of the sea was more violent than usual. "Sea-Storm at Night," I thought, entitlingly. And tried some rhymes slightly deflected: "Sound of sea-dream yonder. The sea is roaring its own sea-monster. It would pound its own waves down under." The next day, cradling over a shoal in the bay, I dozed, while wavelets nudged against my moored rowboat.

P.P.S. To reach this front of sand-topped ridge, we drove over a sunny clop-clop bridge.